Edgewater

"Textured, rich, and evocative. Sheinmel's
Edgewater is a profound story of belonging and pretending,
and of the ways that the past and present become mysteriously
and sometimes dangerously intertwined."

—LAUREN OLIVER, *NEW YORK TIMES* BESTSELLING AUTHOR
OF *DELIRIUM* AND *BEFORE I FALL*

"You will not be able to put the book down."

—ADELE GRIFFIN, AUTHOR OF THE NATIONAL
BOOK AWARD FINALISTS *WHERE I WANT TO BE*
AND *SONS OF LIBERTY*

"A terrific read—smart, sexy, and shockingly scandalous.
Sheinmel is at her absolute best."

—SARAH MLYNOWSKI, AUTHOR OF *TEN THINGS WE DID (AND
PROBABLY SHOULDN'T HAVE)*

"A deliciously decadent story of glamour, family secrets,
and the twisted legacy of a tortured past."

—ROBIN WASSERMAN, AUTHOR OF
THE WAKING DARK

"Riveting and heartbreaking."

—*KIRKUS REVIEWS*

★ "With powerful messages of family and self-reliance,
Sheinmel's coming-of-age tale captivates with its masterful
storytelling style and intricate detail."

—*PUBLISHERS WEEKLY*, STARRED REVIEW

water

COURTNEY SHEINMEL

AMULET BOOKS
NEW YORK

The Library of Congress has cataloged the hardcover edition as follows:

Library of Congress Cataloging-in-Publication Data
Sheinmel, Courtney.
Edgewater / Courtney Sheinmel.
pages cm
ISBN 978-1-4197-1641-6 (hardback) —
ISBN 978-1-61312-828-2 (ebook)
[1. Families—Fiction. 2. Secrets—Fiction.] I. Title.
PZ7.S54124Ed 2015
[Fic]—dc23
2015006547

Paperback ISBN 978-1-4197-2347-6

Originally published in hardcover by Amulet Books in 2015
Text copyright © 2015 Courtney Sheinmel
Jacket photograph copyright © 2018 Getty Images
Book design by Julia Marvel

ABRAMS The Art of Books
195 Broadway, New York, NY 10007
abramsbooks.com

FOR
DORIS V. SHEINMEL

IT'S VERY DIFFICULT TO KEEP
THE LINE BETWEEN THE
PAST AND THE PRESENT.

—Little Edie Beale, *Grey Gardens*

1
THE BET

WHENEVER I LOOKED BACK ON THAT SUMMER, I'D THINK of the bet as what set all the changes in motion. Even though the actual trigger was something that had happened long before. Before Mom left, and before I walked out the door myself—going anywhere I could to escape home.

Maybe there was some unknown event in my mother's childhood that had shaped her into the kind of person who'd make certain choices that resulted in her absence. And maybe it went even further back than that—to who her parents were, and who her parents' parents were, and all that they had passed down through the generations. Sometimes I think you can draw a line from today back to the beginning of time and see how everything that happened was made inevitable by what preceded it.

But it was that bet, on a hot summer night, that I would come back to as the starting point. Like that moment in *The*

Wizard of Oz when things go from black-and-white to Technicolor. A switch was flipped, and things began to unravel in earnest.

When it happened, I was in North Carolina, attending Camp Woodscape, an equestrian program for advanced riders, for the second summer in a row. Thirty-two of us lived in a dorm adjacent to the barn and stables of Raleigh College's south campus. Late June had seen a week of earth-scorching, record-breaking temperatures up the Eastern Seaboard, and Barrett Hall didn't have air-conditioning. The smells of shampoo and perfume barely masked the stubborn odors of hay and sweat and girls radiating warmth and sucking up all the oxygen.

But I didn't mind. I loved anything even remotely related to horses, even the smells. The mustiness of the barn, the freshly oiled saddles, the fields after a summer rain shower—those scents covered me like a blanket and made me feel utterly at home, more at home than I ever felt in New York, in my own house. In fact, the only thing at Woodscape that really got under my skin was my roommate, Beth-Ann Bracelee. Yes, of *the* Bracelees, as my aunt Gigi would, no doubt, have noted. A Bracelee Candies Bracelee. While Beth-Ann might have been heiress to a half-billion-dollar confectionery fortune, as far as I was concerned, there was nothing sweet about her.

Beth-Ann had had it out for me ever since the prior summer, when her palomino, Pacifica, got a stress fracture that made him all but unridable. Foolishly, I let her ride my horse, Orion, in a dressage competition that I hadn't qualified for myself, and then she got it into her head that Orion would be better off with her. She went as far as to have her dad fly in from their Palm Beach home and take us to dinner at the Oakwood Café, the most expensive restaurant in town, where the cloth napkins were folded like origami swans, the butter was infused with different flavors, and the grilled-lobster salad was served with a citrus dressing that you dreamed about long after dinner was over. "Orion's the perfect age, Daddy," Beth-Ann practically cooed. "He's no longer green, and he has all his best years ahead of him." Clayton Bracelee waved his checkbook in front of me. "Name your price," he said. But I told him there'd been a misunderstanding: Orion wasn't nor would he ever be for sale.

Beth-Ann had pouted for the rest of the summer. Frankly, I didn't expect to see her back at Woodscape again, but on the first day, there she was. Already in our dorm room, having taken the brighter side by the window and moved things around so she ended up with more space. You don't get to pick your room-mate at Woodscape, but I wished I'd had the forethought to write on my housing form: *anyone but Beth-Ann Bracelee.*

Beth-Ann had brought her brand-new prized Thorough-bred, Easter Sunday, that she'd purchased after—get this—the horse psychic she'd hired to tour different barns with her said that she and Easter had a special mind-body connection.

But that kind of thing wasn't out of the ordinary among equestrian circles. I was used to riders like Beth-Ann. Back home my tactic was to steer clear of them. It was just that Beth-Ann made it virtually impossible: She lived in my dorm room, and despite her apparent disdain for me, when we were outside our room, she still always seemed to be at my heels.

I had dinner plans that last night with Isabella Reyes, a

raven-haired, olive-skinned rider from Spain who'd had two of her Arabian horses, Razia and Sultan, flown across the ocean to Woodscape. But Isabella was down-to-earth, or as much as a descendant of the Spanish royal family could be.

Unsurprisingly, Beth-Ann had invited herself along to dinner with Isabella and me, and then she insisted we stop at the CVS on the way, so she could junk up our shared sink with more random drugstore purchases. While Beth-Ann was in line to pay for an armload of nail polish and eye shadow, I wandered over to the ATM to get some cash, forty dollars, and I was denied "due to insufficient funds."

I'd purposely waited for the first day of July to make a withdrawal. Years earlier, my mother had set up a trust fund for my sister, Susannah, and me, right before ditching us to move abroad with her British boyfriend, Nigel. My aunt was named our guardian and the trust's flaky executor. By the end of each month, we were usually living off fumes, waiting for the next stipend to be transferred into our checking account. But today was payday, and—I looked down at my watch—certainly by ten after seven the transfer should have been made.

So money, and the lack thereof, was on my mind as the host at the Oakwood Café, where we'd fast become regulars, led us through the throng of other patrons, men in summer sport jackets and women in pearls, to our table. I'd long ago perfected the art of keeping my face straight and impassive so no one would catch on to the meltdown I was having inside, and besides, Beth-Ann was too involved with her own battles to notice even if I hadn't. She flagged down our waiter to demand olive oil for the bread, then flagged him down again when it didn't come fast enough. "This is why waiters are waiters and not brain surgeons," she stated in her slow Southern drawl before he was safely out of earshot. "Because they can't even remember a simple request."

"Quiet," I said under my breath. When I turned, our waiter was looking right at us, and I was certain he'd heard every word. I ducked my head, mortified.

Beth-Ann barely lowered her voice and went on: "Daddy says it takes all kinds of people for the world to function. Some people need to be the ambitious ones and become doctors and lawyers."

"And candy-shop owners," Isabella said with a smile. Her accent made the word *candy* sound foreign and fancy.

"Candy-*empire* owners," Beth-Ann corrected, her face as deadpan as her voice. Humor and nuance were lost on her. "And some people need to be the ones to serve those people and do all the things we don't want to do."

"That guy's handling, like, a dozen tables," I said. "It's not his fault he wasn't born a candy empress."

"That's not the point," Beth-Ann said. "It's simply not my destiny to serve anyone. But clearly I've offended you and your future plans to be in the food-service industry."

Heat rose to my cheeks, and my underarms were suddenly dripping with sweat. Even the restaurant's full-blast air conditioner was no match for the kind of hot it was outside; besides which, feeling self-conscious always made my body temperature rise a few notches.

"I've been thinking, you need a new passion project anyway," Beth-Ann told me.

I fought to keep my voice steady. "I have no idea what you're talking about."

"You and Orion haven't exactly been in sync lately."

Orion had eaten a piece of moldy hay, and it had taken me longer than it should have to figure out the problem. But he'd been better for a week, and Beth-Ann knew it. "People in glass houses shouldn't throw stones," I said.

"I don't have a problem with Easter. No one knows him like I do—and vice versa. He knows I can be a bitch, he knows when I'm sad, and he even knows when he's crossed me."

"Sounds like your horse is the psychic," I said. "And yet the two of you haven't been able to communicate when it comes to clearing the two-foot oxer." Every time Beth-Ann had approached the double-railed jump on the North Course, Easter had slowed, and she'd had to turn away.

"Are you saying Easter's not much of a jumper?"

Isabella's gaze shifted back and forth between Beth-Ann and me, as if she was watching a tennis match. "Come on, you guys," she said.

But I paid her no mind. "I'm saying, I bet you twenty bucks," I said.

And there it was.

At that moment, I was just another entitled teen having dinner at a restaurant that most people went to only for a special occasion. My horse was stabled at an exclusive riding program, and in two months he and I would return to Hillyer Academy, the boarding school I'd attended since the ninth grade. Back home in Idlewild, the small town on the eastern end of Long Island where I technically lived, everything was in ruins, thanks to Aunt Gigi. But I'd used my trust fund to get away and keep up appearances—I'll be the first to admit, they were extraordinarily extravagant appearances—and it had worked: Here, all the other girls thought I was one of them.

They couldn't have imagined how different it really was for me if they'd tried.

"You're on," Beth-Ann said.

"When?"

"Tomorrow morning, before rounds."

"Fine."

"Fine."

It was my turn to treat. As dinner wound down, so did my adrenaline rush from battling Beth-Ann, and I was a little nervous as I handed my Amex over to the waiter. With the "lack of sufficient funds," chances were Aunt Gigi was late on paying our bills again. But, I reminded myself, she did always pay them eventually. The credit card companies knew it and extended our credit anyhow. They were probably happy about how Gigi conducted things; my family was good for the money, and they got what we owed them, along with all those extra interest charges and late fees.

I planned to add an extra-big tip to our bill, to compensate for what the waiter had, no doubt, heard Beth-Ann say, but just as I'd dreaded, my Amex was denied. And then my backup Visa. Before I could ask the waiter to try splitting the bill across both cards, Isabella leaned over and handed him *her* Amex. My cheeks burned as I made a mental note to call home first thing in the morning, apologized to Isabella, and loudly promised that the next dinner was on me.

But there would be no next dinner. By morning, everything had changed.

We were on the North Course, Orion and I, and Isabella and Sultan, and of course Beth-Ann and Easter Sunday. My dark hair itched under my helmet. I could feel the tendrils that had escaped from my ponytail curling at the base of my neck. But if the heat was getting to Beth-Ann, you couldn't tell. She looped around, showing off. Easter was in good form, as if horse and rider really had been communicating telepathically. The bet was on, and Beth-Ann pressed the horse forward, gathering speed. I knew at least five paces in that they'd do it, effortlessly sailing over, clearing the two feet and then some.

"Guess you owe me twenty, Hollander," Beth-Ann crowed as she reined in Easter.

"Lorrie Hollander!"

I turned to see Woodscape's director, Pamela Bunn, waving madly from the end of the fence. She'd walked a long way from the administrative offices, and by the time she reached me, the underarms of her blue oxford were half-mooned with sweat, and her usually pale face had a baked-cherry redness.

"Lorrie, can you hand Orion off and come back with me to Whelan Hall?"

"Okay."

Beth-Ann and Isabella watched as I led Orion to one of the stable hands. I met up with Pamela on the other side of the building, and we cut across the flat pasture to the winding pathway behind the tack room. Pamela was breathing heavily. She couldn't muster the strength for small talk to fill the space between us, and that was fine; I couldn't, either. Something was wrong. I knew it. What had happened at the ATM had just been the first sign, the harbinger of doom.

We finally made it to Pamela's office, and I took the folding chair opposite her large, battered desk. "Lorrie," she began, leaning forward on her arms. As if the weight of what she needed to say demanded the support. "I hate to say this, but it looks as if we're going to have to send you home."

"What? Why?"

"Your aunt has not paid your tuition, and you cannot stay here for free."

"She can get a check to you by the end of this week," I insisted. "She's really bad at managing the money, but the funds are there. I swear."

"I believe you, Lorrie. And if you could get her to transfer the money today, I'd overlook it. But she hasn't responded to any of our calls or e-mails. Today was as far as we were willing to extend the deadline."

"Listen, I know Gigi is . . . erratic," I said. "But she always—"

"Lorrie, please don't make this harder on me. This is a terribly regrettable situation for us, too. We decided to overlook the initial delays because you were here last year and because you're a talented rider. But now we're weeks into the program. It's not feasible for us to provide you room and board free of charge. Not to mention the fact that it's simply unfair to the other girls, whose families *have* paid."

A large drowsy fly had begun to bat the mesh window-screen behind Pamela. I felt the same way. Tired but looking anywhere for a way out.

Pamela Bunn wasn't a cruel woman. I knew that. We were

both a bit like the fly. Trapped in this room, itching to escape. "Surely you've seen these invoices?" she went on, not unkindly. "In your in-box?"

I nodded. And I'd also received a voice mail and had a pointed conversation with Pamela's assistant, John, last week: "We're gonna really be needing that payment soon, okay, Lorrie? If you could call your aunt? Lorrie?"

I *had* called Aunt Gigi, a few times, even before John had tracked me down, to tell her to please make the transfer or send the check or do whatever she had to do to pay up. She'd said she would take care of it.

She always said she'd take care of things.

"My aunt isn't the most together person," I said.

Pamela Bunn stopped me with a raised hand. "You need to speak with her today. Either she arranges for the transfer of funds, or she arranges for your travel home. There's a flight today out of Raleigh at six that would get into New York by half past seven," she said.

Oh God. This was really happening.

"I can recommend a service to transport Orion, which shouldn't be more than a few hundred dollars," Pamela continued. "He could be home with you in two days—three, max, if it comes to that. I think this is the best plan."

All I could do was nod. It was too shocking for us both, in a way. I was going to be kicked out of Woodscape, and Pamela had to do the kicking. We stared at each other, almost unable to breathe through our intense mutual discomfort. But now it was done. There was nothing to say.

I said something anyway. "You're making a big mistake," I told her as I scraped back my chair and stood.

"I am terribly sorry, Lorrie," she answered. "I feel awful about this, truly."

But did she, really? Mostly, she looked relieved as she sat back and folded her arms across her chest.

I left Whelan Hall and headed straight to the dorms. Back in my room I made one last-ditch call to Aunt Gigi, which, of course, went unanswered. And so I began to stuff clothes into my suitcase: underwear, socks, shirts, jodhpurs. I pulled my jeans out of the bottom drawer and dug through the pockets for spare bills. I also had a few dollars on my dresser, and I was pretty sure I'd stuck the change from lunch on Monday in the pocket of my barn jacket.

As soon as I finished packing, I'd call Lennox. My best friend would put my flight on her parents' credit card and pick me up from the airport. And she wouldn't even ask why, because she'd already know.

My final financial tally was twenty-eight dollars, in fives and ones. At that moment, it was all the money I had access to in the world. I folded eight ones into my wallet. The rest I slipped into an envelope and left on Beth-Ann's bed.

Woodscape could go ahead and toss me, but I was still a girl who honored her bets. Even if I was no longer a girl who could afford to place them.

2

ONE FALSE MOVE

LENNOX PICKED ME UP HERSELF IN A CAR I'D HEARD about but never seen, a silver Audi with a tan interior that still had the new-car smell to it. It had been an early summer birthday present from her moms.

Lennox's moms, Allyson and Meeghan, were partners in life and in business, they always said. They'd founded an architecture firm together after graduate school and set up a home office on the Idlewild estate that had been in Allyson's family for two generations. When they decided to start a family, Lennox and her sister, Harper, were carried by Meeghan, using sperm from Allyson's brother, Craig. "My uncle who is also my dad," Lennox sometimes joked. "Just your average American family." Lennox had Meeghan's brown skin, stirred a shade lighter, with Allyson's (and Craig's) angular face and catlike eyes.

Lennox and I had met the first day of Pony Club at Oceanfront Equestrian Center. We were six years old, and neither one of us had ever been on a horse. But somehow Lennox already had the whole place figured out, and she grabbed my hand to show me the peephole in the tack room. In exchange, I gave her a plastic Pegasus key chain. That same summer, we tied for the Marmalade Junior Cup. We'd been best friends ever since, and as we exited the Long Island Expressway, I could feel her restlessness with everything she wanted to ask me. She paused longer than she needed to at the first stop sign, turning to give me a look.

"You're not ready to talk," she said. An observation. Not an inquiry.

"Not yet."

The morning's memories were too fresh—Pamela's sad eyes, the walk to John's truck, head-down like a criminal being led to her cell, the judging stares of the other girls as I'd climbed into the van to the airport.

"That's all right," Lennox told me. "In the meantime . . . maybe you'll come out to Oceanfront tomorrow? Claire has jumps school, and I told her I'd watch for moral support."

"I don't know if I'm ready to see Claire just yet," I said.

Claire Glidewell had started out in Pony Club with Lennox and me, and she never missed an opportunity to ask me about the state of my house. "How did you let it get so dirty?" or, "Why don't you clean it up yourself?" Meanwhile, I was certain that Claire Glidewell herself had never so much as made her own bed. Lennox always said she didn't think Claire meant any harm by her questions. But if you asked me, Claire had a little bit of the Beth-Ann Bracelee Superiority Complex in her.

"Sorry," I told Lennox.

"That's okay," she said. "What if we meet for lunch after? Just you and me. With ice cream."

With ice cream meant: long talk. Lennox and I had had a lot of those over the years. Her goal was to be a political journalist and expose all, but when it came to my life, she guarded my secrets like Fort Knox.

"Mmm," I said. "With ice cream."

"Okay, cool," she said. "In the meantime, want a Twizzler or five?" She produced a fresh pack from her purse. Lennox was the kind of person who always had snacks on her. If ever I were asked to make a list of my favorite things about her, it would be quite long, and that trait would be right at the top.

I took the pack from her and ripped it open. Lennox pressed the gas and a few minutes later made a left off Route 77 onto Richmond Hill Road. Now we were officially in Idlewild.

In the old days Idlewild had been a farming and whaling community, with wide open fields and sunsets over the ocean in all shades of pink. But then a group of investors "discovered" the area and bought out miles of beachfront property. A central village popped up between the bay and the ocean. As the town grew, more well-known (and expensive) retailers moved in. There's an ordinance in place to keep up appearances that Idlewild is still just a small beach town—storefronts have to be red brick with celadon shutters, and no retail building can be over three stories, so as to preserve the views. But the shops on Main Street are all high-end boutiques. We have a Tiffany & Co., a Chanel, and an Armani. You have to turn onto the side streets to find anything practical, like a supermarket or a drugstore. And then you'll never bump into an actual Idlewild resident in them; Idlewilders send their housekeepers and personal assistants out to buy things like orange juice and tampons.

If you walk west of town, you'll hit the bay, and if you walk east, you'll hit the ocean. Everyone who's anyone belongs to the Crescent Beach Club on the ocean side. There are massive homes sporting their own golf courses and helicopter pads and pathways to private beaches. It's not exactly a lemonade-stand and trick-or-treating kind of community. More a community of breathtaking ocean views and bragging rights.

Lennox made another left onto Break Run Road, the most exclusive address in Idlewild and the gateway to my own family's saga.

My grandfather had made his fortune building suburban communities. The kind where all the houses look the same, save for the color of the front door and the shutters. But my grandfather couldn't abide living in one of those cookie-cutter homes. So he designed a one-of-a-kind waterfront estate for his family. Edgewater was set on five acres, with stone walls imported from Italy and a rose garden befitting a castle, which overlooked the Atlantic. When my grandparents died a couple decades ago, the house was left to their two daughters— my mother and Aunt Gigi. Today it remained an impressive property.

From a distance, that is.

"Can we stop at the Point?" I asked Lennox.

The Point is what we called the outcrop of cliff that made a lookout over the ocean, lapping fiercely at the jagged rocks a hundred feet below. If you were intrepid enough to climb over the guardrail, there was just about enough room for two lean picnickers sharing a blanket and a basket.

Lennox obliged and pulled over. As I looked toward the horizon, the water was like a pane of glass, clear and still. But that wasn't the view I was interested in; it was the view of Edgewater I wanted.

I'm sure there are people who like to look at their homes up close, where they can see the things that make them theirs: a last name stenciled on a mailbox, a welcome mat at the front door, pansies in the window boxes. But the Point was the only place from which I liked to look at my home: from a distance, where things were blurry and not at all shameful. I stared out at it now—gray clapboard stretching three stories high. It was wider than it was tall, part of the row of mansions that ran along Break Run. One was owned by Franklin Copeland, the legendary senior senator from New York, another by the actress Miranda Landis, who'd just nabbed her second Academy Award. And then there were those homes that belonged to your run-of-the-mill hedge-fund billionaires. Families who had it all. Families to be envied.

Once upon a time the Hollander family had been one of those families. Now I would trade mine in for any of the others, and the knowledge of that caught in my throat.

"Check that out." Lennox had pushed her sunglasses up into her mass of dark curls, and she peered forward, squinting over the wheel. "Someone's out there, climbing up the rocks."

"Whoa." I eyed the jagged shore break below and shivered. "One false move and he's shark-bait."

We waited until he had gained solid footing, whoever he

was—it was too hard to tell from that distance. He stood there, still dangerously close to the edge of the cliff, facing the ocean as his T-shirt whipped against his body in the sea breeze.

"Ready to go?" Lennox asked.

"Yeah," I said. I turned to keep watching as Lennox pulled away, and kept my eyes on the boy until the moment the road curved and he disappeared out of sight. "I wonder who that was."

"I can't think of any freaks offhand except Brian."

The mention of Susannah's boyfriend made my skin crawl. A user and a loser who, nonetheless, had my sister enthralled. His dad was a local fisherman who supplemented his income working shifts at the Route 8 junction Exxon–Dunkin' Donuts kiosk. But as far as I could tell, Brian himself didn't do anything besides figure out where to cadge a few bucks so he could score his next dime bag. Sometime last year he'd moved out of his parents' apartment by the railroad tracks and become a de facto boarder at our house. I'm sure he thought he'd moved up in the world, flawed as our home may have been.

But Brian was tall, his limbs connecting at awkward angles, like a crane. This guy, whoever he was, looked strong and firm. "No, it's definitely not Brian," I said. "I don't think it's anyone we know."

Lennox wound the car around with the road, and we lapsed into silence. I had that sense of dread I experienced whenever I drew closer to my family's property. We twisted up the driveway, and the knot in my stomach became a fist. I always, always wanted it to be different. And it never, ever was.

Up close, Edgewater was a shocking vision of neglect. A wreck of its former greatness. It didn't help that it was sandwiched between two perfectly manicured estates. On the left, the Gould family's "Cloud House" was a modern structure, all sharp angles and glass, with a sprawling, military-cut lawn. On the right stood the Deightons' stately mansion, "the Ramble," one of the very first homes built in Idlewild. Over the years, Richard Deighton had made regular calls to Idlewild's chief of police, Tim Blum, to report the "nuisance" of Edgewater. But, thankfully for us, being an eyesore did not rise to the kind of thing the police department could do anything about. Finally, two years ago, Richard Deighton had solved the problem himself by having a hedgerow planted. Now it was nearly two feet taller than when it'd been put in. Tall enough to block us out. I couldn't say I blamed him.

Lennox steered the Audi up the final stretch to the house. We were close enough to see that it wasn't actually meant to be gray. It had once been white, but its paint was now soiled and falling off in strips, as if Edgewater was being peeled like a banana. I made myself look up, past the row of broken dormer windows on the third floor, to the heather-colored sky above. The sunset was breathtaking, per usual. You could always count on nature.

Lennox cut the engine. "I'm going to run in and get your money first," I told her. "Wait here, okay?"

"Of course," she said. "I know the drill."

She knew the drill, that I didn't let anyone—not even her—into my house. I opened the car door, and the ubiquitous roar of the ocean sounded off in the distance. Being in Idlewild was like having a conch shell permanently pressed against your ear. It practically made me seasick.

I ran up the porch steps and took one last deep breath of outside air. Then I pushed open the front door. The foyer was dark—darker than it was outside. The bulbs in the chandelier had long ago burned out, so now the fixture hung down uselessly from two stories above, with dust dangling from the prisms like tinsel. In the center of the room was a fountain, dried up for years, and, beyond that, a winding staircase once famous for its mahogany banister and custom-carved pineapple newels. Back in the day, it had actually been pictured in *Architectural Digest*.

Trying to keep the house clean on my own was a losing battle. We had more creatures living in Edgewater than I could possibly keep count of. Despite Claire Glidewell's suggestion to just clean it myself, there was simply no way for one person to keep up with such a massive estate. I'd called in a housekeeper once, but as soon as she stepped inside, one of the cats dropped a decapitated mouse at her feet. She screamed and ran straight back out. That was five years ago. Now the house was even more far gone.

I switched on a floor lamp and crossed the room to the squat Victorian dresser at the base of the stairs. Susannah and I always called the top drawer the Money Drawer, because it was where Gigi stashed the cash she withdrew from the bank. At times the drawer was practically bursting with twenties and fifties and sometimes hundreds. Other times the offerings were a bit leaner. Still, you could count on there being *something*—a couple hundred bucks at least—and Susannah and I were allowed to dip in, no questions asked. Usually I took only what I needed, but this time, I decided, I'd take whatever was in there—all of it. I'd give Lennox the cash for the plane ticket, and if I had enough left over, I'd pay my way back into Woodscape. I could spend the summer there with Orion, after all, and I'd play off my abrupt departure to the other girls as if it had all been a misunderstanding—*Can you believe it? Pamela Bunn is lucky I don't get her fired.*

I yanked open the Money Drawer and rooted around. But all I found was . . . nothing. Not so much as a lone dollar bill. My throat burned with the need to gulp fresh air. I ran back outside and hurried across to Lennox, careful to avoid the plank on the porch that had partially rotted through. I held my hands up to her to signify that they were empty. "I'm sorry," I told her through the car window. "I can't believe this."

"It's all right. Really."

"I can't believe I'm back here," I said.

"I know," she said. "But I have an idea."

"What's that?"

"So you're home, and you don't want to be home, and that blows. But what if you just think of it as starting senior year early? We have a couple extra months together that we didn't think we'd have. We'll make it really good, starting now."

We had talked about that—making senior year the best ever, packing in as many memories as we possibly could before we were off, most likely to separate colleges.

"We can head to town and grab a bite," she went on. "How about a lobster roll on the boardwalk? There are a lot of cute guys in town this summer."

"You know I have no interest in meeting anyone," I said.

"I'm talking people-watching," she said. "Not that there's anything wrong with meeting anyone."

"I don't want a boyfriend." With my house, with my family, it would be too complicated.

"You will," she assured me with the wisdom of an older person who has seen much more. "When you meet the right person."

"You don't have a boyfriend," I reminded her.

"That's because Nathan and I just broke up," she said.

"Well, apparently there are a lot of cute guys in town this summer," I told her.

"All right, point taken. So how about just us and no ulterior motives? It's not like Twizzlers are enough of a dinner. We'll get lobster rolls and waffle fries, and we'll split the brownie sundae. What do you say?"

I shook my head. "Sorry, not tonight," I said. "I have to get this over with. Can you pop the trunk?"

"Done."

"Thanks, Len. I mean, for everything."

"I'm here whenever, Lorrie. A phone call away."

"I know," I told her. "We'll start senior year tomorrow. I promise."

I waited until Lennox's car was out of sight before I forced myself to face the house, to really look at it. In just three weeks it seemed to have fallen into even greater disrepair. Storm-fallen branches crisscrossed the porch, just as they had the driveway, like the start of a game of pick-up sticks. The porch swing hung at an angle, the rope so frayed, it had finally snapped on one side. I dragged my duffel up the steps. It was no use holding my breath this time, and as I pushed the door open, I was met by the trademark smell of Edgewater, something between cat urine and sour milk. It was almost a physical thing that moved through the rooms, up your nose, and into the little crevices of your closed mouth.

I headed back to the dresser by the stairs and rummaged through the rest of the drawers, just to make sure I hadn't missed anything. An enormous Maine coon cat—either Abeline or Carolina; I didn't know and didn't care—squatted on the second step of the staircase to relieve herself. Oh, good: This pee stain would match all the other pee stains on the carpet runner. And if you looked carefully where the carpet had worn thin, you could spy vegetation growing through the floorboards—mushrooms or mold. In middle-school science class, we'd read about how long it would take nature to invade the spaces we'd worked so hard to keep clean, should humans ever cease to exist. Our house could be a case study in that concept. Not exactly *Architectural Digest* material any longer.

From around the corner came a noise I couldn't quite make out, but someone was in there, in the kitchen. Once, I'd heard a kitchen described as the heartbeat of a house, the place where everyone gathered for sustenance and restoration. Ours was more where things went to die.

It was time to find my aunt, and that's where I'd start.

3
HOME SWEET HOME

GIGI WASN'T IN THE KITCHEN, BUT SUSANNAH WAS, bent over a cardboard box on the table. I didn't need to peer inside to know that something frail and sickly was contained within. Instead, I observed my sister, who remained oblivious to me, to the smell—possibly even worse in the kitchen—and to the harsh static of the radio on the counter. Her thick strawberry-blond hair was in its customary braid down her back, her checked dress, while "new" to my eyes, was likely some discard she'd found at a tag sale. Her feet were, as usual, bare and caked with dirt. When we were young, Gigi had called Susannah the "child of light" because of her hair, not to mention her sunny personality. Which I supposed made me the child of darkness.

I cleared my throat, loudly.

"Lorrie!" Susannah said, pivoting to face me, blocking the

box with her body. "What are you doing here? I thought you'd be gone all summer."

"That *was* the plan," I said.

"What happened?"

"They kicked me out," I said.

"You're kidding."

"I'm not," I told her. "Apparently there's a policy against staying at Woodscape for free. Where's Gigi?"

Susannah lowered her eyes. "BP," she said quietly.

That was code we'd come up with when we were kids, for Gigi's Blue Periods.

Some days, Gigi would wake early, push the curtains in our bedrooms aside, and shout out a greeting to the morning sun. She'd coax the deer on the lawn close to the porch with table scraps and get them to eat off the palm of her hand. She held dance parties in the middle of the night when we couldn't sleep.

But then came the BP, seemingly without warning. It generally lasted a day or two, maybe three. The longest one went on for nine days. I was in sixth grade, Susannah was in fourth, and we'd had to stay home from school the whole time while Gigi lay in her room, blackout curtains drawn, sometimes sleeping, sometimes weeping. If Susannah or I went in to ask her for anything—food for us, milk for the cats—she'd groan and cover her ears, as if the sound of our voices pained her. By the time she'd snapped out of it, we were down to the crumbs in a box of Wheat Thins and a quarter of a block of cheese.

There'd be no confrontation until Gigi was out of BP, no matter how riled up and ready I was.

"How convenient for her," I said. "How long so far?"

"I think this is the third day," Susannah said. "Third or fourth. She'll come out of it soon, like she always does. Don't worry."

"I wasn't," I said. "So, what's your excuse?"

"My excuse?"

"Yeah, I only sent you about two dozen text messages in the last few hours to clue you in to the Woodscape stuff, and I've sent you even more going back the last couple weeks."

"Sorry," Susannah said lightly. "My cell phone's been acting wonky. I stuck it in a bowl of rice, because Brian says that cures phones, but it's still not working. He'll fix it soon, I'm sure."

"He really is a jack-of-no-trades, isn't he? Has that guy ever done one thing he promised?"

"Be nice," Susannah said. "That's my boyfriend you're talking about. He'll probably be your brother-in-law someday. The father of your nieces and nephews."

I couldn't think of anything more revolting. "Where is this prince right now?" Not that I wanted to see him. More so I could avoid him.

"At a poker game or something."

"Is that why the Money Drawer is empty?" I asked.

"No!" she said a little too quickly. "Brian would never do that."

"Never steal?" I'd seen him come home with random little gifts for Susannah—nothing she'd asked for or even wanted, but things that were easy enough to swipe off a store shelf and shove into a backpack: lipsticks in various unattractive shades, a tiny stuffed dog, fuzzy socks, a pack of highlighters. "Yeah, right."

Susannah shook her head. "He wouldn't," she insisted. "Besides, he doesn't know about the drawer."

"Really?"

"Really. I swear. I told you I wouldn't tell, and I didn't, but you . . . you don't know as much about him as you think you do, Lorrie. He's not a bad person, and he's important to me."

"I know he is." That was what made it even worse. "You deserve so much more, Susie. Someone who is smart and ambitious, and who isn't using you for the benefit of having a boardinghouse to crash at."

Susannah ignored the last bit. "I guess Aunt Gigi just hasn't had time to go to the bank these last few days to make the transfer," she said. "That's all. I'm sure it's no big thing. She'll go when it passes."

The BP, she meant.

"God," I said. "I can barely hear myself think with all this noise."

"What noise?"

"You're kidding me, right?" I stepped up to the counter and snapped off the radio. Then, for emphasis, I pulled the plug from the wall. "Now, that oughta do it."

But it didn't do it. The stack of dishes in the sink overflowed onto the counter, competing for space with at least two weeks' worth of *New York Posts*. We were surrounded by so much stuff that was old and broken and just waiting to be thrown away. I felt the burning need to deal with it all *right that minute*. I grabbed one of the paper bags on the windowsill and moved toward the refrigerator, a coffin of mildew and decay.

"Here we go," Susannah murmured.

I threw her a look and got on with it. Inside the fridge were the usual suspects: green-gold hunk of cheese, congealed carton of yogurt, milk well past the sell-by date and gone chunky, leaden-gray bar of something in a baggie, rotting head of lettuce, an onion coated in fizzy white mold, countless opened cans of soda long gone flat. My hands were like robot arms, picking and tossing.

"Aunt Gigi will be upset you trashed her chopped liver."

"Was that what that was? Tell her I'm saving her from E. coli."

Susannah shrugged. "Tell her yourself."

I went for the freezer, a fun house of mystery meats wrapped in foil, and I pulled back the wrapping on one, uncovering something fleshy, pink, and unidentifiable. "I bet you can't even tell me what this is," I said.

"That's monkfish, from Brian's dad," Susannah told me. "It's only a couple weeks old."

I put it back, picked up another, and peeled the foil back. "Holy shit," I said as the package slipped from my hands to the floor.

"Oh, my birdies!" Susannah put down what looked like an eyedropper and stepped away from the box at the table. "I found them on a nature walk."

Gigi had started taking Susannah on nature walks years ago, and my sister found beauty in every bone, every carcass.

"Poor little red-breasted robins," Susannah went on. She picked the foil package up from the floor and caressed the frozen feathers. "They were dead when I found them, but I couldn't just leave them there, and I couldn't put them in the ground to decompose just yet. Gigi said we could put them in the freezer, just for a little while."

Of course that was what Gigi had said, and of course my sister had gone along with her. They shared a similar temperament. For years I'd been waiting for Susannah to change. Waiting for lightning to strike and—*poof!*—she'd be turned into the person I wanted her to be. One day, surely, she'd wake up and say, "Oh my God, Lorrie, I just realized that you've been completely right about this all along. This is insane. This is *unacceptable*."

She wasn't ever going to, and I knew it, but still I desperately wanted her to. And every time she didn't, it made me unspeakably sad, as if I'd lost yet another essential person.

"Preserving them on ice isn't going to save them, you know," I told my sister. "Once something is dead, it's dead. You and Gigi must be violating some safety code, having dead things in the freezer next to the food we're supposed to eat."

"The monkfish is dead," Susannah pointed out.

"I know you know the difference," I told her.

Susannah resealed the package with the care of a new mother swaddling an infant, put it back in the freezer, and hugged me from behind. "You've been gone for three weeks," she said. "I don't know why you have to be so pissy the minute you come through the door. I'm happy to see you, Lorrie-Lorrie-bo-borrie. Aren't you happy to see me?"

"Yeah, of course." I twisted around and returned her hug. Susannah's hair was tawny and as thick as a mane. A picture of Orion flashed in my head. His registered name was Hunting Achievement. But his nickname came from the great hunter who, according to Greek mythology, Zeus had placed among the stars.

Was Orion being well cared for? I'd forgotten to tell anyone about the baggie of mints tucked at the back of the shelf just outside his stall. He ate them off my palm, a treat at the end of the day. As thanks, he'd lower his muzzle to the top of my head, exhaling into my hair.

"My big duffel's in the front hall," I said, letting go and blinking back the sting in my eyes. "I have to bring it upstairs."

"I'll help you, if you want."

"Yeah, thanks. That'd be great." I tipped my head toward the box on the table that Susannah had left unguarded. "So, what's the deal?"

"Five kittens. They're Pansy's, and the runt's a calico. We should keep her. It's bad luck to let go of a calico." She moved toward the box again. "Look, isn't she cute?"

I peered in on the squirming mass of furry bodies rammed up against Pansy, and then I saw the one in a corner—a little smaller than all the others. Pansy stared at me through dazed yellow eyes.

"Poor little runt, she's not thriving," Susannah went on, "and she hasn't attached to Pansy yet. But I think she'll come around." She was speaking to me, but she was looking at the kitten and talking in her baby voice, a voice meant to soothe. Broken things were so easy for my sister to love.

"That's great, Susannah," I said. "Now come give me a hand."

We lugged my bag, as large as a man's body and nearly as heavy, up to my room. It had once been Mom's childhood room, but I'd long ago removed all traces of her. Hard enough to have a mother who'd left voluntarily; I didn't want to look around and be reminded of that. So Mom's watercolors and Limoges figurines, her old schoolbooks and poetry collection, were all boxed up and stuffed in the attic. I liked my room to be clutter-free anyway. As I entered it now, it appeared unchanged in my absence. Clean and sparse. No piles, no knickknacks. Even my horse ribbons were displayed in a perfect line along the top of the window frame, not a single one crooked or frayed. But they were looking a little dust-coated. I knew I wouldn't fall asleep until I'd wiped them clean.

"Aren't you coming back down?" Susannah hung in the doorway, picking her cuticles. "We could name the kittens."

"Name them before you take them to the shelter, you mean?"

"Sure." Though we both knew it was a lie. Susannah never delivered to shelters, only retrieved from them. She shopped at animal-rescue centers the way old ladies prowled department stores.

I shook my head. "Sorry," I said. "I'm not really in the mood. All I can think about is my showdown with Gigi. This whole thing seems like some kind of brutal mind game to force me to come home. Or maybe she's just lost her mind for good this time."

"Shh, lower your voice," Susannah warned, even though Gigi's room was at the other end of the house.

"She can't hear us. But she's such a shitty guardian or executor, or whatever she wants to call herself, that she can't be bothered to make a simple payment. What do I care if she *does* hear us?"

It wasn't lost on me that I was acting a bit like Beth-Ann Bracelee. But I didn't care.

"I told her a bunch of times that you needed the money," Susannah said, her own voice hushed, just in case. "The last time I said it, she just started crying. It was really sad." I rolled my eyes. "No, really, Lorrie. It was. Did you ever think that maybe she needed you at home?"

"Whatever. You could've at least clued me in to her melt-down."

"I just figured it had all worked out."

"You knew she hadn't gone to the bank to replenish the Money Drawer. In what world do you think that means things are 'all worked out'?"

"What I know is, you don't want to be home, and you're taking it out on me. I'm going to go downstairs and take care of my babies."

"Kittens. Not babies. You didn't give birth to them. But that's not . . . Fine." My last word was spoken to an empty space, as Susannah had already jumped away in her usual quick-silver fashion. She was never the girl who would duke it out, but rather was always hiding around a corner, under the table, or, most often, up in a tree. One hard-flung word was all it took. I might not see her again for a day.

I'd been harsh, but I'd been right. My brain was sizzling with anger at both my aunt's uselessness and my sister's indifference. And right now the most important thing for me was to get myself settled, physically and emotionally, in the safe space of my own room. My only refuge in this sorry excuse for Home Sweet Home.

4

LET ME HELP

I WOKE UP WITH RENEWED ENERGY. LIFE SOMEHOW feels easier to manage in the morning than it does at night. Even if your problems are the same old clothes, you can put them on fresh and feel new possibilities.

So here it was: I had two months before I was due back at Hillyer, and I had a plan. I'd go along with what Gigi apparently wanted and stay at Edgewater for the summer. I would bring back Orion and board him at Oceanfront. I didn't think Orion would mind; for my horse and me, home was wherever we were together. Meanwhile I'd cozy up to Gigi, make her really comfortable, and help her realize how much easier things could be if I were in charge. I'd get her to sign over the rights to my trust, and I'd pay everything that needed to be paid. I'd make sure Susannah was taken care of—bonus if I could manage to extricate her from Brian while I was at it. And then I'd pack up my stuff and head back to Hillyer for senior year, secure in the knowledge that nothing like Woodscape would ever happen again.

Of course, I wasn't yet eighteen, and I'd probably have to petition to be an emancipated minor first, like those child actors. But if judges were willing to declare boozing, partying Hollywood teens free from their parents and in control of their own money, then certainly I would meet the requirements.

I climbed out of bed to unpack. We'd just had our white-glove laundry service at Woodscape, so nearly everything I'd brought home was clean and pressed. I settled the stacks neatly in my dresser drawers and headed into the bathroom. I swept open the shower curtain to discover a dead silverfish, belly-up, and one of the cats had apparently used the tub as a litter box. There were four squares of toilet paper left on the roll and no spare rolls in the cabinet under the sink.

Just when you think you have it all figured out, you're out of toilet paper, I thought to myself.

But a roll of toilet paper could be replaced—in fact, I'd buy enough to keep the whole house stocked for the rest of the summer. A little gesture to show Gigi just how on top of things I was.

With the last four squares of tissue I picked up what the cat had left behind and dropped the mess into the toilet, then I turned on the shower and watched the silverfish swirl down the drain before stepping in myself. A few minutes later I was washed up and dressed for the day, in a white shirt with an eyelet collar and a denim skirt. Clean and casual—perfect for a little quality time with my aunt and lunch afterward with Lennox.

I stuck my cell phone into one pocket and my entire eight-dollar fortune into the other. In the hall outside my bedroom, I stepped over a few cats on my way to the staircase. Gigi's door was still closed. But even if the BP was over and forgotten, she'd still be fast asleep. On a good day she was rarely up before most people were thinking about their lunch plans.

But that was fine. Better than fine, even: It was ideal. I'd go over to Idlewild Fidelity and find out everything I needed to know about the trust—specifically, what I needed to do to get my hands on it—and I'd be armed with information by the time I saw Gigi.

According to my watch, it was just after nine o'clock, which meant the bank was open. Operation: I'm in Charge of My Own Goddamn Trust could officially begin. I jogged down the stairs and practically skipped into the kitchen, then rooted through the piles of flotsam and jetsam on the counter to find the keys to Gigi's black hearse of a Mercedes. And I was off.

IT WOULD'VE BEEN TOO MUCH TO EXPECT A FULL tank of gas—or any gas at all, for that matter. When I turned the key in the ignition, the needle on the gauge lifted to just above empty, and the fuel-indicator light turned red. I was going to have to stop at the gas station before I went anywhere else, and I only had eight dollars, which wasn't going to buy me very much. But just as long as it got me to the bank, I didn't care.

I pulled up at the Exxon–Dunkin' Donuts kiosk self-service pump, behind a vintage Porsche, black with the top down to reveal a perfectly restored charcoal-gray interior. You have to prepay at the register, and when I walked in, there was Brian

Beecher's dad. The name TRAVIS was stitched into his front pocket. "You're, ah . . ." he said, his voice trailing. "Ah . . ."

"Lorrie," I supplied. "Susannah's sister."

"That's right. My wife said Brian came by the other day and cleaned us out of fish patties to bring back to your place. I hope you enjoyed them."

"I just got home last night," I said. "I haven't had a chance to taste them yet."

"Better act fast before Brian inhales them," he said. "My wife says the season seems shorter every year on account of his appetite."

"But the season's not over yet, right?"

"Things are slowing down. But I'll be back on the boat tomorrow."

I regarded Travis Beecher. He was an older version of his son, tall and bony, just balder and more weathered. Travis Beecher hadn't come into the world with an enormous inheritance. He worked hard, he worked *two* jobs, and maybe that would never get him an estate on Break Run Road with an ocean view, but he kept at it, because that was what needed to be done. It made me admire him, and I wondered: Shouldn't the apple not fall so far from the tree? "Do you ever take Brian out on the boat with you?" I asked.

"I did when he was a kid. It's not really his thing."

"What is his thing?"

"I'd say it's your sister."

Gross.

"It's good for him to stay at your place—he gets more room, and we get more room. A win-win."

This conversation was making my stomach turn. "So, I'm at pump number four," I said. I pulled the bills out of my pocket and counted them again, as if by magic they might have multiplied, which, of course, they hadn't. "Can I put in eight dollars of regular, please?"

Travis Beecher glanced out the window at my car. "You sure that's all you want for that gas-guzzler?"

"It's all I have on me right now," I said. "And, actually, can you make it seven, and I'll take a can of Coke, too?"

I hadn't had so much as a sip of water before I'd left the house; in fact, I hadn't had anything to drink since I'd left Woodscape. The realization made me suddenly, incredibly parched, as if all the spit had been sucked from my mouth. Soda isn't supposed to quench your thirst, but right then it was all I wanted.

"Coke is a buck-fifty," he told me.

Subtract that from eight dollars, and I'd barely have enough left for two gallons.

"Actually, would you mind letting me fill it with eight dollars of gas?" I asked. "I'm headed to the bank now, so if you can just give me the soda on credit, I'll come straight back with cash when I'm done. I promise."

I was asking for a loan of a dollar and fifty cents, which was just about the most pathetic thing I'd ever done.

Even more pathetic—Travis Beecher turned me down.

"Sorry," he said. "We don't sell things on credit."

I felt a rush of anger, and I wanted to shout: *You must be kidding me! Your son is living at my house, rent-free, and probably even raiding our cash supply! You should be handing me a case of Cokes— and throwing in bags of Doritos!* Instead, my mouth set straight, I pushed the eight dollars toward him. Keep calm, and game on. I'd be an actor to everyone this summer. "All for gas?" he asked.

"Yes," I said.

"If you come back later with more money, you can buy the soda then," he offered.

I didn't bother to reply. From behind me came a rustle, then someone's voice: "Here, let me help."

I turned around, and there, in the flesh, was Charlie Copeland. As in Charlie *Copeland*. The son of Senator Franklin Copeland, and the grandson and great-grandson of a couple former presidents.

If America had a royal family, the Copelands were it. Though lots of people said the line of succession would stop with Charlie. Like the other members of his family, Charlie often had his picture show up in the papers, but not for the same reasons. Charlie was usually snapped while out partying, with an arm slung around Shelby Rhodes, his rock-star girlfriend. A few months ago he'd been arrested for picking a fight with a photographer who'd had the temerity to take a picture of him and Shelby making out in a hotel lobby, when Charlie was supposed to be in lockdown in his dorm at Grosvenor-Baldwin Academy for some other school-rule infraction. GBA was quite possibly the most exclusive boarding school in the country. It basically had a one-hundred-percent Ivy League matriculation record for graduating seniors. Charlie was summarily kicked out, even though generations of Copelands had attended the school. Half of its buildings were built on the Copeland dime and named after the family. I remembered talking to Lennox about it at the time, as if the trials and tribulations of the Copelands were things that actually affected us. "Who would kick out a Copeland?" she'd said, incredulous. The incident was, according to the gossip columns, a major blow to the entire clan.

Now Charlie was just standing there in the Exxon–Dunkin' Donuts kiosk, like anyone, with a cup of coffee in his hand. I hadn't known that anyone else was there. But of course someone was; I'd pulled up behind another car, a Porsche.

Charlie Copeland *would* drive a Porsche.

As far as I knew, the Copelands rarely used their Idlewild home. Though even when they weren't there, it was still well kept and fully staffed. Mrs. Copeland's hairdresser spent at least a few weeks there every year. That was according to Lennox, whose moms had been called in to submit blueprints for a new yoga studio in one of the guest cottages while we were away at school. (They didn't get the job.)

I'd only ever seen Charlie in person once before, back when he was a chubby, towheaded five-year-old and the Copelands used the estate for themselves, not just for guests. I'd been five then myself, too young to know who the Copelands even were. Instead, I'd been focused on the fact that Gigi was delivering a cake to a party, and it was my job to hold it steady in my lap. Charlie and I had both grown up a lot since then. He had slimmed down, and his chest and shoulders had filled out. I'd never seen anyone wear a plain gray T-shirt quite so well. He had khaki shorts, cinched with a rope belt. His hair was fresh-from-the-shower wet and combed back from his forehead. It looked dark brown, but I knew from all the pictures in magazines that it was actually lighter, sandy-colored. In the mug shot seen 'round the world, it was long and hung partly in front of his face.

"So, could I?" he asked me.

At that moment I realized my mouth was a gaping O. I closed it, but then I opened it again to speak. "Could you what?"

"Help you out? It'd be no problem." He smiled, eyes crinkling. In his free hand he held up a brown leather wallet.

Suddenly it was like Woodscape all over again, having a witness to my humiliation. I deeply regretted being all principled and making good on my bet to Beth-Ann. If I had that extra twenty bucks right now . . .

"So," he said to Travis Beecher, who seemed unruffled by Charlie Copeland's presence. Perhaps he didn't know who Charlie was. "I'm at pump three, and I'm going to fill up with premium unleaded. And I have the coffee, and I'll take a soda, too." He turned back to me. "You said a Coke, right?"

"Yes, I said a Coke, but—"

"And do you need to fill up?"

"Don't worry about what I need," I told him. "I can take care of it."

"I'm sorry," he said. "I didn't mean to imply that you couldn't. I was just aiming for Mr. Nice Guy." He paused for a beat. "I guess I missed the mark."

I took a deep breath. "No, I'm sorry. You caught me on a bad day."

"How about this—we'll make it a loan. I'll front you the money now, and you can pay me back at my party tomorrow night. It's actually my parents' party, so there'll be loads of old men with trophy wives talking about the stock market and their golf handicaps. You can't tell me you're willing to turn all that down."

Wait, I just told off Charlie Copeland, and now he was inviting me to a party—a party his parents would be hosting?

"Hold this, please." He thrust his coffee at me and opened his wallet to retrieve the bills. When he turned back to me, man, his jaw was square. I felt like I was in a trance, watching him.

"What?" Charlie asked.

"Nothing," I said, blinking fast.

He rattled off the address of the Compound—that was the name of his family's estate, a smattering of smaller houses like planets orbiting around one enormous, sprawling, stone building known as the Main—as if it were possible I wouldn't have known it. Even if I'd never been there, I would've known it. Everyone did.

"So, you'll come? Eight o'clock, tomorrow night. It's the Fourth of July, you know."

I nodded. "And thanks for the loan," I said finally, sheepishly. "I'm Lorrie."

"You're welcome, Lorrie. I'm Charlie." Like he had to tell me his name. "I'll see you then."

5

IT'S REALLY NOT THAT SIMPLE

THOUGHTS OF CHARLIE COPELAND PERSISTED IN spite of the task at hand. I tried not to dwell on lingering impressions of his smile, his crinkly eyes, the perfect break of his broad shoulders . . .

Concentrate, Lorrie, I admonished myself silently. *Think about your money.*

The bulk of the Hollander estate was fairly depleted by the time my grandparents died. Grandpa's communities had long since been divided up and sold off. Even so, Mom and Aunt Gigi had each inherited a wad of money, in addition to joint ownership of the house, which they used on weekends. During the week, my mother worked as exhibits director at a museum in Manhattan. She lived off her salary and invested her inheritance wisely. But of course Gigi was foolish about her share; she'd wanted to be an artist, and she'd invested in a gallery that went belly-up. She'd wanted to act, and she'd spent thousands on lessons of the craft but never earned back a dime. She didn't work a day in her life, and when she ran out of money, she moved into Edgewater full-time and relied on Mom to help keep up with her bills. Further evidence that Mom's trust should now be in my hands, not hers.

When I walked into Idlewild Fidelity, I made a beeline for the customer-service desk at the back, chin up and gaze unfixed so as not to make eye contact with any of the other customers. Idlewild was a small town, and there were a lot of people I wanted to avoid.

"What can I do for you?" the woman behind the counter asked pleasantly.

"Is there a manager I can speak to?"

"Take a seat," she said, waving toward a row of chairs, her voice now a little sharper. I hadn't meant to offend her sense of competency, but I wanted to start at the top of the food chain. "I'll see if anyone's available."

Twenty minutes later I was finally ushered into a small back office by a man whose name tag, JIM TRAYLOR, had me thinking about all the drives out to Idlewild we'd taken from the city in Mom's Volvo, her James Taylor CD the soundtrack to our ride. Our favorite was "How Sweet It Is to Be Loved by You" because Mom would put Susannah's and my names into the lyrics. I had no idea what had happened to that car. Had Mom shipped it across the ocean? Or driven it to the airport and left it there?

Jim Traylor listened as I recited my information—name, date of birth, social security number—and he punched keys on his keyboard as I explained my objective. "I'm not trying to be spiteful or hurt my aunt or anything like that. I just want what's mine, and I'd like to get the ball rolling. So, if you could tell me exactly what needs to be done and how to do it . . ."

"It's really not that simple."

"I know, I know. I'm under eighteen. But aren't there cases where minors can get control of their own money? Is that power of attorney? Is there a form for it?"

"That's not the problem," he said.

"So, what is? Do I need to bring my aunt in? I can probably make that happen within a few days."

Traylor tapped one last tap on his keyboard, then pushed the screen so that I could see it. "Miss Hollander, your checking account, your joint checking account with your sister, and your savings account are all at a negative balance."

The screen was a spreadsheet, each column in the red. My chest tightened in fear.

Years before, Gigi had taken Susannah and me to a meditation class. The teacher taught us to close our eyes and repeat a mantra—a private, nonsense word he gave each of us—to calm down and become Zen. Predictably, Susannah was all into it, and I thought it was hokey and strange. But right then I closed my eyes for a couple beats longer than a blink and said my mantra in my head—*yim, yim*—while Jim Traylor waited for me to respond.

Finally, I did: "This is precisely why I need to have control of the trust," I told him. "Because my aunt is not responsible enough to keep track of bills and bank balances on her own. Once I'm in control, I'll transfer money over, and Susannah and I can get out of the red."

"I suppose that's what I'm trying to explain." Jim Traylor's hands, skimming over his computer keyboard, were pale, as if they'd known only this windowless office, time unending. "There is no trust."

"That's ridiculous," I said. I laughed, and it sounded strange, as if I were making the sound from underwater. "Of course there is."

I'd seen the letter from Mom, explaining it all. She needed her freedom, Mom had written to Susannah and me; in exchange, she was leaving us, her two daughters, all the money her father had given her, now augmented with the interest she'd earned over the years. She'd start fresh in England with Nigel. She'd included a bunch of syrupy, Hallmark-card assurances about what wonderful daughters we were, how she wanted only the best for us. *I love you forever and ever, my lovely Lorrie and my sweet Susannah. Love, Mom.* I had clung to that letter, along with the cards that came on Chanukah, our birthdays, and occasionally on random holidays like Valentine's Day or Halloween. She ended them the way she'd always ended the notes she'd stuck in my kindergarten lunchbox: a stick drawing of her, Susannah, and me. Mom in the middle with her arms around her two girls. "The Three Musketeers," she'd called us. But we weren't a threesome anymore, at least not that one.

As time went by, notes from Mom arrived less and less frequently, and the ones I'd saved seemed to mock all she'd taken away. Up to the attic they went. Out of sight and out of mind.

Jim Traylor's voice broke me from my thoughts. "Is there anything else I can help you with?" he asked.

"But . . ." I began. "But the trust is there. I know it is—at least

I know it *was*. My mother set it up. It was supposed to last us . . . oh, I don't know how long it was supposed to last, but certainly at least until I finished high school."

But sitting there, across from Jim Traylor, I realized how implausible that was. Gigi hadn't been able to make her own trust fund last; how could she have managed ours?

"According to our records, Miss Hollander," he said, "there's no trust. And I have no record of you ever having one."

"You're making a big mistake," I told him.

With that sentence came a horrible sense of déjà vu. I'd said those words before, just about twenty-four hours ago, when I sat in front of Pamela Bunn and her battered desk.

But Pamela hadn't made a mistake, and it was entirely possible that Jim Traylor hadn't, either. The common denominator in all of it was Aunt Gigi. What had she done with our money? And how had she managed to erase all record of its existence?

Was this all just a game to her?

I didn't know. What I knew for sure was this: I had no money to my name, a horse stranded five hundred miles away, and a tank of gas bought on credit from a stranger, and I had to get to the bottom of it.

6

WE REGRET TO INFORM YOU

MY HANDS WERE SHAKING AS I FUMBLED WITH MY cell phone to call Lennox. It took me three tries to press the right buttons, but then instead of ringing, a mechanical voice informed me that my phone bill was past due. It went on to recite a phone number for AT&T. "Press one to be connected now, or call back at your earliest convenience." Digits were recited, but I hung up before the recording was done. The cell-phone issue would have to take a backseat to all the others.

I went straight home to confront Gigi, storming into the house and not even noticing the smell. Maybe because I hadn't bothered to inhale; I just screamed, "Gigi! Gigi!" BP or not, she was going to have to give me some answers. Right now.

"GIGI!"

"Lorrie?" came a call from the kitchen.

Gigi was standing by the counter when I walked in, all

dressed up in a flapper dress, low-waisted, with fringe on the bottom. Behind her, the radio was plugged back in, and I could just make out her favorite oldies station coming in through the static.

"Darling girl!" she exclaimed, and she swooped toward me, arms wide open.

I ducked out of her embrace. "I just came from Idlewild Fidelity. They said all our accounts are in the red."

"Mmm-hmm." A L'Eggo My Eggo waffle popped up in the toaster, and Gigi turned back to grab it with her bare hands. "Ouch, ouch." She dropped it straight onto the counter—no plate.

"What's going on?" I asked.

"How am I supposed to know the ins and outs of how they conduct business at that bank—if they keep accounts in the red or in the green or in the mauve? That's their business."

"According to them, it means we don't have any money."

"It's nothing for you to worry about," she said, bending down to adjust the strap on one of her shoes. "Worrying is pointless. Worrying is negative goal setting."

"Give me a break," I said. Gigi barely lifted her head. "Look at me," I demanded.

When she looked up, she lifted a foot to show off a five-inch heel, as delicate as a Cinderella slipper, crystal-detailed, with a black patent-leather strap. "What do you think?" she asked.

"I don't care about your goddamn shoe," I told her.

"This isn't a shoe," she said. "It's a Louboutin." She drawled the word out as only Gigi could: *Lou-bouuuu-tahhhhn.*

But I knew the brand from its trademark red sole, and I knew that a pair of them cost upward of a thousand dollars.

"I got them for my party," she said.

"What party?"

"My birthday party, of course." She shook her head, as if she couldn't believe I was so dense. "You only turn forty-two once, and I'm planning a big celebration. It'd be a shame to limp around my own party because I didn't have the forethought to break in my new shoes. Though sometimes shoes don't break in no matter how hard you try. I could write a book about it—*When Bad Shoes Happen to Good People.* I have a feeling this strap will be a problem. A design flaw I'd never—"

I cut her off. "Do you even hear yourself when you speak?"

"I'm an excellent designer," Gigi said with a bit of indignation. "I used to design all my own clothes. You were just too young to remember."

"Jim Traylor at Idlewild Fidelity said there isn't a trust at all," I told her. "Design your way out of that."

"The trust isn't at Idlewild Fidelity anymore," Gigi said. "I moved it."

"You *moved* it? Why?"

"It's not good to stay in one place," said the woman who barely left the house anymore.

"So, where is it?"

"Enough of the twenty questions," Gigi said. "What I do with the money is not your concern."

"It's the very definition of my concern," I said. "Susannah's, too. Mom set up the trust for us."

"I had plans of my own, you know. I put everything on hold to raise you girls, and you just keep hitting me up with your demands."

"My demands?"

"Boarding school, a horse," she said.

"That's what Mom's money was for. I'd like to use some of it to at least get my horse home."

My voice cracked at the last bit, but Gigi didn't take notice. "And I was never good enough for you," she went on. "And the house was never clean enough."

It was a choice between screaming and crying, and I picked screaming. "Because the house is filled with junk and filth! How can you stand it?"

I reached out and yanked the radio cord from the wall again, so hard that the radio shook and sent an avalanche of yellow-stained mail onto the floor. A picture flashed in my head: Beth-Ann Bracelee showing up here for a "surprise visit." It was a horrible game I played with myself sometimes, when I imagined people from my outside life coming into my inside one, and I could almost hear myself, shrill in my effort to be lighthearted: *What, you've never seen envelopes stained with cat urine before?*

"Lorrie," Gigi said stubbornly, "you know I like my radio in the mornings."

"It doesn't even work right!" I picked it up and stuffed it into an already stuffed garbage can, pushing it down with the force of all my weight—I'd make it fit. Then I went for the soiled mail on the floor. Three Pottery Barn catalogs—because just one wouldn't be enough. Those catalogs always made me so damn jealous. Sure, Edgewater's rooms had once been grander, but I'd kill to live within those pages, where everything looked so neat and orderly. Beds were made, tables were set, floors were swept clean, and not a shit stain or a hairball in sight. I stuffed them in on top of the radio.

"Don't get rid of things I need," Gigi said.

"One day we'll all be dead, and it'll be someone's job to come in here and clean this place out. I'm just getting a head start."

"Why do you have to be so morbid, Lorrie?" She tapped her waffle, testing the temperature, then picked it up and took a bite.

"Why do you have to be so insane? Why can't you just talk straight and tell me where the money is?"

I was squatting on the floor, sorting and tossing and looking for anything that might offer a clue to where Gigi had moved the trust. Mostly there were just old bills, still sealed. I ripped envelopes open and looked at the due dates.

"These are all late," I told her.

"I'll take care of it," Gigi said flippantly, wiping her hands on a dish towel that had probably never seen the inside of a washing machine.

I ripped open another envelope. "Here's the summer show schedule Woodscape sent out. Guess you won't be needing it now." Into the garbage it went. I reached for the next envelope—thick, cream-colored stock with HILLYER ACADEMY written in the return address corner—and took a deep breath.

Oh God. Hillyer.

When Lennox's older sister, Harper, was headed into ninth grade, the moms had decided she needed a proper preparatory education, one she couldn't get at our local high school. Two years later, naturally, Lennox was all set to join her. I filled out my own forms and sent them in without asking Aunt Gigi's permission. I even forged her signature and told her the application check I'd requested was for an after-school program. She hadn't asked for more details, and I hadn't come clean until I'd been admitted.

For three years Hillyer had been my real home base. This was just about the time of year that the housing administration sent out September dorm assignments. I knew Lennox would be my roommate again, but it'd be nice to see it in writing, along with our building and room number—a tangible reminder that my summer at Edgewater had an expiration date.

My chest filled with icy dread: *Please let this be the dorm assignment.*

The envelope was addressed to Aunt Gigi; since she was my guardian, Hillyer sent all relevant correspondence directly to her. Not that she cared. I slipped a finger under the envelope flap and pulled it upward.

Gigi was chattering away, oblivious: "I'm thinking I should have a theme for my birthday party. I went to a Christmas-in-July party once. Not that I want a used theme. Maybe the theme should just be me, since I'm the birthday girl. Either way—"

Dear Ms. Hollander, We regret to inform you . . .

I swear, my heart stopped frozen in my chest for several beats. My voice—when I could speak—was smaller, more scared than I'd anticipated. "What the hell have you done, Gigi?"

She blinked. "Darling, I know it's old-fashioned, but I do prefer *Aunt* Gigi."

"What kind of aunt are you?" I began softly. But I cut myself off and started again. "I don't know why this is shocking to me—that you managed to find money for those ridiculous shoes but can't be bothered to make a DOWN PAYMENT ON MY TUITION!"

Gigi blinked. "Do you really think these shoes are ridiculous?"

"Goddamn it!" I cried. "I can't believe you're worried about the shoes, of all things. I'm embarrassed to be related to you. That's why I don't call you *Aunt* Gigi. I don't want to remind myself that we're related at all!"

Gigi's shoulders slumped. Even in her towering heels, she suddenly looked very small. "I've been doing my best," she said, and tears spilled over her cheeks, as if she was a child. "It was only me, all this time. This wasn't the plan. This wasn't the plan."

She moved past me, a sobbing comet of gold stars and swishy blue satin. I pulled the car keys from my pocket and slammed outside, gulping air, dying for escape.

7
NO STRINGS ATTACHED

SATURDAY MORNING, I WOKE UP IN THE MIDDLE OF a dream. I was at Oceanfront, and a jumps course had been freshly set up for competition. A trailer pulled into the circular dirt driveway in front of the stables, and I raced out to it, because I knew my horse was in it. Sure enough, Charlie Copeland jumped out of the cab and opened the back to lead Orion down the ramp. But with each step they took, the ramp seemed to grow longer and longer, and I woke up before they could reach me.

I wasn't ready to be awake just yet, and I closed my eyes and tried to slip back into sleep—back to the possibility of reaching my horse and his handler. But it was futile.

I twisted around in bed to face the window. The shade was down, but there was a thin band of early-morning sunlight, pinkish yellow, streaming through the sliver of space between the bottom of the shade and the top of the windowsill. This was my favorite time of day to ride Orion, before most other people in the world had so much as swung their legs out of bed and had a first cup of coffee. My heart ached from missing him, and I hoped he was handling our separation better than I was.

Yes, he was a horse. Just a horse, some people might say, but we'd barely been apart since the afternoon I'd spotted him, four years earlier. Lennox and I had been taking lessons at Oceanfront for years, but we were at the Hampton Classic as spectators, not riders. Orion was standing in the main corral. Chocolate brown, except for the blaze on his nose, a small spot on his neck, and matching snow-white markings on each of his legs, as if he was wearing knee-high stockings. He was three years old and sixteen hands high—almost as tall as he'd be full-grown—but he still had the bony awkwardness of a colt. He reared up, and I watched his trainer stumble back, then step forward and tug on the reins to regain control. Orion came down, nostrils flaring. He whipped his head, and when he did, he looked straight at me, as if he somehow knew who I was. The two of us held each other's gaze for at least five full seconds, until the trainer tugged on the reins again to lead him away, and even then, Orion turned to glance at me once more before he was pulled around the corner to the stables.

In the days that followed I couldn't stop thinking about him. It made me believe maybe there was such a thing as love at first sight, if not between a girl and a boy, then at least between a girl and a horse. I told Aunt Gigi I needed to have him. She made the arrangements, even though my birthday wasn't for two more months.

It's not an exaggeration to say that Orion had finally plugged up the hole that had opened in me when Mom left. I think it was about having something in my life that made me feel worthy. There were times, approaching a jump at twenty miles an hour, my legs tense against Orion's abdomen, when his powerful, muscular body felt like an extension of my own. I knew that horseback riding came with tremendous risks. We'd all heard horrible stories, and that was why we wore the latest helmets and learned how to fall as safely as possible, and even then we knew we were putting our lives into the figurative hands of creatures over which we ultimately had no control. But Orion always got me safely to the other side.

I swung my legs out of bed and got dressed for a morning run. Just as I opened my door, I heard something scampering away and my eye caught the tip of a striped, bushy tail turning at the end of the hall. A raccoon. For all I knew, it was one Susannah had purposely taken in and named.

What, Beth-Ann? You don't have raccoons in your house, too?

Gigi had shut herself in her room after our fight in the kitchen, and her door was still closed. I wondered what my mother was doing at that very moment. Breakfast in Piccadilly Circus, perhaps? Actually, with the time change it was already lunchtime in London. Maybe Mom and Nigel had eaten shepherd's pie in a pub. Or maybe they'd taken the Eurostar train to Paris and were eating croque monsieurs on the banks of the Seine.

Must be nice, a life with no strings attached.

Meanwhile I'd driven to every other bank in town over the past twenty-four hours, inquiring about a trust or accounts for Lorrie and Susannah Hollander. Everywhere I hit had no record of any money in our names. I knew I had to expand my search, but I didn't want to waste the gas on a wild-goose chase. Gigi could've moved our money to any bank on Long Island, or in New York City, or even beyond. The list of possibilities was nearly endless. I felt like one of those old, wild-eyed people on the beach, combing the dunes with a metal detector. I could spend the rest of my life looking for our money. And there was still the possibility that there was nothing left to find at all.

The clock was ticking for me to figure it all out. I'd called Hillyer Academy from Brian's cell phone—that's how desperate I was: I'd asked *Brian* for a favor—and inquired about financial aid for the fall semester. "I'm sorry, but those funds are already committed to other students," Ms. Strafford, the director of admissions, had told me. "And I can't guarantee your spot will be open much longer. We've already reached out to the waiting list."

I'd used Brian's phone for one more call, this one to the North Carolina Equestrian Transport Company, to make arrangements for Orion. "And your credit card number?" the woman on the other end had asked. I faked a call on the other line and hung up. For now, Orion would be staying put.

And that brought up another issue: The longer it took for me to come up with the money to spring Orion from Wood-scape, the higher the bill for his food and board would be.

There were so many bills to keep track of. None of my friends realized what a small miracle it was that each month their parents had the money on hand to pay them. My body felt heavy as I headed downstairs. I didn't even notice the stench of the house anymore. That was the worst part of living at Edgewater: knowing that the smell was still there but that I'd become immune to it.

Brian looked up from the table when I walked into the kitchen. He was wearing his trademark low-slung jeans and a red T-shirt, both so wrinkled that I was sure he'd slept in them. For a second his face reminded me of Susannah's when I'd surprised her the night I'd come back from Woodscape and she'd been bent over a box of new critters she'd brought into the house. A look of *Oh, crap, I've been caught.* But then it was back to his regular, disaffected stoner face. "Wassup, Lorrie?" He picked up a bottle of Corona and took a swig.

"It's a little early in the morning for that, isn't it?"

"Hangover," Brian said. "Best cure is more alcohol."

"Is that so?"

"What bothers you more about this—that I'm drinking before noon, or that it's beer and not something fancy like you private school kids like—gimlets, or Grey Goose vodka, or whatever?" He put down the beer and lifted a delft china teacup to his lips. "Chaser," he explained.

"That's an heirloom. You're not supposed to actually use it."

"The regular glasses are dirty," he said, nodding toward the sink, which was overflowing.

"Doesn't make them disposable," I told him. "Clean them, and you can use them again." I grabbed a glass from the sink, turned the water to hot to rinse it, and wiped it with the bottom of my shirt—no way I'd be using a dish towel—before filling it with water again.

"I *am* cleaning," Brian said. "I'm polishing the silver." He held up one of the heavy Hollander-family dinner forks.

At bedtime, Mom used to tell Susannah and me stories about her parents, the two of us pressed against her like the newborn kittens pressed against Pansy. I liked to curl a lock of Mom's hair around my finger. There was one story about our grandmother and the acquisition of her prized Tiffany sterling set: When they were first married, my grandparents didn't have much money. But Grandma saved up whatever she had left over each week from her secretarial wages and began buying one utensil at a time. After Grandpa made it big in real estate, she was able to quit her job and buy the rest of the set in one fell swoop.

"I noticed they were pretty badly tarnished, and I found some polish under the sink," Brian went on. "The cap was missing, and it was hardened on top, but I scraped off the layer, and there's fresh stuff underneath. See?"

I barely gave it a glance. "Why are you doing this?"

"I told you. I'm cleaning."

I wasn't buying his fake happy-helper story. Brian was up to something. But I knew I might need his cell phone again, so my hard gaze was his only clue that I was on to him. I drank my water, rinsed the glass out again, and shoved it deep into the back of the cabinet. There, that could be my safe glass.

From their box in the corner, Pansy's kittens were mewing softly. The larger cats began to gather, as if out of nowhere, multiplying like gremlins. I knew that meant Susannah was awake and on her way down to feed them. Somehow they were always able to sense her impending presence. Sure enough, she walked in, the little calico cradled in her arms. "Hi, babies, hi, babies," Susannah crooned to the rest of them. "Hey, Bri-Bri French fry."

"Morning, babe," Brian said. Ugh. I hated hearing that word in his voice, especially when it referred to my sister. He rose from his seat and patted Susannah's head as if she herself was a kitten. She leaned back into him for a couple seconds. There was something so intimate in that moment, I had to avert my eyes.

"Good morning, Lorrie-glory," Susannah said.

I turned back toward her and tipped my head toward the kitten in her arms. "Hey," I said. "How's he doing?"

"She," Susannah corrected. "Better, I think. Here, hold her." I took the kitten from her, a minute morsel. As soft and weightless as a bunch of cotton balls. "I named her Wren, because she's so tiny, and the way she purrs, it's like a song. Can you feel it?"

"Mmm-hmm." Like cotton balls vibrating in my cupped hands.

Susannah moved toward the back cupboards and began pulling out several varieties of cat food: a bag of kitty kibble, plus assorted tins of chicken and liver paste. She mashed dry and wet food together in bowls, enough to accommodate the now dozen or so cats weaving through her legs, pressing their bodies against her calves and arching their backs in complete cat-satisfaction. When she was done with the food prep, they all moved to the sliding glass door, where she placed their bowls in a line. Pansy was at the end, getting her own nourishment before she stepped back into the box to feed her kittens. But cats are fickle, and their attachment to their young is fleeting. In a few months' time, I knew, Pansy would be so over them. She'd pass her formerly beloved kittens in the hall without so much as a glance of recognition.

Kind of like another mom I knew.

"How do you always manage to have a gourmet buffet for the cats on hand when there's nothing in this house fit for actual human consumption?" I asked Susannah.

"You wanna come for breakfast with us?" Brian asked. "We're going to Declan's. My treat."

Declan's was a restaurant on Main Street. The breakfast menu came vaguely close to reasonably priced. Still, I couldn't believe Brian was offering to foot the bill. In fact, I couldn't recall his ever offering to treat anyone to anything. "You're kidding, right?"

Susannah had started to fill an eyedropper with milk for Wren, but she turned away from the counter and gave Brian an almost imperceptible shake of her head. "I don't think Lorrie will be up for it."

"What?" Brian asked. "Too good for dine and dash?"

I glared at my sister. "Don't tell me that's what you're really planning to do."

"There's no food, like you said."

"You know, Lorrie," Brian added, "you'd enjoy life so much more if you just killed the bug you have stuck up your ass."

"I want you out of this house," I told him.

"She's just under a lot of stress," Susannah said quickly. "She doesn't mean it."

"You're worried about him right now?" I asked my sister, incredulous. "Did you hear how he just spoke to me? He is not welcome here."

She turned to me. "He is, Lorrie."

Brian grinned as if he'd just won some dumb carnival prize. "I love how you think you can just make a decision like that," he told me. "Like your name is on the deed or something. Meanwhile, you're never here, and when you are, you'll do anything to avoid facing up to the fact that you're no better than anyone else."

"Get. Out."

But if Brian's expression was gleeful, Susannah's was of a girl destroyed. "Please stop it now. It hurts me too much when you fight like this."

"I'm sorry, babe," Brian said. "Let's go. We'll get something to eat, just you and me."

"Yeah, okay." She swiped at her face, actual tears. Susannah didn't make gestures just for effect.

"Got everything you need?"

"Uh-huh."

They started toward the back door. Brian had his arm around my sister, steering her away. Two of Grandma's silver forks were sticking out of the back pocket of his jeans.

"Wait!" I'm sure they both thought I was only about to make a last-ditch effort to get Susannah to stay. But I knew that was a lost cause. "Over my dead body you're leaving with those."

Susannah turned around. "What are you talking about?"

"He has the silver he was 'polishing' in his back pocket."

Brian reached around before Susannah could check and pulled the forks out of his pocket. He yanked open a drawer by the stove and dropped them inside. They clanged against whatever else was thrown in there. We didn't have a designated utensil drawer with one of those organizers to separate everything into neat little sections. Nope—the utensils were subject to the same chaos as everything else in our house.

"Don't think I didn't know what you wanted to do with those," I said.

"You think you know everything about everybody, don't you?" he asked me.

But he didn't stick around to hear my answer. The screen door slammed shut behind them.

That was my life these days: a series of doors slammed shut.

With Susannah and Brian gone, I went around the kitchen opening various drawers, on the hunt for whatever other pieces I could find of Grandma's silver. I think there'd originally been twelve each of the forks, knives, and spoons, plus serving pieces. I found maybe half, buried under a hundred other things—a screwdriver, a paperback book with the cover torn off, a broken pair of scissors, a stretched-out Slinky, an old photograph of my parents looking young and happy. I paused for a second, staring at them. Susannah had inherited the recessive blond gene, but my hair was chestnut brown, like both of my parents'. My face was mostly my mother's—same eyes and arched brows, same small space between our upper lips and our noses.

I dropped the photo back in and slammed the drawer shut. Somewhere in the house was the velvet-lined wooden box that the silver was meant to be stored in, to prevent the blackened tarnish Brian had so diligently been cleaning off. God, he never did anything without an ulterior motive. But Susannah was an ostrich with her head in the sand about all things Brian Beecher. About a lot of things, actually.

Where the box was hiding was anyone's guess, and I didn't have the time or the inclination for that game of hide-and-seek. I collected all the silver I could find, put my loot in a paper bag, and ran it up to my bedroom closet. Only then did I finally leave the house for my morning run.

I RAN ALONG THE BEACH WITHOUT A SPECIFIC DESTINA-tion in mind. But somehow, instinctively, as my heart pounded and my legs ached, missing a thousand pounds of horse between them, I ended up at Oceanfront, the only place in Idlewild I ever really felt comfortable. I went into the barn, greeting the horses in their stalls as I made my way back to the one that had last been Orion's. The stall was empty, but there was a fresh bedding of cedar chips on the floor, which meant someone was boarded here in Orion's absence, probably a horse out on its own morning ride. Around the corner came a voice: "Not to worry, Ma. I'll get you a check tonight."

When I peeked around, I spotted Jeremy Gummer, a cell phone pressed against his ear, at the far end of the corridor. Gumby Gummer. That had been his childhood nickname, he'd once told me, and it fit. He was tall and lanky but with a softness to him. Not sharp like Brian, and not solid and square like Charlie.

Everyone knew Jeremy's story: He used to be a weekender in Idlewild, who boarded a horse at Oceanfront. But a couple years back his father was convicted of insider trading. The family managed to hold on to their Idlewild home, which had been on his mother's side for years. But otherwise they were wiped out. Everything had to be sold, including Jeremy's horse, to pay legal fees and penalties. Now Mrs. Gummer ran a bed-and-breakfast out of their main house, and she and Jeremy lived in the caretaker's cottage. Jeremy himself had to put college on hold and get a job, and Oceanfront's owner, Naomi Ward, had hired him as a part-groom, part-trainer. Multiple times I'd seen him ease his way into the stall of a snorting, stomping animal, get up close, and speak in low tones to calm all the wildness right out of it.

Jeremy had left a bucket of grain just outside the stall of a horse named Kismet, who whinnied from within, hungry for lunch. It's tough to be a horse and always be at the mercy of humans when you want your food. "Hey there. I got you, I got you," I told him. I unlatched the stall door and carried the grain in, unhooked the old feed bucket, and replaced it with the fresh one. Kismet hardly waited for me to move my hand before he nosedived in. I dropped the old bucket, and it clanged onto the floor. Jeremy ran over to investigate and was clearly startled to see me.

"Sorry," I mouthed sheepishly. I had the bucket back in hand, and I slipped out of Kismet's stall and redid the latch.

"Listen, I have to go," Jeremy said into the phone. "Yeah, you, too. See you later."

"Hey," I said, once he'd clicked off. "I was just trying to help. I didn't mean to interrupt your call."

"No worries." He reached toward me with a hug hello. "Oh, no, I'm too sweaty," I told him. "I ran all the way here."

"Sorry." He backed up awkwardly and propped an elbow up against the window of the stall across from Kismet's. "I heard you'd be away all summer."

"I had some family stuff to get back for," I said.

"I hope everything's all right."

I hesitated for the smallest moment. I was certain Jeremy didn't notice. "Oh, yeah," I said. "Of course. Everything's great. My aunt just wanted some quality time."

"I get it," Jeremy said. He tugged at the goatee on his chin. Facial hair was not really my thing, but there was something about Jeremy's that I found fascinating, because it always looked like he'd just started to grow it. Did he trim it that way, or was that the most he could get? We did not have a close enough relationship for me to probe these things. "Where's Orion?"

"On his way. His return is just a bit delayed because my friend Beth-Ann had a competition and she needed a good jumper."

As if Beth-Ann and I were friends. As if I'd make the mistake of lending her Orion again.

Behind us another horse whinnied a lunch demand.

"Orion will be back soon," I said. I needed to say it out loud to make myself believe it. "So I need to talk to someone about his board. Is Naomi around?"

"Later today," he said. "But I can ask for you and call you back."

"Thanks," I said. Except I didn't have a working phone. "Or I'll call you."

"Either way."

"Thanks," I said again. "And, uh, maybe you can ask Naomi if she needs more help around here. You know, as long as I'm back." And as long as I was destitute. Working at Oceanfront, I'd have money on hand to bring Orion home, without having to rely on Gigi and the missing trust fund, and be able to board him at a discount. But I certainly wasn't going to tell Jeremy all that and blow my cover. "I can't spend every single waking hour with my family, and I'd like to feel useful."

"She mentioned we needed someone," he said. "I'll let her know you're looking. And I'll tell her how you helped out today with Kismet."

"Oh, that was nothing," I said. I twisted my hands together. They were even sweatier than the rest of me.

"So, uh, I heard the Copelands are hosting some blowout party tonight."

My heart skipped a beat at the mention of the Copeland name. "Yeah, I heard that." I hoped my voice sounded cool, as if a Copeland party was completely unremarkable to me.

"People around here have been trying to get invites, but it's some political thing. Really exclusive. Apparently Gucci is doing the fireworks."

He meant Grucci. It was a fireworks company that did the pyrotechnics for the Olympics and presidential inaugurations. Hannah Mayberry, who went to Hillyer with Lennox and me, had invited us to the New Year's display over the Statue of Liberty a couple years before. Her dad's law firm did the deal, so we had VIP passes and shook hands with the Grucci brothers themselves. And now they'd be in the Copelands' backyard.

"You'll be able to see them from the beach," he went on.

Lennox had been the first of the two of us to notice that Jeremy had a crush on me. I sloughed it off, telling her I was sure he was nice to me simply because I was nice back—which was more than you could say for a lot of the girls who boarded their horses at Oceanfront. But even after I came around to agreeing with her, she didn't push me to pursue it. There was an element of "us and them" when it came to Jeremy Gummer and the Oceanfront regulars; not just because he was the only guy at the barn—most riders were girls—but also because he wasn't wealthy like the rest. From my end, I liked Jeremy a lot, but not *that* way; besides, I didn't want to get too close to him. Getting close to him would be something everyone around us would notice. It'd be yet another thing they'd talk about.

From down the corridor the horse whinnied again and stomped a foot. "I think you're being paged," I told Jeremy. "And I've got to get going. But tell Naomi I can start Monday."

"Monday," he repeated. "See you then."

8

GRAVESIDE CHAT

ON MY WAY BACK HOME I RAN ALONG THE ROAD instead of the beach, figuring pavement versus sand would make the running easier. The houses I passed looked like paintings in their perfection, but I only got as far as the Point before I had to stop and drop to my knees, my breaths coming in short, ragged bursts. My legs felt like they were made of Jell-O. It was a few minutes before I stood back up and walked over to the guardrail. The ocean was roaring below, and there on the lip of the cliff was a bouquet of flowers—roses, at least a couple dozen of them, tied together with a satin ribbon, the petals browning from being left out in the sun. I knew it wasn't the smartest idea to walk out to the edge of a cliff to get them, but we'd seen that guy out here in the same spot the night Lennox had picked me up from the airport. God, that seemed like ages ago.

If he could do it, then I could.

Just as I stepped forward, a gust of wind came up and swept the bouquet off the rocks. The water below was too rough to hear a splash. I stepped back again. Why did I want withered flowers anyway? We had more than enough things that were dead and dying back at Edgewater already.

Behind me, a car was coming down Break Run, and I heard the sound of gravel crunching as it slowed, and then a honk. "Lorrie!" Lennox called.

"Hey."

"You looked like you were thinking of going over."

"There was a bouquet of flowers," I told her.

"Huh. Maybe the freak put them there."

The breeze blew again. It was pushing ninety degrees, but a chill suddenly went up my spine. "Oh my God," I said. "You don't think someone left them here for him, do you? Like, because he fell or something?"

"Oh, no," Lennox said quickly. "If that had happened, we would've heard all about it."

"Yeah, maybe." I paused. "So where are you headed?"

"Just coming back from the nail salon."

I looked at her hand on the steering wheel, nails free of polish. "Going for the natural look?"

"Diana double-booked, if you can believe it. And the only reason the other customer got there first was because I held the door open for her. Which just goes to show that no good deed goes unpunished. Diana doesn't have another opening today, but she said maybe, *maybe* she could squeeze me in later this afternoon—like she'd be doing me a favor. I'd have to go all the way back there, and she wouldn't even be able to do my toes, too."

I had a flash of a mean thought in my head: *Oh, the hardship of Lennox Sackler-Kandell, having to paint her own toenails.*

But then I felt bad for being begrudging. Hardship is all relative. "That's annoying," I said.

"Yeah. My next manicure better be on the house," she said. "But the good news is, I ran into you. I just tried calling to see if you wanted to have brunch. I've been calling you for days, as a matter of fact."

"Sorry about that. Cell-phone issues."

"So, brunch?"

I shook my head. "I don't have any money on me."

"No prob," she said. "I do. I can add it to your tab."

I didn't want to owe Lennox any more than I already did. Besides, I was too sweaty for the club and too mortified to appear at any of a half dozen places in town where Susannah and Brian previously might have left their waiter in the lurch when the check came. "I'm not that hungry, actually," I said as my stomach turned over in hunger. I wondered what treats Lennox had in her purse right then. A candy bar? A power bar? "But I will take a lift."

"Hop in."

I walked around to the other side and pulled open the passenger door.

"Where to?" Lennox asked.

"Let's just drive around for a bit, if you don't mind. I'm not ready to go home yet."

"Your wish is my command."

"Did you tell the moms about my plane ticket?" I asked as Lennox pulled out onto Break Run.

"Yeah," she said. "They'll get the credit card statement, and I didn't want them to open the envelope and just find out like that. But don't worry—they were completely cool about it. They know there's a cash-flow issue out of your control and you're in a tough spot sometimes, and obviously they wouldn't want you stranded in North Carolina until the funds cleared up. You're practically another daughter to them."

"Thanks, sis," I said.

"Besides, they know you're good for the money."

Ah, there was the rub—the difference between *practically* being another daughter and *actually* being one. An actual Sackler-Kandell daughter would get to take a lot for granted, like having the money to get home from wherever it was she'd gone, and like not opening mail to find out her tuition hadn't been paid. Like knowing she was, in fact, good for the money.

"You're not mad, are you?" Lennox asked.

"No, no, of course not. I knew you had to tell them. I just wondered if you had yet, that's all."

"But there's something you're not saying," she said. "I don't mean to go all therapist on you, but we never did have that ice cream chat."

I turned away again, took a deep breath, and exhaled out the window into the wind.

"I don't think it's healthy to keep too much inside for too long," she said. She looked away from the road for an instant and put her free hand on my knee. "I'm serious about this. You can tell me anything."

"I know I can," I said. "I'm just still processing everything."

"Process with me," Lennox said. "I'm a journalist, you know."

"What does that have to do with it?"

"I'm good at information intake, that's all."

"Soon," I told her. "I promise."

"All right," Lennox said. "I'll take a hint, even though I don't want to. I have something really exciting to tell you anyway."

"Oh, yeah?"

"The Copelands are back, and there's a party at the Compound tonight. I got a Google Alert about it."

"You have a Google Alert for a Copeland party?"

"For anything Copeland," she told me. "So I can be the first to know."

"Well, you're actually the third person to tell me about the party," I said. "I was at Oceanfront just before this, and Jeremy said he'd heard there'd be fireworks."

Lennox gave me a sly smile. "Let me guess what kind of fireworks Jeremy had in mind."

"You're incorrigible," I told her.

"Nice use of an SAT word."

"I try."

"Anyway," Lennox went on, "Claire said the usual crowd will be at the club tonight."

I stiffened in my seat. It was hard enough to hang out with Claire Glidewell and the usual crowd and pretend to be like everyone else on a good day. If I told Lennox I didn't want to join them, she'd have to choose between them and me. I knew she'd choose me. But Lennox liked those kids. I think it was fun for her to have some Idlewild friends who were normal. Making her choose wouldn't really be fair to her.

"Wait a second," she said. "You said I was the third person to tell you. So, Jeremy and I are two. Who's three?"

"There's my journalist."

"Am I supposed to investigate this further or just take some wild guesses?"

"You'll never guess."

"Brian?"

"Ew! Why'd you pick him?"

"I was going for Person Least Likely to Have Any Intel on the Copelands."

"Actually, Brian's so weaselly, I wouldn't put it past him to know everything," I said. "But you're wrong on this, and you should just give up so I can tell you and watch you freak out." She nodded for me to go ahead. "Charlie."

"Charlie? Who's Charlie?"

"Franklin Charles Copeland the Third," I said. "Otherwise known as Charlie."

"Wait! What?"

The car swerved and I gasped. "Eyes on the road, Len!"

"I can't," she said. "I should pull over for this." We happened to be on Lamb Avenue just then, the road that ran alongside the Idlewild Cemetery. When I'd said Charlie's name, Lennox had nearly driven into the white picket fence that bordered the property. Now she slowed to a stop, and I glanced out the window at a row of headstones.

The cemetery had never been my favorite place. When Susannah and I were young, we held our breath whenever we drove past it, so we didn't inhale any of the dead's souls. That was the old wives' tale that Gigi had told us, and of course it was bullshit, like most other things to ever come out of her mouth. The dead were harmless, and better for us to pull over here than in front of someone's house. These residents wouldn't look out and wonder what Lennox and I were doing on their front lawn.

"Okay, go," Lennox said.

"I met him at the gas station," I said.

"When?"

"Yesterday."

"You met Charlie Copeland? At the gas station? Yesterday?"

"Are you going to repeat everything I say in question form?"

"It's just . . . I'm just . . ."

"I can't believe I've rendered Lennox Sackler-Kandell speechless."

"I can't believe the first I'm hearing about this is right now."

"I've been wrapped up in family stuff, so, honestly, I hadn't really thought of it since."

Which wasn't true. I had thought about it. I'd thought about it a lot—and about Charlie's strong jaw and square shoulders. Everything about him was square, even his hands. I'd noticed that when he held out his wallet and offered to buy my gas and soda. Gas and soda that, pathetically, I couldn't afford to buy myself.

"And I figured I wouldn't go to the party anyway," I said.

"Hold up. You were *invited* to this party?"

"Charlie invited me."

"What? Why have you been holding out on me?"

"Sorry," I said. "It's complicated."

"You have a complicated relationship with Charlie Copeland that I don't know about?"

"Okay, 'complicated' is the wrong word. It's just embarrassing."

"Lorrie, this is me you're talking to. Your best friend. You can tell me anything. So spill the Copeland deets, please, or we'll be sitting in front of this graveyard all day."

"I needed gas and I barely had any cash on me. Charlie offered to fill my tank. But I felt weird letting him, so he said it could be a loan, and I could pay him back at this party. Except Gigi moved our trust to some secret location and locked herself in her room. I can't get any money out of the ATM, but I can't show up to his party and not pay him back, right?"

"His father is a billionaire."

"So? Doesn't mean he owes any of it to me."

"Ah, Lorrie, is this what you've been processing?"

"Yeah, pretty much," I told her.

"Well, don't worry," she said. "This isn't a problem."

"But—" I began.

"No 'buts,'" Lennox said. "It's a money problem, and Ma says problems don't count when you can spend money to fix them. That's what money is for. It's the other problems you should really be worried about."

I knew what she was saying—it wasn't an illness or a death or anything. But still, it was an easy thing for Allyson Sackler-Kandell to say: She'd always had money. Up till now, so had I.

"I think you should go to this party," Lennox said. "And I think I should come with you. I'll give you the money for Charlie."

"You're not my personal bank."

"Just think of it as my admission fee to the best party of the year. You don't even have to pay me back."

"Charlie probably doesn't even remember he invited me."

"So what? He'll remember when he sees you."

"If he notices me at all. He probably invited every girl he's spoken to this week to this thing."

"It's still a holy-shit-big-deal thing to go to the Copelands' house. I wonder if his parents will be there."

"He said it was his *parents'* party," I told her.

"Oh my God," she said. "My knees are shaking. Look at them. They're actually shaking." I looked; they were. "I've never met a president-to-be before."

"You don't know that he'll ever be president," I reminded her.

"The senator *has* been keeping a low profile lately," Lennox said, speaking as if she were reporting to a crowd at large. "But my suspicion is, he's gearing up for the big announcement. Even his wife is working the campaign trail these days, giving lots of speeches. You know the First Lady is one of the most visible people in the world, and she doesn't even get to be on the payroll. But the voters have to like her, too. People vote for the family, not just for the president."

"You know, Len, I adore you. I really do. I love how you're passionate about stuff like this—like what's going on in the world. I love how completely unapologetic you are about what a nerd it makes you."

"It'd be a landmark thing," she insisted. "The first time we'd have a third-generation president in the White House. Do you think he'll announce tonight?"

I shrugged. "Charlie didn't say."

"Charlie," she said incredulously. "You keep calling him Charlie."

"What else am I supposed to call him?"

"Did he pump his own gas?"

I nodded. "The stars, they're just like us," I said. Lennox made a face. She hated those tabloid newspapers. She wanted to be a serious journalist. "I've never seen you so starstruck before."

"Are you kidding? You just lived my dream. Did he say you could bring a friend to the party?"

"He didn't say I couldn't."

"Good. Because I'm definitely coming with you."

"It's just . . . what if someone says something? You know, about my family."

"They wouldn't at something like this."

"You don't know that."

"If anyone does, I'll take a page from the Charlie Copeland Behavior Handbook and punch them out. Then we'll make a run for it."

I waited a few seconds before responding, just to torture her a bit more. "All right," I said finally.

"'All right' we can go?"

"Yeah."

Lennox grinned and put her non-manicured hands back on the wheel. "You know what I'm thinking?"

"What?"

"You and Charlie Copeland—you'd make a cute couple."

I waved her off. "Oh, please."

"Come on, it's Charlie Copeland," she pressed. "Don't tell me he's not boyfriend material."

"He's not."

"Are you crazy?"

"*You* are," I told her. "Copeland crazy."

"Don't pretend you're not, too. Every time I say his name, your cheeks get redder."

"They do not."

"Charlie Copeland, Charlie Copeland," she said. "Ha! You're scarlet!"

"It's just that he's . . . he's . . ." I searched for the word. "There was something familiar about him."

"Familiar is a start."

"Oh, come on, Len. We've all seen his face on a thousand magazines. Everyone thinks he's familiar."

"But everyone didn't have a conversation with him and get a personal invitation to his parents' party."

"It doesn't matter. He'd never be interested in me."

"Why not? You're beautiful."

"You're biased."

"And smart," she went on, ignoring me, "and funny, and kind."

"And I have too weird of a family for someone with Charlie Copeland's pedigree. Besides, he's dating Shelby Rhodes."

"They're doomed," Lennox said. "Everyone knows they're doomed. His parents don't want him around such a train wreck."

"So they'll want him around Edgewater with me and my thousand cats?" I asked.

"Maybe he's a cat lover," Lennox said. "You don't know."

"And the raccoons," I went on. "And the mice. And there are a few groundhogs making their home in the basement. It's our own personal Groundhog Day when they come up from hibernation."

"That boy is no better than you are," Lennox said, firm in her conviction, even though mere minutes prior her knees had been knocking at the thought of being in the same vicinity as his parents. "I just think you're screwed up about guys because of your parents."

I thought of that picture of my parents that I'd found in the kitchen drawer. Who would've ever predicted the future of that smiling, earnest-looking couple: that the man would go on a bender and walk out when he found out his wife was pregnant with her second baby, because he realized he didn't want one kid, let alone two; and that the woman would leave a few years later, when she decided her new boyfriend was more important than her kids? "I certainly won the parental lottery, didn't I?" I asked Lennox.

"Yeah, but . . ." she said, and I could tell she was trying to be careful now, as if each word was being measured before it left her mouth. "Susannah didn't let it stop her, and you shouldn't let it stop you, either."

She'd hit on something right there, something that I hated thinking about, because it made me feel too awful. As wretched as Brian was, he seemed to be committed to my sister, and she was to him. He brought her presents. She gave him a place to live. They called each other "babe." My younger sister had managed to make a relationship work. She was ahead of me that way.

But at least I was tapped into reality, I told myself. Susannah lived in the same house I did, overrun with dirt and mold and critters, and she didn't see anything wrong with it. That couldn't count as well-adjusted.

"There's always an excuse why you're not interested in a guy," Lennox said. "He kisses too sloppily, or he littered in the movie theater, or smacks his gum too loudly."

"So you're saying I should go out with guys I'm not interested in?"

"I'm saying I don't want you to keep hiding behind your past or your house as a reason not to."

A silence settled over us. I sat there stewing over the truth of it: Susannah was happy. And I was not.

"It's not a reason not to go for it," Lennox said softly. "Especially when we're talking about Charlie Copeland."

It was easy for Lennox to think that's how simple it was— that I'd charm Charlie, and none of the rest of it would matter. All the same, it was fun to pretend I had a shot with Charlie Copeland.

"Who has two thumbs and is going to a party at the friggin' Copeland Compound tonight?" I asked her.

She made two thumbs-up and pointed to herself. "These girls! I just have to hit the ATM before we go."

"I still feel bad," I said. Lennox made a face. "I can't help it. I really hate turning to you for this sort of stuff."

"That's what best friends are for."

"I highly doubt most best friends have had to shell out as much money as you have for me in the last week, and I'm really sorry about it."

"Listen," Lennox said, "if you hurt my feelings, or you skip out on something important to me, or screw up in some way—then you can apologize. But don't apologize to me over something that's easy for me to do and in my self-interest."

"But I can't pay you back for any of it, at least not for a while." I paused, and for a moment I felt very, very sorry for myself. Lennox reached out a hand and squeezed my knee. I offered her a small smile. "Can I at least say thank you?"

"Yes," she said. "That's entirely allowed."

"Thank you. I don't know what I'd do without you."

"Yeah, well, ditto. I can't believe we're going tonight! You'll stay over after, right?"

I hesitated, because I didn't want to go to Lennox's house and face the moms while I owed them money; but after the conversation we'd just had, I didn't even want to try explaining that to her.

"Come on," she said. "The moms will be happier to know I'm not on my own anyway. They're in Kiawah till Monday."

"Sure, I could use some time away from home."

"Should I drive you by Edgewater now so you can pick up what you need?"

"I don't need anything from there," I told her. "As long as you have something I can borrow tonight."

"Of course, straight back to Dream Hollow then," she said. Dream Hollow was the name of the gated community Lennox's family lived in, on the bay side of Idlewild. "It's a plan."

9
WELCOME TO OUR HUMBLE HOME

OF COURSE, YOU COULDN'T SIMPLY DRIVE UP TO THE Copelands' house to go to a party. Lennox followed signs to beach parking, where guests were loaded onto shuttle buses for the ride up to the Compound.

But first you had to get name-checked against the list that a woman in a headset was holding. "And you are?" she asked when Lennox and I approached.

"Lorrie," I told her.

"And your last name?"

"Charlie invited me," I told her. "He doesn't know my last name."

She shook her head, not even trying to hide her disdain. "Lorrie, Lorrie," she said, running her finger down a few hundred names. "There's no Lorrie on the list."

"It was a last-minute thing. Probably after the formal list was printed."

I put a hand on my hip as I spoke. A power pose, Gigi called it. She'd taken a class in body language several years earlier—not an actual class in a physical school but one she'd signed up for online and paid for with money from our trust, no doubt. For weeks afterward she'd talked about the importance of positioning your body to look powerful. Then, she said, you were more likely to feel so. If I felt powerful, then I'd act powerful. And if I acted powerful, Headset Woman might just think I belonged.

"And she's with me," I said, putting my other hand on Lennox's shoulder.

Headset Woman looked utterly exasperated, but she pressed a button on the side of her headset. "Brittany, there are a couple of kids down here who say they're on Charlie's personal list." There was pause. "Yeah, if you can find him, ask him. One of them says her name is Lorrie." Another pause. "All right, I will." Back to us, she said, "You two will need to wait right here."

We stepped aside while other guests gave their names and were ushered onto a bus. Most of them looked vaguely familiar, and a few of them looked very familiar. There went Miranda Landis, Idlewild's resident Academy Award winner. Though no one seemed to care who she was. In this crowd, everyone was important. Everyone except Lennox and me. I kept my hands on my hips; even so, with each passing second my confidence waned. Headset Woman was throwing irritated looks our way, and I felt my imposter status on total display. We should turn around and get back into the car. That was the plan that made the most sense. I'd give it two more minutes.

Okay, two more minutes.

"Lorrie," I heard Headset Woman say. I turned to her. "Apparently Charlie just vouched for you. But you'll have to wait for the next bus."

A few minutes later the shuttle bus was back, and Lennox and I climbed in. We had seats near the front, and I watched out the windshield as we drove through the sculpted iron gates of the Compound, up a long, private road flanked by trees forming a canopy above us.

"They're Norway spruce trees," Lennox whispered to me. "The Copelands had them imported."

Minutes passed, and finally the road opened up into a driveway as big as a parking lot. Boxwoods formed an intricate pattern in the center, and an American flag flapped in the breeze in the middle of it all. Beyond it was the Main, an opulent limestone mansion with huge Corinthian columns that stretched up all three stories. You know when you're a kid, and things seem so big, but when you go back to them, it's like they've shrunk just as you've grown? This was the opposite of that. The house was even more impressive to me now than it had been twelve years before.

I was five years old, and the Copelands were hosting a party. Gigi had somehow managed to wangle an invitation for herself, along with invites for Mom and Nigel. Since it also happened to be Gigi's thirtieth birthday, she'd made her own three-tiered buttercream cake. I was enlisted to drive over with her earlier in the day, so I could hold it oh-so-carefully in my lap. We drove up to the front of the house, and a woman in a maid's uniform came running out to the car. Gigi came around to my side, opened the passenger door, and lifted the cake gingerly from my lap. Her dog, Katie, along for the ride, jumped to the front and onto me.

"You're from the catering company?" the woman asked.

"No, I'm Gigi Hollander," she said, her voice full of superiority. "I'm an invited *guest*." I climbed out of the car, Katie in my arms. Gigi prattled on her instructions of how to handle the cake with care but stopped in midsentence as the front door opened again and the tallest man I'd ever seen walked out. He had silver hair slicked back, not a strand out of place, and he looked old enough to be someone's grandfather, but the little boy trailing him was calling, "Dad? Dad?"

"Not now, Charlie," the man said, and he got into his car.

On the drive home Gigi told me what a lucky girl I was, that I'd gotten to see the legendary Senator Franklin Copeland.

Now I looked toward the Main, half expecting the senator to walk out again, but all I saw was a line of guests headed up the steps. Everyone looked coiffed and beautiful and in the middle of their own happy lives, and I looked that way, too. Lennox had called the concierge service on her moms' black Amex card and scored spa appointments for us both to get blowouts and manicure-pedicures. ("I don't know why I didn't think to go to the spa in the first place. It's so much better. I'll never go to the nail salon again.") Back at her house, I'd raided Harper's closet—Lennox was too tall to be an ideal clothes-sharer, but her sister and I were the same height—and found a black and gold Diane von Fürstenberg wrap dress, never worn, tags still on. I'd asked Lennox if we should call Harper for permission, but Lennox said she'd bet money that Harper had forgotten she owned it. The neckline had a deep V, and along with one of Lennox's push-up bras, it gave the illusion that there was more to my chest than there actually was. Lennox herself was in an elegant sundress the color of a blueberry. It stopped just at her knees in the front but sloped longer in the back, skimming the ground as she walked. "I'm so excited, I feel like my head is about to fly off!" she said.

"Lorrie! You made it!" a voice rang out.

And there was Charlie Copeland, headed toward us. My heartbeat picked up its pace. He was in khakis and a white oxford shirt, the sleeves rolled up. His hair was dry and blond-ish brown, just like all the pictures I'd seen, and his bangs had settled in front of his eyes. He pushed them back. It worked for a second, and then they fell back down again.

"Hey," I said.

Charlie leaned toward me and kissed me hello on either cheek, very breezy and European, and his lips on my skin made my cheeks heat up. He smelled good—like, really good. Fresh and citrusy like a bergamot orange. Voices buzzed around us, "Charlie, Charlie," whispered under people's breaths. If he noticed, you couldn't tell.

I introduced Charlie and Lennox. "Nice to meet you," Charlie told her.

"You, too," Lennox said. I could feel her enthusiasm, like a horse at the starting gate raring to go. "Is it all right that I tagged along tonight? Lorrie said she was coming out, and I thought it'd be fun. I didn't realize what a big-deal party this would be."

She didn't realize? Liar.

"Any friend of Lorrie's is a friend of mine," Charlie assured her. "Welcome to our humble home. Come on in."

We stepped through the metal detectors that were set up on the front porch. These were not your everyday, gray airport metal detectors. They were painted a soft white, almost an ecru, and they blended in, as well as possible, with the house's columns and window frames. I handed my purse over to the man in a suit and tie who was reaching for it. He had a little earpiece behind his ear. A hired guard, or maybe even a Secret Service agent. He snapped open my purse to look inside. It was also on loan from Harper's closet, and I deeply regretted leaving the house without removing the loose tampons swimming around in there.

Lennox was stepping through an adjacent metal detector, handing her purse over to another man in a suit. Mine was handed back, but hers wasn't. "Miss, I see you have a cell phone in here."

"Yes, of course I do," Lennox said.

"The Copelands are requiring that all devices that can take pictures or be enabled to post onto social media not be brought onto the premises unless you have a press pass. It was stated plainly on the invitation."

"Hey," Charlie said, sticking a hand out. "I'm Charlie Copeland. I'm the son of the people who hired you tonight."

"I know who you are, sir."

"Call me Charlie, please. What's your name?"

"Philip."

"Philip, good to meet you. I agree with you that this girl

looks awfully suspicious, but I assure you, she's harmless, and I don't mind if she brings her phone in. She promises not to use it, right?" He looked at Lennox.

"Sure, of course not," she said quickly.

"All right?" Charlie asked. He leaned toward Philip. "I'm trying to make a good impression here."

As if he had anything to worry about where Lennox and I were concerned.

"All right," Philip said. He handed Lennox her purse—phone and all. Charlie ushered us forward, into a foyer as big as a wedding hall. The floor was patterned marble, and several gilded chandeliers hung down from a frescoed ceiling. Standing below, it looked three-dimensional, and I couldn't imagine that the Sistine Chapel itself was any more awe-inspiring. The back wall was a window that stretched up two stories. Sliding panels at the bottom were thrown wide open, and the crowd was moving toward them, headed outside. Charlie kept getting intercepted by people wanting to say hello and tell him it was good to see him back in Idlewild.

Lennox steered me toward a waiter with a silver tray of drinks balanced precariously on one hand. "That's a poppy in his lapel," she told me.

"So?"

"It's the Copeland family flower," she said. She nodded toward the cocktails on his tray, which looked a bit like liquid candy. "Pick a color, any color."

I reached for a glass of red, but the waiter pulled the drinks back from me. "Miss, I'm going to need to see some ID."

"Sorry. Never mind."

"You, too," Charlie was saying to an older man with a much younger blonde on his arm. "It was great to see you both. I'll see you around."

The three of us finally made it outside, onto an expansive deck featuring a human-size chessboard at the center. Guests were milling about on the black and white squares, resting the butt ends of drinks and appetizers on the crowns of giant king and queen game pieces. Lennox moved toward the railing. "Look," she said. "That guy in the orange tie over there by the pool—that's the Speaker of the House!"

"Wow," Charlie said. "You've done your homework."

"I read the *Washington Post* every day," Lennox said. "And I have my own blog—Capitol Teen. You can look it up."

"Between you and me, the Speaker's a total asshole," Charlie told her.

"Really?" Lennox leaned over the rail again. I did, too—to see if there was anyone out there I had to avoid.

"Oh my God," Lennox said. "I see your mom. Oh my God, she's looking right at us!"

Julia Copeland *was* looking right at us—well, right at Charlie. Tall and slender, she was wearing a sleeveless white dress that showed off her sculpted arms. Four thick gold necklaces were layered around her neck, and her blond hair was pulled back into a tight ponytail. She looked as perfect and symmetrical as the Eiffel Tower. People were reaching hands out toward her. She would reach back and give them a squeeze or occasionally lean in for a hug or an air kiss. She was mesmerizing to watch.

"Shit," Charlie said. "We've been spotted." His mother came up the stairs, a woman in a navy suit at her heels. Lennox grabbed my hand and squeezed it hard. This was the moment she'd been waiting for; one of the moments, at least. I could practically hear what she was thinking: *Now I get to shake the hand of the next First Lady.*

"Charlie," Julia Copeland said when she reached us, leaning in toward her son and taking the opportunity to sweep his bangs from his forehead. "I've been looking for you."

"I've been with my friends," Charlie said.

"I thought you said you hadn't invited anyone," she said.

"Surprise," he said.

A few steps away a crowd had gathered in parentheses around the two of them, people trying to look oh-so-casual, as if they just happened to be standing right by that very spot.

Julia looked Lennox and me up and down, then looked back at her son. "Aren't you going to introduce me?"

"Sure," he said. "Lorrie, Lennox, please meet the Famous Talking Julia Doll."

"Charles, please," Julia Copeland said. She took a step toward us and shook my hand, then Lennox's. "Good to meet you, girls."

"It's nice to meet you, too," I said.

"Thank you so much for having us, Mrs. Copeland," Lennox said. "I've actually seen you speak before—at the Rally for Women in DC last year. My entire American Government and Law class attended. You were so inspiring."

"That's kind of you to say."

"I'm excited to see your husband tonight, too."

"Unfortunately, he was called away. No such thing as a holiday weekend when there's a bill on the floor."

"But I thought . . . I thought the Senate wasn't in session right now."

"Julia!" We all swiveled our heads. "Julia!" A woman rushed toward us; well, rushed as well as she could on five-inch strappy sandals. Beth-Ann Bracelee had the same ones in multiple colors: Yves Saint Laurent.

The woman in navy bent toward Julia's ear and whispered helpful information: "That's Jill Whitley-Ford. Platinum sponsor this evening."

"Don't go anywhere," Julia told Charlie. She raised her hand to wave.

"Julia!" Jill Whitley-Ford said, pushing Lennox and me out of the way. She grasped Julia Copeland's arm.

"Jill, what a pleasure to see you again."

"The pleasure is mine," Jill Whitley-Ford said. "And this gorgeous young man?" She looked up at Charlie adoringly. "My daughter's still in elementary school, but I'm reserving you right now. Sloane is all yours in about ten years, okay?"

"Gross," I whispered to Lennox.

"The Senate's not in session right now," Lennox whispered back.

"What?"

"It's not in session. There can't be a bill on the floor."

"You look simply divine, Julia," Jill said.

"This old thing?" Julia Copeland flashed a glorious smile. "I just threw it on."

Jill threw her head back and laughed, as if it was the funniest and most original joke she'd ever heard.

Charlie stepped away from them and grabbed my hand.

"Now's our chance," he said. My palm felt slippery against his, which was as cool and dry as a piece of paper. I grabbed Lennox's hand with my left, and we raced down the steps. Hundreds of guests were mingling on a lawn as vast and well kept as the rolling fairways of the club's eighteen-hole golf course. Charlie led us to the catering tent set up by the side of the tennis courts. He told us to wait while he ducked inside.

Of course Lennox was dying to look inside, and she did. "An assembly line of food prep is going on," she reported back.

"Behind the Scenes at the Copeland Compound," I said into an imaginary microphone. "By Lennox Sackler-Kandell."

"Stay tuned for an in-depth interview with Charlie Copeland himself," Lennox said. "When he talks about his father's run, his own summer plans, and how much he loves Lorrie Hollander in that dress."

"Now you sound like a tabloid," I told her, my cheeks warming. "And you don't even know him. You can't tell what he loves."

A few minutes later Charlie reemerged, a big box in his arms. Lennox and I followed him even farther away from the house and the lawn and all the action, into the woods on the property. It occurred to me that if I didn't have Lennox with me, this would be getting a little too close to a scene out of some teen horror flick: Girl meets boy, boy seems too good to be true, girl gets all dressed up in a sexy dress and learns that when someone seems too good to be true, he usually is; in the middle of the fabulous party he's brought her to, he leads her into the woods and, well, everyone knows the end of that story.

Charlie stopped at a big oak tree. Steps spiraled around the trunk. "Here we are," he said, gesturing upward. I looked up, and there, partly hidden by branches, was the biggest tree house I'd ever seen, its girth expanding well beyond the tree. The corners of the house were on wooden stilts, built to blend in with the trunks of the trees surrounding it. Up we went to a wraparound deck. "After you," Charlie said as he pushed open the door. Lennox and I stepped inside, into a large room designed to look like the interior of a log cabin. I remembered something I'd read years earlier, in elementary school: Abraham Lincoln had been born and raised in a single-room log cabin. Though I doubted Abe's childhood home had been so spacious and well-appointed, with thick Oriental rugs and built-in bookshelves. The trunk of the tree went through the center, from floor to ceiling, with a custom bench built around it. Charlie deposited the box of food on a large round table. "I've been up here a few times since we've been back in Idlewild, and it's totally secure. I tested all the floorboards."

"Why are you back in Idlewild?" Lennox asked.

Maybe she didn't have a press pass, but the journalist hat was on.

"It was always my mom's favorite place," Charlie said. "We haven't been back in years, but she had some work she wanted to do here, and I think she finally wore my dad down. I guess marriage is about compromise, right? Anyway, if we weren't back, I wouldn't get to hang here with you."

"I think it's great," I said quickly, afraid that Lennox would have a bunch of follow-up questions. But her cell phone buzzed.

"Oh God, it's Nathan," she said.

"Her ex," I told Charlie.

"Is it all right if I answer?"

"Of course," Charlie said. "Consider this the safe house."

Lennox pressed a button and held the phone to her ear. "Hey there."

Charlie turned to me. "You hungry?"

"Sure," I said.

"God, Nathan. It's not like that at all, and this is exactly why." She paused. "Just hold on a sec. Actually, I'll call you back." She dropped the phone from her ear and turned to Charlie and me.

"Everything okay?" I asked.

"Fine, fine," she said. "I'm sorry, guys, I know this is super rude, but would you mind terribly if I step outside, just so I can call him back? I promise I won't take any pictures or post anything."

"Go on," Charlie said. "I'm really not worried about it." Lennox went out to make her call, and Charlie turned to me. "How long did they go out?"

"Not long," I said.

"Tough breakup?"

"For him, I think. Personally, I wasn't sad to see him go."

"Oh, no?"

"He was so possessive of Lennox. When he couldn't get her on the phone, he'd text me to check up on her. It was always so excessive. Plus, he used the word *literally* wrong. When he said it, he almost always meant *figuratively*."

"I heard they changed the definition of the word so it really means both now."

"Yeah, Lennox said that, too. But that kind of thing would normally have driven her crazy—that they changed the dictionary to accommodate people who were saying things wrong. I never understood what she saw in him."

"People are complicated," Charlie Copeland told me.

"Yeah," I said. "So . . . I brought money with me, to pay you back for the other day."

"Oh, please," Charlie said. "You don't really think I was serious about that being a loan, do you?"

"I don't want you to pay for my gas," I said.

"We're talking about sixty bucks," Charlie said. "It's nothing." I knew sixty dollars wasn't nothing to a lot of people. Right then, it wasn't nothing to me.

"But—"

"I believe the words you are looking for, once again, are *thank you*."

My cheeks burned. He didn't even know about the moment with Lennox in the car, that the money was really hers, and he wasn't the only person I was indebted to. "Thank you," I said.

"Good. That's settled. Now, would you like the VIP tour?"

"Yes, please," I said.

"So, this is the east wing," Charlie said. He pointed to a model train set running through a model town. "And that's the Copeland and Carrigan Railroad Station."

"Okay, Copeland I get," I told him. "But who was Carrigan?"

"My nanny, Mona," Charlie said. "Until she was unceremoniously fired."

"Why?"

"She secretly arranged for her photographer boyfriend to get pictures of me in the park that they could sell to put a down payment on a boat. Or something like that."

"Whoa."

"Yeah, but before that she logged a few hundred hours up here with me." He gestured toward a love seat and a pair of matching plush chairs. "Over here is the sitting room that I basically never sat in, though Mona liked it best. Check out the view."

I looked out the window. A break in the line of trees allowed a direct look onto the Point.

"And now, come with me," Charlie went on, and I followed him around the tree trunk. "Voilà! My art studio." Against the far wall was an easel and shelves of colored paper, paints, brushes, and clay. Drawings were tacked up to the tree trunk, a sort of kid's art exhibit of painted spaceships, airplanes, and a few not-so-easily identifiable things.

"What's that one?" I asked him. "A submarine?"

"Nope, a coffin," he said.

I stepped closer and saw that it did, indeed, look like a coffin. "Wow," I said. "So it is. Man, all I drew when I was little were horses. I pinned them all over my bedroom walls."

"Do you still have them?"

"Nah," I said.

Mom used to draw animals for Susannah and me all the time, pretty good ones, but I hadn't inherited the artist gene. Horses looked like works of art to me. On the page, though, they looked messy and misshapen. At some point I stopped even trying to draw them.

"I guess you think it's pretty immature that I still have these."

"Not at all," I said quickly. "Actually, I think a coffin is pretty advanced for a little kid."

"My school was having its centennial, and they told us to draw ourselves in a hundred years, wherever we thought we'd be. Even at six years old, I knew I wasn't likely to be alive that long. So, behold—my coffin. When my mom saw it, she said it was totally creepy and I had to redo it. I told her I didn't have any other ideas, and she said I should draw myself as an old man at a desk, writing my memoirs. Naturally she thought I'd have the kind of life other people would want to read about."

"If you lived to a hundred and six, you'd have a lot to write about," I said.

"I doubt that's in the cards for me. My grandfather died at seventy-six."

I didn't tell him, but I remembered watching the funeral on TV in Lennox's den. We were in eighth grade. Charlie had been in a black suit, hands hooked behind his back as he walked beside his dad, behind the casket. He hadn't shed a tear, but Lennox had. "This is a loss for our country," she'd said, her voice thick with mourning.

"And my other grandfather, my mom's father, died in his fifties," Charlie went on. "Massive heart attack. So there's my DNA. But I was proud of the coffin. I looked up pictures of real coffins on the Internet so I had something to base it on. I even got the beveling right—see?"

I did see; he'd drawn the lid with rounded edges. I lifted a hand to trace them with my finger.

"I like your watch," Charlie told me.

"Thanks."

"My dad gave a speech a couple years ago about how you don't see kids wearing watches these days, because they're just single-function devices, and kids expect more—a timepiece, a camera, a phone, a twelve-piece orchestra—all rolled into one. Guess you proved him wrong."

I smiled. "It was my mom's," I explained.

"Was," he repeated. "Oh, shit." He looked to the coffin picture and back to me. "I didn't mean to be so insensitive."

"No, no," I said. "My mom's fine. She's alive and well."

"You guys are close?"

"Not exactly."

Charlie raised an eyebrow.

"My sister can do that," I told him.

"What?"

"Raise one eyebrow. When I was a kid, I practiced in front of the mirror for about a hundred hours. I couldn't do it."

"My dad can do it, too," he said. "It's genetic."

"I know that now," I said.

"So, which of your parents can raise an eyebrow, and which can't?"

I shrugged. "I couldn't tell you."

There went Charlie's eyebrow again.

"My mom and I, well, we have a birthday-card and holiday-card kind of relationship." That was the line I often gave to explain Mom away. Though at this point the cards had all but disappeared. "And my dad left a long time ago."

Now Charlie's expression was full of pity. God, why couldn't Lennox finish her call already and get me out of this conversation?

"It's not a big deal," I assured him. "I don't remember him. I don't even have his last name."

He'd had a drinking problem, my father. I was fuzzy on the details, on account of being so young when he'd fallen off the wagon and left us behind. Mom had changed our last name back to her maiden name, because that's how incidental he was.

"So, who do you live with?" Charlie asked.

"During the school year I go to Hillyer, and on vacations I stay here with my aunt."

"Do you miss your parents?"

I shook my head. "I don't think parents should automatically be the center of their kids' worlds simply because they produced them. I think they need to prove themselves, like in any other job. My mom proved she's not such a good mom, and my dad proved he's not a good dad. Why should I miss them?"

"That's fascinating," he said. I made a face. "Sorry, that came out wrong. Believe me, I know what it's like when people think your life is fascinating and you just think it's your own shitty life. What I meant was, the way you talk about what happened to you, it's really fascinating."

"I hate talking about my family," I admitted.

"Oh, come on. You know all about mine."

"That's different," I told him.

"Why? Because everyone does?"

"Well, yes."

"I like your honesty," he said. "You're a cool girl, Lorrie. And your parents are crazy for not wanting to be a bigger part of your life."

"You don't have to say that."

"I mean it, and I've officially decided to hate them both on your behalf. I hope I never meet them."

My last memory of my mother was her leaving Edgewater to go to that party at the Copelands', on Gigi's thirtieth birthday, after we'd dropped off the cake. Mom's usually stick-straight hair was in waves like a Botticelli angel's. She was wearing a new dress, long and white, gauzy and ethereal. I didn't want her to go, and I actually attached myself to her leg in an effort to make her stay. It was as if I'd known in advance that I wasn't ever going to see her again. But of course that's the kind of thing you think in retrospect. It's not as if I really had any sort of premonition. Mom put her watch on my wrist and told me I could stay up an extra half hour and keep track of my bedtime myself. Then she called to the babysitter to take me from her.

Certainly that night was unremarkable for Charlie; his parents always had parties, and he always had both of them back when the parties were over. It was possible Charlie had already met my mom, that night, a random woman in a beautiful dress. But he wouldn't remember, and she wasn't around to ask.

"The thing is," Charlie went on, "I know practically everything there is to know about my father, and my grandfather, and his grandfather. Hell, anyone with a library card can get all that information if they want. Sometimes I fantasize about knowing a little bit less. I know you said you don't miss your parents, and maybe you mean that. But just in case you have mixed feelings on it, I'm here to tell you, the whole family thing, it can be a bit overrated."

I had to hand it to Charlie Copeland. He wasn't at all like I expected him to be. "Thanks," I said.

"So you live with your aunt, huh? She have any kids of her own?"

"Nope, just me and my sister."

"Your sister who can raise an eyebrow?"

"That's the one," I said. "Is that fascinating, too?"

"It is for someone who's spent his whole life as an only child. I always wanted a sibling, just to have someone who could roll his eyes along with me whenever my parents did something insufferable. We'd suffer together, you know?"

"Safety in numbers."

"Exactly," he said.

"Susannah and I are really different," I said.

"I guess that happens." He paused. "Any pets?"

"Just my horse." As far as I was concerned, Orion was my only pet. If it were up to me, I'd serve every cat and critter making their home at Edgewater their eviction notices.

"You're a horse girl. I should've known."

"Why do you say that?"

I knew he couldn't smell it on me. I'd only spent twenty minutes at Oceanfront and I hadn't even mounted a horse. Besides, I'd taken a shower after. I was certain I didn't have so much as a single piece of hay on me. I missed it, too. The barn smells, the stray pieces of hay—they were my trademarks. Who was I if I wasn't around horses?

"Your palm," he said. "I felt the callus. It's from the reins, right? Shelby rides when she's not touring, and her hands feel just like yours."

Now my hands were being compared to Shelby Rhodes's hands. "Orion's a bit headstrong," I said, and I pictured my horse nodding his head vigorously. I could practically feel the reins straining in my hands. "He fights the bit."

"So does Ambassador."

"Is that Shelby's horse?" I asked.

"Yup."

"Is Shelby coming tonight?"

Please, God, let the answer be no.

Though who was I to keep Shelby Rhodes away from her own boyfriend? I didn't want a boyfriend, and I certainly didn't want to be the girl who got mixed up with someone else's.

"No," Charlie said. "We're taking a bit of a break this summer. She's filming a movie with Hayden O'Conner. She didn't want to be tied to too many things."

"I didn't know she was an actress."

"Now she is." He paused. "Let's talk about something else."

Charlie had been the one to bring up Shelby, but I didn't point that out. He pushed the hair from his eyes. Of course his bangs fell right back down again. I had the urge to reach out and sweep them from his forehead myself. My fingers actually tingled at the thought. But I didn't do it. I wasn't his girlfriend or his mother. I wasn't allowed to touch him that way. I turned away to look at the coffin picture again.

"Lorrie?"

"Yeah?" I said, turning back again. And then Charlie's lips were on mine, just barely, as if he wasn't sure he was allowed to press any harder. My whole body was trembling. His lips were soft and dry. I took the smallest of steps closer, to let him know it was all right. I could feel something buzzing between us, as if my body and his body together created an electric charge.

"Hey, guys," Lennox called right then. Charlie and I broke apart just before she flung the door open. "The view is incredible. Let's eat out here."

10

I SPY

CHARLIE HAD DUG UP AN OLD PAIR OF BINOCULARS, and Lennox and I passed them back and forth over the remnants of our dinner. The sun was going down, but tiki lanterns were strung up around the Copelands' lawn, crisscrossing above the guests' heads. The drinks in people's hands glowed red and blue, very patriotic. Somewhere out there a stage must've been set up. I heard snippets of lyrics I recognized from a song by the Jessarae Band, which had been at the top of the charts all spring.

Just like the journalist she aspired to be, Lennox grilled Charlie on everything from what his plans were for the rest of the summer to whether he'd be allowed back at Grosvenor-Baldwin Academy in the fall.

"I think that ship has sailed," Charlie said to her. His knee bumped accidentally against mine. Or maybe it wasn't accidental, because he made no attempt to move it away. I didn't move my knee, either, and there was a wave of heat running through me, from my heart thump-thumping in my chest to the place where our bodies touched. I picked up my glass of wine and took a sip—Charlie had produced a bottle from the box of food, explaining that his parents were only strict about the underage-drinking thing when they thought other people might be watching.

"Being a politician is mostly about managing people's perceptions," Lennox said with authority. Then she went on about Charlie's school choices. "You should check out Hillyer. It's only four hours from here, *Forbes* named it one of the top ten boarding schools in the Northeast, and as a bonus, Lorrie and I go there. He should come, don't you think, Lor?"

"Oh, yeah," I said. "Sure."

I made my voice sound light, but a heaviness had settled in my chest as I thought that maybe Charlie Copeland would get the spot I'd be leaving open. I forced myself to take a deep breath. *Yim, yim.*

"More wine?" Charlie asked.

"I have to drive later," Lennox said.

"Lorrie? I'll top you off?"

"No, thanks. I'm good," I said.

"Lorrie's always only good for one glass," Lennox said. "Unless it's champagne—then she can't resist."

"If only I'd known," Charlie said.

"This is good, too," I said, and I picked up my wineglass and took another sip to prove it.

"When does your dad get back from DC?" Lennox asked.

"I'm not sure," Charlie said.

"What bill is he voting on?"

"Lennox," I said, "I don't think Charlie wants to talk about all that."

"It's all right," Charlie said. "You can have one more question. Make it a good one."

Lennox bit her lip, thinking. "All right," she said finally. "What's something your dad always tells you? Like, not in a sound bite, but something he'd say to you personally over dinner."

"I don't have many dinners with my dad these days," Charlie said. "But after the whole expulsion thing, he kept going on about how today's stupid decisions will ruin your life tomorrow."

"I read his NYU commencement speech," Lennox said. "He said you can't ignore the past if you want to step boldly, confidently into the future."

"That sounds like him."

"Does he really have the highest IQ of anyone in the Senate?"

Charlie shrugged. "I don't know."

"He said one question," I reminded Len.

"Right," Charlie said. "And anyway, the time has come for me to teach you my favorite party game."

"What's that?"

He smiled wickedly. "Watching everyone else."

"Oh, I've got that covered," Lennox said, swinging the binoculars around on their cord. "I spotted your mother, and the Speaker, and the guy who does the political commentary for Channel Four."

"Gimme those," Charlie told her. He raised the lenses to his eyes. "When I was younger and my parents hosted things in the ballroom that I wasn't invited to, I'd sit up on the balcony and pretend I had telekinesis, and just by zeroing in on someone and concentrating really hard, I could control the person's next move. Sometimes I'd convince myself that it actually worked."

"Are you doing it now?"

"Naturally. There's a guy in a blue shirt by the lion statue next to the pool house—he keeps grabbing multiple appetizers off each tray. Here." He handed the binoculars to me. "Can you see him?"

"Yup. He's got a napkin full of crab cakes in his hand."

"Right, now watch. He's going to take one more crab cake, and then he's going to step to the left."

"His left or my left?"

"Um, my left. I mean, your left. Our left."

Our left.

"Sorry, Charlie. He just moved right," I said, and I felt disappointed about it.

"Shit."

"Don't be so hard on yourself," Lennox said. "You're just not as good at this as you thought you were."

"You think you could do better?" he asked.

"I know I could," she said.

Charlie took the binoculars back from me and leaned in toward Lennox. In the process, he moved his knee from mine. The spot of heat now felt strange and empty.

"I spy with my little eye . . . I'm looking for someone political," Lennox said.

"Pick a douchebag, any douchebag," Charlie told her.

"Okay, fine. I spy with my little eye an old man's bald spot."

"That describes, like, fifty percent of the heads at this party," Charlie said.

"Well, this bald spot is in front of the topiary garden, and its owner is at least six foot five, I'd say. He's interested in a woman about ten feet away. She's standing next to a grizzly-bear topiary, and he's built like a grizzly bear himself. But he's a gentle giant, just working up the nerve to go talk to her."

"All right, I'm testing you on this," Charlie said. "Hand those over, and tell me when he's going to make a move."

"In three, two—"

"He just turned," Charlie said.

"Nice!" I said to Lennox, and I held out my fist for her to bump it.

"It's Victor Underhill," Charlie said. "I can't believe he's here."

"Who's Victor Underhill?" I asked.

"This guy who used to work for my dad," Charlie said. "But they had a falling-out years ago. I haven't seen him since I was a kid."

"Can I see what he looks like?" Lennox asked.

Charlie handed the binoculars over. I leaned forward, toward the rail on the deck, straining to get a closer look myself, but we were too far from the topiary garden. When Lennox lowered the binoculars, I took them for myself. "Is it okay if I look, too?"

"'Course," Charlie said.

"He's big," Lennox told me. "Hard to miss."

"I see him," I told her. Even from a distance, Victor Underhill looked a little bit more menacing than the other guests. Not quite the gentle giant Lennox had described from the view of his back. His feet were planted in a wide stance, as if he was daring someone, anyone, to approach and just try to mess with him. I put the binoculars down on the table. The game was done.

The music had drifted off, and suddenly a man's voice was coming from the speakers. A smattering of clapping followed, and then another voice, a distinctly female one, took over.

"Ah, the Famous Talking Julia Doll, in all her glory."

"Don't you want to go down and hear her?" Lennox asked.

"I've heard it all before," Charlie said. "But I know you want to go."

I started to shake my head, but Lennox had scraped her chair back. "I do, if you don't mind," she said.

"By the time you get close enough, her speech will probably be done," I said.

"Nah, she'll go on for a while," Charlie said. "You should go if you want. She always puts on a good show, and she has a special announcement planned for tonight."

"A special announcement?" Lennox asked, her eyes widening. "*The* announcement? Oh my God, is your dad *here*?"

Charlie grimaced and shook his head. "No," he said a bit too quickly. "It has nothing to do with him."

"Methinks you doth protest too much," Lennox said. Her voice rose with excitement. "You'll come watch with me, right, Lor?"

I tried to telepathically let her know that I didn't want to leave the safety and privacy of this tree house, where no one would possibly recognize me. But somehow, it wasn't working.

"Please?" she begged.

"All right," I said. To Charlie, I added, "We'll be back soon, and we'll help you clean up."

"Of course we will," Lennox said. From the distance, we heard a pause, then laughter, but we were too far away to hear the joke itself. Lennox grabbed my hand. "Come on, before we miss too much."

We raced down the steps of the tree house, through the woods, and out onto the lawn. The crowd was packed near the stage, but we found a little pocket with an only partially obstructed view of Julia Copeland, who was giving thanks to a long list of donors and volunteers. "I bet the senator is here," Lennox whispered. "That he's been here all along, hiding in the wings. History is going to be made right now. Just watch."

"One of the greatest privileges of my life is that occasionally I get to be the host of events like this one," Julia Copeland said. "Though I don't deserve any of the credit for the incredible display Mother Nature offered up. When you plan an outdoor party, the recurring nightmare is that the weather won't cooperate. But tonight, well, I don't think I've ever seen the moon so bright or the sky so filled with stars. It's like a night out of my dreams, giving us the perfect setting to enjoy the beautiful music of the Jessarae Band."

Julia paused for an obligatory burst of applause. "And I am thrilled to have had the pleasure of your company, and I'm honored that each and every one of you took time out of your busy schedules and gave up this coveted summer evening to come to our home."

Lennox was standing on her toes, listing first to the left and then to the right, trying to see around people's heads.

"Your support means so much, not only to me but to count-less others, as well. Particularly on a night like this, when we have so much to enjoy, it is important for us to remember those who are less fortunate. I think of them every time I look in the mirror. Yes, I am the wife of a senator, and I've enjoyed many privileges in my adult life. But I am also a sister, a daughter, a mother—that last label is the one I hold most dear. My love for my son matches the love that each and every one of my fellow citizens has for his or her children. I may be standing here under the stars with you tonight, but I grew up in a small apartment in a rough town, and when I study my reflection up close, I see not only myself but also the child I once was. I see my own mother, who worked two jobs in order to lift her children out of the life we were living. I see other mothers, just across town, doing the same thing right now. It is their collective dream that their children get the very best shot at living long, healthy, productive lives. And it is that very dream that has inspired me to realize one of my own. Tonight I am announcing my candidacy for the United States House of Representatives."

She barely got the words out, and the applause was thun-derous. You could feel the ground trembling from a thousand hands clapping at once. "She's running for the senator's job?" I asked.

"No," Lennox said, still slapping her palms together. "For a seat in the House of Representatives. She'll be a congress-woman."

"I promise you," Julia Copeland said, the applause dying down. "I promise you that I believe in the dreams of everyone in the First District of the great state of New York—those of you here tonight and those who could not be here, those we encounter every day, and those we may never meet. I do not plan to rest until we create a space where everyone has a chance to see their dreams for their children come true. And the key to that is education."

More applause, hooting, and whistling. Lennox's eyes were gleaming. "Isn't this exciting? I can't believe it!"

I felt the tears pricking behind my own eyes, because I was suddenly thinking about those parents in the First Congressional District. Parents who cared enough to dream about their kids. Parents who didn't leave them.

"You okay?" Lennox asked.

"I'm fine," I said. "I'm just getting it now, what you always said. Politics is really moving—the way it affects all of us."

Lennox believed me right then, because she so genuinely believed it herself. When she got excited about something, she wanted you to feel it just as much as she did. She squeezed my hand, and we listened to the end of the speech. The Jessarae Band took the stage again to sing a song they'd written just for the occasion. The lights that were strung up all over the property dimmed until we were all standing in the dark, with just the glow of the stars above us. From the direction of the ocean came a loud bang, and then another, and another. Streaks of light were shooting up, high into the sky above the water. When they were maybe a thousand feet above us, the streaks exploded into fireworks of red, white, and blue. The crowd gave a collective gasp. Even the wealthiest and most jaded people could still be awed by fireworks.

But right then there was somewhere else I wanted to be. "Let's head back," I told Lennox.

"Do you realize how remarkable this is?" Lennox said as we walked away from the crowd. "The wife of a senator running for Congress. I think they'll be the first spouses in the legislative branch."

"If she's elected," I reminded her.

"Of course she'll be elected. And if he runs for president . . . Can you just imagine? The First Lady has never been a congresswoman herself!" She pulled out her phone. "I have to take notes on this."

"Press only," I reminded her.

"I'm not going to live tweet any pictures," she said. "But they can't stop me from posting something on my blog later, right?" She stopped in her tracks and pulled my arm. "Hang on. I want a selfie of us all dressed up—I promised Nathan."

"You promised Nathan?"

"We're trying to be friends," she explained.

"Oh, really?"

"Relationships are complicated," she said. "You'll find out when you and Charlie start getting serious."

"I thought you'd given up on getting Charlie and me together."

"What gave you that impression?"

"You made me leave him to go watch Julia Copeland's speech."

"That was part of your political education," she said. "Which temporarily sidetracked the fix-up plan, but it's still on."

"He said he and Shelby were on a break."

"A 'break' is code for break*up*."

"Not that it matters."

Lennox rolled her eyes at me. "Here, approve this picture."

She handed me the phone, and I looked at the photo she'd snapped. The lighting wasn't great, but I liked the way our cheeks were pressed against each other's, so close that in the fuzziness of the picture, you almost couldn't tell where one of us stopped and the other started. "I approve. Send it to me when you send it to Nathan."

I didn't remember that my cell phone wasn't working at that moment until she was pressing buttons. I wondered if my first paycheck from Oceanfront would cover that bill. But of course, even if it would, I hadn't even started working there yet, and there were other bills to pay first.

"You got it," Lennox said.

We didn't notice the ear-pieced security guard walking briskly toward us until he was upon us. "The presence of cell phones is strictly prohibited at this event," he said.

"We're friends of Charlie's," Lennox said quickly. "Charlie *Copeland*. He worked it out that it was fine for me to keep my phone. You can ask the security guard out front. He okayed it. Right, Lor?"

I nodded. "His name was Philip," I added.

This guy either didn't believe us or didn't care. "You're going to have to leave the premises with that immediately," he said.

"We were just going to say good-bye to Charlie," I told him. "We're leaving right after that."

"I'm happy to confiscate your phone and then you can say whatever you want to whoever you want." He held out his hand.

Lennox turned to me. "You go say good-bye to Charlie for both of us," she said. "It's even better this way. You'll get some alone time. All part of my plan."

"Let's go, miss," the guard said. "And I'm going to need to take that phone from you in the meantime."

"I'll meet you out front," I told Lennox.

She gave the phone to the security guard, gave me a quick hug, and then turned to follow him to the Main. I kept moving toward the woods, picking up my pace a little, though it occurred to me then that I hadn't planned to do this walk on my own, and I wasn't exactly sure where to go. I should've looked for some landmarks when we'd left. It was darker now, but the sky was still illuminated by the fireworks, and, remarkably, I found the oak tree with the stairwell wrapped around it. I took the steps two at a time up to the porch landing.

I guess I'd expected Charlie to be right where we'd left him, but he wasn't. Perhaps he'd gone back inside, to the art studio or the sitting area. My heart started to beat a little bit faster. I was about to be alone with Charlie Copeland. This time, without Lennox to interrupt us. And there I was, all dressed up in Harper's dress with its sexy neckline. This was it; this was my moment. I felt all lit up inside.

I peered through the window and scanned the room. Charlie wasn't on the love seat or in either of the chairs, and he wasn't by the table. Then I saw some movement on the other side of the tree trunk, in the corner by the model train tracks. The tree was blocking most of his body, but I saw one arm extending, a hand on the engine, rolling it up a felt mountain. It was kind of cute that Charlie was so in touch with his inner child, playing with his trains.

His body inched out from behind the trunk. I saw his forearm, and then his shoulder, and then the crown of his head.

But wait. The man in the tree house had gray hair. It couldn't be Charlie.

He turned his head, and I could see his profile.

That famous profile. That profile that everyone in the world knew. The one belonging to Senator Franklin Copeland.

I could hardly believe what I was seeing: The senator was on the floor in his son's childhood tree house, playing with toy trains. I wanted to leave before he caught me watching, but I couldn't tear myself away. He stood up, with effort, putting a hand against the tree trunk to lift himself.

And then he turned so he was looking straight at me. I saw the shock register on his face, and I was sure my expression matched his.

"S-sorry," I stuttered. "Excuse me."

The senator stepped toward me, stumbling over a train car. Panicked, I turned and ran down the steps as fast as I could. I raced across the lawn to the front of the house to find Lennox.

11

A PEACEFUL SLEEP FOR OUR FRIENDS

BACK AT LENNOX'S HOUSE, SHE WAS IN JOURNALIST mode, pacing around the den, trying to put together the pieces of the night. She stopped and raised her pointer finger in the air, which was what she always did when ideas struck. "I've figured it out," she said.

"Tell me," I said.

"The senator was hiding because he wasn't supposed to be there tonight. That's why Underhill was there."

"Underhill?"

"Victor Underhill. The guy we saw through the binoculars."

"I know who you meant," I said. "But what I don't get is what you think he has to do with Senator Copeland being in the tree house."

"Didn't Charlie say they had a big falling-out?"

"Yeah, years ago," I said.

"Right, so my guess is, Julia Copeland invited Underhill back on the scene because she wants him to work for her now, and she didn't think the senator would be there."

"But the senator *was* there," I reminded her.

"Julia didn't know that. He told her there was a vote in DC."

"If you knew that wasn't true, then I'm sure she did, too—especially since she's running for Congress. It doesn't make any sense."

"Maybe she knew there was no vote, but she asked him to stay away so he didn't steal the spotlight."

"I would think his spotlight would be good for her political career."

"You're right," she said, and she started pacing again. "Okay, so maybe I'm wrong about a few details."

"It was so weird, Len. You should've seen the look on his face when he saw me. And then he tripped over a train set."

"I wish I had seen that," she said. "I'd love to see Senator Franklin Copeland in person."

Lennox's cell phone vibrated against the coffee table, and she picked it up and looked at the screen. "It's Brian," she said.

"Brian? Brian Beecher?" Lennox nodded, and the phone buzzed again. "Shit. I hope he and Susannah didn't get arrested or anything."

She pressed the button to answer. "Hello?"

She listened, and I heard muffled sounds of Brian talking, explaining why he was calling. I imagined the worst: They'd dined and dashed again, and Brian hadn't stuck around long enough to see Susannah get arrested, but she was in a holding cell across town, and if I could just come up with the money for bail . . .

It'd be more money that I'd have to borrow from Lennox, and how would she explain that to the moms?

"Lorrie," Lennox said, holding out the phone to me. "It's Susannah."

I took it and pressed it to my ear. "Susie?"

She spoke softly, but I knew what I heard.

Mom's dead, I heard her say.

Something dropped inside me. A feeling I'd never had before. Maybe it was relief. What kind of person feels relieved to hear that her mom is dead?

I guess the kind of person for whom it doesn't matter if her mother is alive or dead. My cheeks went hot. Goddamn her. "It's my fault!" Susannah wailed. "I shouldn't have gone out tonight. She'd attached to Pansy this afternoon. I thought it would be okay. I thought if Brian and I went out . . ." She choked back another sob.

Her fault? Attached to Pansy?

Oh! It was *Wren*, Susannah's morsel of a kitten, who had died. My mom was still alive and well, wherever she was. Inside me, the space of relief filled up with rage.

"I should've stayed home with her," Susannah said, choking back sobs. "It's my fault. It's my fault."

"It wasn't your fault," I said. "No one can be there every single moment. And she probably wouldn't have made it no matter what you did."

"I'm a terrible mother."

It wasn't the time to remind her that she wasn't actually a mother; although, truth be told, she was more of one to the animals than our mother was to us.

"Can you come home?" Susannah asked, her voice as plaintive as Wren's sweet, soft mews.

"Yes, of course," I said. "I'm on my way."

THE NEXT MORNING, WE WERE ALL DRESSED UP IN OUR somber best to bury Wren in Edgewater's pet cemetery on the south end of our property. Brian's baseball cap was off, and his jeans were pulled all the way up to his waist for once, which was basically his version of wearing a suit and tie. Susannah wore a simple gray shift dress. Gigi was in a layered black cloak of a dress, the sleeves attached in such a way that when she lifted an arm to press a yellowed handkerchief to her face, she looked like a bat.

No joke, we had some of those buried in the Edgewater pet cemetery, too.

My sister knelt on the ground beside Brian, one hand inside the shoe box that held Wren. I knew she'd lined the box with cotton before she'd laid the kitten inside, and I knew she was waiting until the very last possible second to put the lid on, so that she could get in as many final strokes as possible. Brian went on about Wren's short and meaningful life as the breeze blew through the thin wisps of grass like strands of hair. "And now Susannah wants to say a few words," he said.

Susannah was crying softly as she rose from the ground. Brian hooked an arm around her, as if he were a stake holding up a fragile flower. "My sweet baby Wren is gone before her time," Susannah said. "Though Brian said maybe we're all here for some predetermined period, by God or whatever, and we should be grateful that Wren's time was spent with us." Susannah paused to take a shaky breath. "I don't know if that's true. Or if it's all random and Brian was just trying to make me feel better." At this she looked away from us and back down at the box, addressing it directly. "Either way, Wren, I'm sorry I didn't do more for you when you were here. I'll never forget you."

Susannah bent down to the ground again and gave Wren one last pet before finally placing the lid on top of the box, picking it up with the care one might use when holding a crystal ball, and placing it gently into the ground. Then she took the shovel and did eight scoops of dirt to symbolize the eight letters in *I love you*, as she had done for every creature she'd loved and lost. Watching her, my mind flicked to the one and only creature that mattered to me: Orion. But the idea of losing him was so unbearable I had to push it out of my head.

Susannah passed the shovel around so we each got a turn, which was also part of her ritual. When it was over, she wasn't quite ready to leave the graveside. "You don't mind if I get going, right, babe?" Brian asked. "I promised the guys I'd meet up with them for . . . uh . . ." He glanced at me for a split second. As if I cared where he was going. I only cared when he was taking my sister, dragging her down with him. "For a thing. Is that all right?"

"Yeah," Susannah said. "I want to be alone with Wren for a bit anyway."

Brian squeezed Susannah's shoulder. "I won't be too late," he told her, and then he was off.

Gigi reached toward Susannah with her bat arms, but Susannah shook her head.

"I really do just want a few minutes by myself," she said.

"Of course, darling girl," Gigi said. She turned to me. "Come, let's prepare lunch."

I met Susannah's eyes and looked for a signal that she secretly wanted me to stay behind. But she nodded and said she'd be in soon but she wasn't really all that hungry.

Gigi and I walked back toward the house, around the other gravestones and various fallen branches, and a quartet of sculptures that my grandparents had long ago imported from Tuscany. Now they were lying cracked and ruined on their sides. Gigi bent to clear the graves of dried wildflowers. She dusted each stone, using a fingernail to get any dirt out of the crevices where Susannah had tried to carve their names with sticks and rocks. If only Gigi attended to our house with the same level of care.

I walked ahead of her. Dandelions sprouted up everywhere, even in the patchiest parts of our lawn. When we were kids, Susannah and I loved to pick them once they'd lost their petals and transformed into translucent white cotton balls of seeds. "Puffer flowers," we'd called them, and we'd snap them up and blow hard to make wishes, hundreds of seeds for identical dandelions dispersing with our breaths.

I bent to pick one now, took in a deep breath, and concentrated on my deepest wishes: *I wish I could find my trust, and I wish Orion was already home, and I wish we could both count on going back to Hillyer this fall.*

What were the rules, where puffer flowers were concerned:

one wish per cotton ball, or one wish per seed? If it was the former, I had more dandelion picking to do. I picked a few more, just in case. Gigi caught up to me and reached over to grab the bunch of them. "Oh, good," she said. "We can blow some wishes for a peaceful sleep for our friends." She took a loud breath in and blew it out, scattering seeds on the nearest graves. "There you go, Freddie and Flossie. Sweet dreams for you both."

I rolled my eyes at myself for even thinking up stupid dandelion wishes; I didn't actually believe those things came true. If they did, then all those wishes for my mom throughout my childhood would have brought her home long ago.

"Pick some more," Gigi told me. "We should cover all our friends."

I glanced down at the closest gravestone. GINGER, carved in all caps. "I don't even remember who Ginger was," I said.

"Silly," Gigi said. "Of course you remember Ginger. She was the rat Susannah found at the wildlife center."

I shook my head. I had absolutely no memory of it. Not that I particularly wanted to remember a rat.

"Go on, give Ginger some flowers," Gigi said.

"It feels too weird to put flowers on the grave of something I don't remember," I told her. "Maybe because it's vermin and didn't belong in our home in the first place."

"A rat is just a squirrel without fur on its tail," Gigi said. "You wouldn't call a squirrel *vermin*, would you? That wasn't poor Ginger's fault."

"I have nothing against rats, or squirrels, or whatever other member of the rodent family you feel like defending. As long as they stay in their space and don't come into mine."

"You know, Lorrie," Gigi said, "being strong-willed is a good thing, but it doesn't mean you should always be so stubborn and so cold. There's so much out there to love. If you'd just let things in."

"I love Orion," I told her. "And I loved that poodle you had— Katie."

It occurred to me right then, standing on the edge of the pet cemetery, that I had no memory of Katie's death. How didn't I remember the death of the one childhood pet I'd actually cared about? Maybe Gigi was right. Maybe I was hardened, just a little.

"I'll put flowers on *her* grave, all right?" I said a little more softly. "Just tell me where it is."

But Gigi's face had changed, and now she was the one who was stony.

"What?" I asked.

"Your mother took Katie with her when she went."

"Mom took Katie?"

How had I not remembered that?

I guess if your mom up and leaves you and your little sister without so much as a kiss good-bye, you have bigger issues than a missing dog.

"Why?"

Gigi shrugged. "I couldn't tell you," she said, her voice thick with despair.

"God, I can't believe it," I said. "I can't believe *her*. You know, it's not even easy to take a dog with you to England. They quar- antine them first, for like six months. Did you know that?"

There was paperwork and red tape for Katie, which, appar- ently, my mom had been more than willing to deal with, but she couldn't be bothered with her own kids? And now she had no idea what had become of us.

"I don't know why anything I hear about Mom surprises me at this point," I said. But I was speaking to Gigi's back. She'd walked past me toward the house, not bothering to leave flowers on the rest of the graves.

In the other direction, there was Susannah, sitting on the ground by the freshly turned dirt of Wren's grave. If Mom had stayed, surely my sister would be a different kind of girl. And Gigi wouldn't be headed back to the house of horrors in tears. And I wouldn't be standing here, lost between them. All while Mom was gallivanting around London with Nigel, strolling through Hyde Park and Kensington Gardens, maybe pretending to be a tourist and taking in the changing of the guard at Buckingham Palace.

"Was it worth it, Mom?" I asked.

But of course I was asking it to the air, to no one, because my mom had long ago abdicated the job of giving me any answers.

12

ACCLIMATION

I HADN'T OFFICIALLY CONFIRMED MY NEW JOB AT Oceanfront with Naomi Ward, but I showed up bright and early Monday morning, hoping that Jeremy had taken care of the logistics and that everything was set.

My cell phone still didn't work, my horse was still stranded, there was next to no food or toilet paper in my house and absolutely no money to get any more, but I walked with as much confidence as I could muster into Naomi's office behind the main stable. Pictures of every horse Oceanfront had ever boarded covered the walls like wallpaper. As with Susannah and her cats, if you pointed to a random shot and asked Naomi to name the horse in the picture, she'd be able to do it.

"Well, aren't you a sight for sore eyes?" Naomi said, standing to embrace me. She could've been a model—that was what everyone said when they saw her: tall, with deep red hair down to the center of her back and cheekbones that could cut glass. Plus, she was model-thin. Though I'd seen her down cheeseburgers plenty of times. It was just that she was almost always in motion; when she wasn't riding a horse, she was grooming one or mucking a stall. Every inch of her body was pure muscle, and her sinewy arms gave me one last squeeze before she released me. "I hear we get to put you to work this summer."

"I'm glad I can be of use," I said. "I told Jeremy I don't want to cramp your style."

"Nonsense," she said. "We can always use another pair of hands—especially since Sara Nichols left us in the lurch. Got a nanny job in the French Riviera, if you can believe it. All sorts of perks, along with not killing her knees and her back and her shoulders and not smelling like horse shit all day long."

"I love the lingering smell of horse shit," I said.

"I was counting on it," she said. "How many days a week are you good for?"

"How many do you want me?"

"Five?" she asked. I nodded. "And a rotating schedule is all right with you? I'm sure you know, weekends are often our busiest days, so I can't guarantee you'll get every Saturday and Sunday off, but I'll do my best."

"It's fine," I said. "I'm totally flexible. I could even work more days if you want—six . . . or even seven."

"I don't want you to burn out. But I can count on you for five days—at least until something better comes along? I mean, I know how these things work. Like falling dominos."

"You know I'm not going to think anything is better than being around horses all day," I said.

"It's good to have you," she said. "So, you'll officially be a stable hand, but if you want to assist some of the young-riders groups, I'm sure Jen and Altana would love it." Jen and Altana were the riding instructors, former Olympians both. Jen had once brought her medal in to show us—bronze, not gold, but still as heavy as a doorstop. "And I'd love it if you could help exercise some of the younger horses. They're too green to use in lessons, but they do need to get out more."

"Of course," I said.

"We're nearly at full occupancy. Forty stalls, two pastures."

"*Nearly* full means there's still room for Orion, right?"

"Yes, of course. We always have room for Orion."

"Oh, that's great. Thank you. And, um . . ." How should I say this? I'd never had to ask for anything like this in my life. I put my hands on my hips. My palms were clammy. The power pose wasn't having its intended effect. "If I'm working here, his board is at a discount, right?"

"That's right," Naomi said.

"And there's a salary?" I asked. Because until I figured out where the trust was, I was going to need it.

"I think we can work something out," Naomi said.

"Cool. I'm conducting a little experiment this summer, trying to pay for everything myself and not rely on my family. It's all part of my attempt to feel useful, which is partly why I want this job. But the other part is, I really do want to be here at the barn. You know, it's basically my favorite place. I shouldn't have left to go to Woodscape anyway."

I was nervous, and I was rambling. I didn't need to explain so much.

"Anyway"—I took a breath and slowed down—"Orion's still in North Carolina, and I want to pay for his transport on my own, so if there's any way to advance me a little bit . . ."

"No worries," Naomi said. "I'll cut you a check today."

"Actually, maybe you could even wire the money directly to the transport service. The faster they get the money . . ." The faster my horse would be home with me.

Naomi looked at me funny. Like everyone else in Idlewild, she knew my family was different, but all she said was, "Consider it done."

For a few seconds an awkward silence hung between us like something you could touch, a mist in the air.

"Thanks," I said. "I just want to, you know, feel useful."

Shit, I'd said that already. I blushed lamely.

"I think we're set," Naomi said. "Now I'm putting you to work. There are horses that need to be tacked before morning lessons, and after that, if you could turn Allegria out, maybe even put her on a lead line, that'd be great. Tesa hasn't been in to ride her for a month, although rumor has it she's flying back from Aspen at the end of the week and will come by then. I'll believe it when I see it."

"I'm on it," I said.

"Great, let's check in with each other around lunchtime, and I'll take care of the money wire."

"Thanks," I said again.

A PART OF ME HAD BEEN RETICENT TO BE AT OCEAN-front without Orion, even for a couple of days, because I feared I'd miss him too much. But as soon as I walked back to the barn, I felt better. The day flew by, both my body and my brain engaged the whole time. I couldn't worry too much about the trust or my house; I had these creatures to attend to. I cantered Allegria on a lead line, and I tacked a dozen horses. Later in the day Lennox came by to take a private lesson with her horse, Pepper. From a distance Pepper looked gray, but up close you could see he was white with a thousand tiny black flecks peppering his coat. They came out more in the sun, like freckles. Afterward, we showered him together. I had to muck out his stall, so Lennox turned him out for me. Then she came back to help me. I used a shavings fork to remove the bigger droppings and wet spots, and Lennox sifted through the rest with a pitchfork.

"Did you see my blog about the Copeland party?" she asked.

The mention of the Copelands made something involuntarily burst inside me. *Charlie!*

Not that I needed Lennox or anyone else to mention the Copelands for me to think of him. I'd wake up in the morning wondering if he was still sleeping. I'd squirt ketchup on a hot dog and wonder about his favorite condiment. Back at Wren's graveside, I'd wondered if Charlie had ever had a pet he'd loved.

Thinking about Charlie was a little bit like dreaming: I just couldn't help myself.

"You didn't post anything about what I saw, did you?" I asked Lennox.

"Of course not," she said. "I blogged about what *I* saw—Julia's announcement, which is all over the place now anyway. And even if it wasn't, they couldn't be mad about it. I didn't use any unauthorized pictures or anything, and even the Copelands can't violate the First Amendment and issue a gag order on all their guests."

"That probably wouldn't be good for her political career," I said.

"I got a hundred comments," Lennox said. "That's a record for me. I underestimated how polarizing the Copelands are—people either love the idea of Julia running or they hate it."

"I can see that," I said. "Here, push the rest of the shavings aside."

She did, while I swept the floor. "The haters say she lacks political experience."

"I imagine she's had a lot of political experience being married to Franklin Copeland all those years."

"That's what I wrote in reply," Lennox said. "And then a dozen other people wrote back that she should've spent more time at home and then maybe Charlie wouldn't always be getting into trouble. Speaking of whom—have you heard from him?"

I felt my cheeks flush, and I looked down and shook my head. "I don't have a phone that works, remember? But it's fine. We were just playing for a night."

It was a version of Cinderella—I was dressed up for the night and out at a fancy party, complete with a handsome prince, as if I belonged there as much as anybody else. But the clock had struck midnight, and the magic had ended. Charlie remained in his proverbial castle, but I was here, back in reality, mucking a stall and wondering what the hell was going to happen to me. No fairy godmother was going to pop in to solve things. My heart began to race, and my breathing quickened. I didn't want to let on to Lennox, but I had to pause and press a palm against the stall door to steady myself for a moment, while I repeated my mantra in my head.

"There could be something real between you and Charlie," Lennox said, oblivious to the shit-storm of terror going on inside me. "If you want there to be."

I did. Of course I did. More than I'd ever admit. My heart pounded like hoofbeats in my chest, and I honestly didn't know if it was due to Charlie or my missing trust fund.

"I have so much family stuff to deal with right now."

"Even more of a reason—you deserve something good to take your mind off things."

I shook my head. "Actually, I need to stay focused. You know Gigi's never going to grow up, and Susannah may never wake up. Figuring out my family's finances is up to me."

I stepped out into the corridor, and Lennox followed. "It's all going to work out," she said. "I know it will."

"How do you know?"

"Because it always has."

"I hope so," I managed.

"You know, I'm pretty sore from that lesson earlier. Altana had me riding without stirrups." I knew from experience that was one of Altana's favorite exercises—she swore it was the best way to strengthen your legs and improve your balance. "Wanna come with me to the club for massages—my treat?"

"Can't," I said. "I have to do Charger's stall."

"All right," Lennox said. She rolled her shoulders and wiped her brow. "Let's do it."

"You don't have to," I said. "Naomi's paying me to do this, but you're paying her so you don't have to."

"Today Naomi gets two for the price of one," Lennox said.

"What about your massage?"

"I'll get it later," she said. "Right now I'd rather be with you."

We headed down the corridor and started over, in Charger's stall, picking out the droppings and wet shavings. Horses may be majestic works of art, but they're also a bit gross. "So," Lennox said, "you want to know something weird?"

"Always."

"I Googled Victor Underhill, and I didn't find anything. Not one single thing about him."

"He's not a politician," I said as I swept shavings to the side of the stall. "He just worked for one."

"But everyone has a footprint on the Internet these days," Lennox said. She picked up Charger's water bucket and dumped the old water out through the drain in the floor. "Even Pepper has one. I think it's strange that there's not a trace of him—strange and suspicious."

I leaned against the stall door. "You're always looking for things to mean something," I told her.

"That's because they usually do."

MY SECOND DAY ON THE JOB WAS MORE OF THE same, sans Lennox. In the morning, I fed and groomed and tacked. In the afternoon, I helped Altana corral the bunch of ten-year-olds in her young-riders class. Basically I was just a safety blanket for one particularly anxious rider who was sitting atop Donut, the most docile horse boarded at Oceanfront. You practically had to cattle-prod Donut to remind him to breathe. I held the lead line as Donut plodded around the ring, and my mind wandered to the letter I could write to Kathleen Strafford in the Hillyer Admissions Office:

Dear Ms. Strafford,

As we discussed last week, my aunt has not sent in my tuition check for my senior year. Please know it does not reflect a lack of my commitment to Hillyer, just that my family is in a bad financial state right now.

I recently heard Julia Copeland give a speech about quality education, and as I listened, I couldn't help but think about how choosing to attend Hillyer in ninth grade was one of the best and most important decisions I have ever made for myself. I know you said there's no money left for scholarships, but would a loan be possible? I just want to spend my senior year at the school I think of as my home. I promise to pay you back as soon as I can.

Sincerely,

Lorrie Hollander

A little hand tapped mine. "Excuse me. Excuse me," a shrill voice said.

"You're doing great," I told Lyle. "Keep it up."

"Okay," he said shakily, clearly not convinced. "But I think someone wants you."

I'd been so busy composing the letter in my head that I hadn't heard Jeremy calling me from outside the ring. He waved me over to him.

"I'll be right back," I told Lyle.

"You're leaving me?" he asked, eyes widening.

"You're fine," I assured him. "Totally fine. Just do what you're doing. Follow the line. Let Donut know who's in charge. He's looking for a leader. That's you."

Lyle clutched the reins so tightly his knuckles turned white, and I jogged over to the fence.

"Naomi was looking for you," Jeremy said.

"Can you tell her I'm in a lesson?"

"She needs you now. You have a phone call in her office."

I'd never gotten a call in Naomi's office before. I'd always had my cell phone for private calls. Not that my cell phone was working, but who would need me so badly that they'd track me down at the barn? My stomach muscles tightened in fear.

"Help!" Lyle called.

"I'll deal with him," Jeremy said. "You go on."

13

GOOD-BYE
AND HELLO

MY TERROR ONLY INCREASED DURING THE WALK across the pasture to Naomi's office, and with it came a horrible sense of déjà vu: I'd starred in this movie before—the girl heading from the stable to the administrative office, where the rug was about to be pulled out from under her. My mind raced as to who might have called Naomi with news so important that she had to summon me. The distance to her office seemed endless, and yet all too soon I was standing at her door. I said my mantra in my head: *yim, yim.* All these dumb Aunt Gigi lessons, and I was hanging on to them for dear life, like a drowning man to a life raft.

Naomi's door was slightly ajar, but it opened all the way with the lightest knock. Naomi was sitting back in her beat-up red leather wing chair, her feet propped up on the reconditioned barn door that served as her desk, ankles crossed. She looked perfectly at ease. She wouldn't be sitting like that if she was about to deliver really bad news, right?

When she spotted me in the doorway, she winked. "Lorrie just walked in, so I'll put her on," she said into the phone, and she paused, listening to the response on the other end. "It was great talking to you, too. And anytime you or your family need anything, seriously, you just give me a holler."

She covered the mouthpiece and lowered her voice to a stage whisper as she handed me the receiver. "It's Charlie Copeland!"

Now, of all the people I thought might possibly track me down and call me at Oceanfront, Charlie had to be the absolute last person on the list.

"You can have my office to chat," Naomi told me. "I've got to tend to a few things." She winked again, and then she was out the door, closing it behind her.

"Charlie?" I said into the phone.

"Lorrie?"

My cheeks went hot at the sound of my name in his voice.

"Do you have any idea how hard it is to track someone down without a last name?" he asked.

"I knew you were up to the challenge."

"What is your last name?"

I hesitated. "Holl . . . *Hall*." I said. I didn't know I would lie about it until the moment it was out of my mouth. "Lorrie Hall." It came out more easily the second time. It had a nice, no-baggage ring to it.

"Lorrie Hall," he repeated. I liked the sound of it. Especially in his voice. I could tell by his tone that he was smiling, and something inside me relaxed like an exhale. I wondered where he was right then. Whenever I was on the phone with Lennox, I'd picture her where she was calling from—her car, her room, the sunroom that looked out on the moms' prized rose garden. And I knew exactly what image to call up in my head, because I knew what all those places looked like in real life. But in Charlie's case, save for his Porsche and his tree house and the ballroom-size foyer at the Compound, I didn't have any notion of his possible surroundings. I think because of the state of my home, I wondered a lot about everyone else's.

"Where are you right now?" I asked him.

"Home."

"Where in your home?"

"In my room," he said.

Charlie in his bedroom!

"Where are you?" he countered.

"I'm at Naomi's desk, in her big chair, which I've always wanted an excuse to sit in, so thanks for that."

"Happy to be of service."

"It used to be such a rare thing to be called to Naomi's office. It only happened if you did something really special, like the time I was youngest rider to win gymkhana."

"I don't know what that is," Charlie said.

"It's a series of timed games you play while riding. Naomi invited me in here and said I could put a picture of my horse on the wall. It's still up there now." I spotted it from the vantage point of Naomi's chair—a gray mare named Spice. "You know, over the past couple days, I've been in this office more than I've been in it in the last decade."

Naomi's office was an extension of her home, with a private

entrance so she didn't have people traipsing through her living room to get to it, and it was so unlike the home offices of my friends' parents. Those had been designed and decorated by professionals: chairs set at carefully measured distances from the desks and covered in fabrics that coordinated just so with the rugs and the curtains. Everything was expensive, and nothing was personal. But Naomi herself had chosen whatever was in her office, likely possessions she'd accumulated over time. Everything in the room had a reason for being there, and she managed to make it all look cozy without being cluttered. I imagined that the rest of her house was the same way. Since Naomi lived alone, the place wouldn't bear the stamp of anyone else's personality. She had been married and divorced years before, and now she said that tending the horses was like having a few dozen equine husbands, so she didn't need another human one.

"I remember seeing her in this chair and thinking she was the most amazing woman I'd ever known," I told Charlie.

"And to think I got to speak to her—what's her last name?"

"Ward," I said. No reason to lie about that one. "Naomi Ward. She owns and runs this place."

"Naturally," he said. "When I called, I asked to speak to the woman in charge."

"The *woman* in charge?"

"I'm a feminist. Are you surprised?"

"Yes, actually."

"Well, I am. But that's not really what I said when I called— the woman-in-charge thing. I called and asked for you, and when I said my name . . ."

"Right. Of course, in that case they would transfer you to whoever was in charge."

"It's a curse sometimes."

"You could've just said 'It's Charlie calling.'"

"Ah, but I did," he said. "Oceanfront has some pesky privacy policy whereby they won't confirm or deny if someone is boarding a horse there, so I couldn't even get them to agree to give you a message. That is, until I said *Copeland*."

"The magic word," I said. "Like *open sesame*."

"Yeah, I suppose it is." He paused. "So, Ms. Hall. There you are at Oceanfront."

"Here I am," I said. "How'd you know where to find me, anyway?"

"You mentioned your horse the other night, and I knew you had to board him somewhere around here, so I started calling barns. I figured, if I at least hit the right place, I could leave you a message."

I couldn't believe he'd made the effort. "I'm glad you found me," I told him.

"You could've just given me your number the other night," he said.

"I didn't want to make it too easy for you."

"I've earned it now, though, haven't I?"

He had. But I didn't have a phone number to give. I was always bumping up against the fact that I was actually Lorrie Hollander.

"Not quite yet," I said coyly.

"Well, when you decide I've earned it, I'll be happy to take it," he said. "And I wanted to call because we didn't get to say good-bye the other night."

"Sorry about that," I said. "Lennox got caught taking pictures with her cell phone. Just a selfie, but zero tolerance and all that. We were escorted out."

I left out the part in the middle. The part about seeing his father playing with the model trains. I didn't really have the vocabulary to describe the experience.

"No worries," he said. "We can say a proper good-bye now."

"Oh, okay. That's why you were calling—to say good-bye?"

"And other things, like 'Hello.'"

"Hello," I said.

"Hello," he said again. "Hello. How's Orion?"

I loved that he remembered the name of my horse. "He's on his way back from North Carolina as we speak, but I've gotten to ride a couple of the green horses in the meantime."

"A horse of a different color! Are they Irish or something?"

"Figurative green," I said, thinking of Nathan. "They call them that because they're too green to put new riders on."

"But you're advanced enough."

"Yes," I said. When it came to riding, I didn't believe in modesty. "I've been doing it for years. Statistically, I *should* be pretty good at it by now."

"You don't have to explain," Charlie said. "I like the confidence."

At least there was one thing I was truly confident about.

"So, when will Orion be back?" he asked.

"Tomorrow," I said. "Hopefully."

"Do you have plans for the rest of the day?"

"Just a few things to finish up here," I said.

"Do you want to come over and have dinner with me when you're done?"

The night before, I'd stopped by the break room at the end of the day, pretending to be oh-so-casual as I picked at the left-over food on the long wooden table. I'd planned to do the same tonight, since there was nothing at home besides food frozen next to the dead birds. But now here I was, being asked to have dinner with one of the wealthiest and most eligible of teenage heartthrobs.

Did Charlie qualify as eligible if he was on a break from dating Shelby Rhodes? I didn't want to think too hard on that one. And Shelby aside, I was a little nervous at the prospect of being back at the Copeland house. What if someone recognized me as a Hollander? What if I had another weird meeting with the senator?

Still, I was pretty sure there was only one answer to the question Charlie had asked. "Yes," I said.

14

OUT OF SIGHT

I SHOWERED IN THE BATHROOM BEHIND THE TACK room and then opened the cabinet Naomi kept stocked with supplies and used the spray-on deodorant and some moisturizer. That was when I spotted the extra toilet paper. Rolls of it, there for the taking. Except not really. This would be a new low: toilet-paper thief.

I'll replace the rolls, I promised Naomi silently. *The minute my bank account is replenished, I'll buy even better toilet paper—three-ply, if there is such a thing—and restock the cabinet.* That would make me a borrower, not a thief. Still not great, but definitely better.

I stuffed a few rolls into my oversize bag and walked out of the bathroom. "Hey, Lorrie," Jeremy said.

"Oh, hey," I said. I pulled my bag closer to me, as if Jeremy were a security guard at the Copelands', about to insist on see-ing what was inside it.

"Nice bag," he said.

"Thanks." It was a Goyard. The past fall, Lennox and I had purchased matching versions of the Parisian shoulder bags that were *the* thing to tote your books in from class to class at Hillyer. Hers was orange, and mine was green.

"It looks good on you," he said. "Matches your eyes."

Which was, in fact, why I'd picked that color.

"My mom used to have one like it," he went on.

"Thanks," I said again. In all honesty, I didn't particularly like the Goyard bags, but it would have made more of a statement *not* to get one when they lined the halls of Hillyer. Now I felt simultaneously angry at myself for charging a thousand dollars to be like everyone else, and nostalgic for the time when I could do so and not give it a second thought.

But really: What seventeen-year-old needs a Goyard book bag? What forty-year-old needs one, for that matter? At least it was deep enough to hold a few rolls of contraband toilet paper. I squeezed the bag closer still, feeling the puff of rolls inside it.

"Well, I guess I'll get going," I told Jeremy.

"Wait," he said. "What are you doing?"

It sounded like an accusation. "Nothing," I said. He couldn't possibly know about the toilet paper, could he? "Why do you ask?"

He shifted from one foot to the other. "I just thought maybe, if you were free tonight, we could grab a bite."

I shook my head. "Sorry, I can't."

"Why not?" he asked, uncharacteristically persistent. "If you're not doing anything."

"Who said I wasn't doing anything?"

"You did," he said. He tugged at his goatee. "You just did."

"Sorry, I meant . . ."

I'd meant it as, I was most certainly *not* stealing toilet paper from our boss.

"I'm actually on my way to a friend's house."

"Oh. Don't worry about it," Jeremy said quickly, as if he was the one who should be embarrassed. "Maybe another time, then."

"Yeah," I said. "That'd be great."

THE IRON GATES WERE CLOSED WHEN I GOT TO THE Compound, and I had to roll down my window and speak into a microphone to announce myself. "I'm Lorrie Hall," I said. It sounded a little bit more natural every time I said it. I hoped I wouldn't have to provide my license or any other kind of verification.

"Your business here?" a woman's voice asked.

"I'm here to see Charlie."

"One moment, please," she replied. The seconds seemed to tick by in slow motion as I waited. What was happening on the other end? A background check? Much as I wanted to see Charlie, I couldn't help but think how much easier my life would be if I just stayed home, out of sight.

But then the gates swung back on their hinges. And despite my instincts telling me to do otherwise, I pressed the gas pedal and drove up the long, private road to the Copeland home.

At least a half dozen other cars were parked in the driveway. I pulled up next to a Toyota and grabbed my bag, tossing the rolls of toilet paper onto the floor before heading outside.

Charlie met me at the door, in well-worn jeans and an untucked button-down. "Hey," he said. He hugged me hello, and I breathed in the smell of him—soap mixed with something warm and sweet. As I walked into the barn each day, the smell of it had always done something to me, relaxed me in the way that I guessed scented candles or chamomile tea did for other people. I'd feel my shoulders drop and my limbs loosen. The smell of Charlie had a physical effect on me, too: I felt my knees weaken.

"Thank God you're here," he said as he pulled away. He whipped his head, and his bangs lifted up, then settled down again. "I was worried I'd have to eat on my own."

"Your parents aren't here?"

"Mom's on a road trip of the district, shaking hands and holding babies."

Oh, good. One Copeland parent down. "Sounds like fun," I said.

"Oh, she'll douse herself in Purell when all is said and done," Charlie said. "My dad always says the campaign trail is the best place to pick up a MRSA staph infection."

"I guess you really have to want it badly."

"She does," Charlie said. "My dad always did, too."

I noticed he used the past tense to talk about his dad, which seemed odd. I wondered if that meant something. Back when Nathan and Lennox were an item, he'd say something offhand, and she'd spend the next couple hours analyzing it for hidden meanings. I always told her she gave more thought to his words than he ever did. Now there I was, doing the exact same thing. But mostly I was worried about whether it meant Franklin Copeland was home. "Did your dad go with your mom?" I asked.

Charlie shook his head. "He had a doctor's appointment in Manhattan."

"Is everything okay?"

Charlie's face registered something—the slightest discomfort—for a split second. But he recovered quickly. "He's fine," he said. "Just his annual physical."

"Won't he be back in time for dinner?"

"You ask just as many questions about my parents as your friend Lennox does. Do you have a blog, too?"

I shook my head, and I could feel my cheeks reddening. "No," I said. "I have about as much politics in my whole body as Lennox does in her pinky."

"The irony is, I do, too," Charlie said. "And to answer your question—no, my dad won't be back for dinner. He has a bunch of meetings lined up for the next few days, so he's staying at our apartment in the city. Which means tonight it's just us. That all right with you?"

"It's better," I told him.

"Good. Now, come in already."

INSIDE, THE MAIN WAS NO LESS GRAND JUST BECAUSE I'd seen it before. In fact, without the crowd, it looked like an exhibit hall in a museum. Of course I'd been in nice homes before, even some magnificent homes. Lennox's house in

Dream Hollow was all white and immaculate. The moms collected architectural plans of famous buildings, and original blueprints flanked each side of the double staircase. In her room, Lennox had a blueprint for the White House and a painting that Andy Warhol had done of George Washington.

But the artwork the Sackler-Kandells owned was nothing like this. I recognized at least two pieces from my art history textbook, and we'd barely made it past the front hall. If your house told your story, then the story this one told was: We have more money than God.

Charlie led me down a corridor, vaguely pointing things out as we went. "That's the parlor, that's the music room." The latter had not one but two grand pianos, along with a harp. I heard muffled voices in the background, which got louder as we walked deeper into the house, and when we reached the dining room, I could see why—ten people on ten different phones. The table was piled with papers, but not like the piles at my house. These were neat and purposeful. Thick, scalloped drapes in dark jewel tones hung by the windows, held back with gold tasseled ropes. An Oriental rug was spread across the floor, clean and vibrant, and there wasn't a single cat in sight. "Campaign headquarters is supposed to be in the West House, but it spilled over into the Main," Charlie explained to me.

"Yo, Charlie," a guy called. "Wait up."

Charlie bent toward my ear. "They try to speak my language when they want something from me," he said.

The guy jogged up to us. He was short—shorter than I was—with thick dark hair and horn-rimmed glasses, and he slapped Charlie on the back as if they were pals. "We think it would be great if you could come to Riverhead next week for the town hall your mom is doing. You know, reach out to the eighteen to twenty-four vote."

"I'm seventeen."

"Brock," someone else called out. "Did the Speaker get back to us on that appearance next week?"

"His office said no."

"Get his office on the phone."

"I'm on it." He turned back to Charlie. "I can count on you for that town hall, then?"

"I'll let you know," Charlie said. He took my hand. "Come on."

We turned down another hall. "Luckily you have another dining room," I said as we passed a second one with gilded walls—rococo style, like the one in Edgewater, except without the mold. A crystal chandelier, round and somewhat reminiscent of the ball that drops in the center of Times Square every New Year's, hung down over an enormous mahogany table.

"This is the formal dining room," Charlie said. "My mother would never let a war room be set up in here."

"I can see why. It's beautiful."

"I thought we'd eat outside, but we can eat in here if you want."

I may have cleaned up back at Oceanfront, but all I'd had to change into was a spare T-shirt and jodhpurs. "Outside is perfect," I said. "It's a little too formal in here for me."

"My kind of girl." Charlie picked up a phone on the sideboard. "Annalise, we're headed to the portico." When he hung up, he turned to me. "Right this way."

I followed him through double doors and onto an expansive terrace, where oversize hunter-green wicker chairs were set up around a glass table. Charlie took the seat next to me, not across from me. The chairs had enormous beige pillows on them, but I wished they were a bit smaller, because it felt like we were each sitting on our own private island.

"So, I'm guessing you didn't cook dinner yourself," I said.

"Did you honestly think that was a possibility?"

"I wasn't going to rule out cooking as a secret Charlie Copeland skill."

"It's true, I have a lot of secret skills," he said. "But Felipe cooked tonight."

"Let me guess," I said. "The chef."

"Yup," Charlie said, "and it's your good fortune that he's on staff, because if I cooked for you, I'd likely kill you."

Two women in uniform—I assumed one was Annalise, but I wasn't introduced to either—came out with food on big silver platters: an enormous quiche; a frisée salad with goat cheese, croutons, and pomegranate seeds on top; and a bottle of champagne, which was immediately poured into crystal glasses.

"You said you liked champagne," Charlie explained.

"Lennox said I liked it," I reminded him.

"Well, I took her at her word."

"I do like it," I said. "But I have to drive home."

"What do you normally drink when you have to drive?"

"Anything," I said. "A Coke."

"Of course! Annalise?"

"Oh, no, it's not necessary," I said. But Annalise was already scurrying back to the kitchen.

"I just want you to be comfortable," Charlie told me.

I smiled. "I am."

A minute later, Annalise came back out with another silver tray, with an ice-cold can of Coke, a bucket of ice, and a small plate of lemon wedges. Charlie served me a bit of salad and a wedge of quiche. I took my first bite and had to hold in the sigh of happiness that welled in my chest. You forget how good food can taste until it's hard to come by. I could've inhaled everything on my plate, but I knew I should pace myself. Charlie was watching me.

"Tell me something, Lorrie Hall," he said between bites.

"What?"

"What was the best thing about your day?"

"That's so strange that you just asked me that," I said. "My mom used to ask us that."

"So did my dad."

"Really?"

"Well, he did a few times. When he was home."

"I imagine the man who would be president has a lot of places he has to be," I said.

Charlie popped a crouton into his mouth, chewed, and swallowed. "Something like that."

"So, what was the best part of *your* day?" I asked.

"Oh, no, I asked you first."

"It may be this meal," I said, polishing off the last bite on my plate. I wanted to wait for Charlie to take a second slice of quiche before I did, but now I couldn't help myself, and I reached for more.

"Not the guy eating it with you?"

"I thought present company was excluded from the question. Otherwise, the food is merely a distant second."

"Nice save."

I grinned. "Now what about you—best part of the day?"

"Present company excluded?"

"Present company excluded."

"The drive I took down the coast this afternoon."

"In the Porsche?" I asked.

"Naturally," he said. "Top down, radio blasting, ocean roaring. Perfection. That is, until I got pulled over."

"You got pulled over?"

"It wasn't my fault. I mean, you've seen that car—that thing is practically begging to be driven over the speed limit." Charlie smiled.

"I don't think that means you're *supposed* to."

"Ah, come on. Cars like that—they need to get out, show off what they're made of. And my dad isn't going to do it."

"Maybe he's worried about getting pulled over."

"Nah, he just doesn't drive anymore. Not since I was a kid. If it wasn't for me, his cars would just stay cooped up in a garage their whole lives."

"I get it," I said. "You were doing it for the sake of the car."

"What can I say? I'm a giver."

"Did you explain that to the police officer?"

"Didn't have to. I just handed over my license and registration, and he let me go with a warning."

"The Copeland name works again."

"Have you ever been in a car going over a hundred miles an hour?"

"No," I said.

"Well, maybe we can remedy that."

OUR PLATES WERE CLEARED, AND ANNALISE CAME OUT with dessert—a freshly baked blackberry crumb cake. But we'd barely tasted it when Brock came onto the terrace with a message for Charlie: "We scheduled a haircut for you tomorrow."

"No, thanks," Charlie said.

"Sorry," Brock said. He shifted from one foot to the other, and I could tell this wasn't exactly a message he wanted to deliver. "Your mother said to tell you it wasn't a request."

"Unfortunately, I'm busy tomorrow," Charlie said. "But can you give her a message for me?"

"Certainly."

"Tell her not to staff out my hair. I can take care of it myself. Now, if you don't mind." He nodded his head toward the sliding glass door. "I'm being a bad host."

"My apologies," Brock said, and he slunk away.

Charlie stood up and reached out his hand to me. "Let's go for a walk."

We headed down to the beach on a pathway made of old driftwood. Charlie punched a code into the padlock by a gate and pushed it open to his family's private stretch of ocean. We took off our shoes and walked down to the part where the sand was stiff from recent ocean waves and our feet left footprints.

"I've barely been at the beach so far this summer," I told Charlie. "When we were kids, Lennox and I practically lived at Crescent."

At Crescent, attendants brought over beach chairs and thick towels striped white and gold, and you could order fresh-baked cookies and sweetened lemonade to be delivered to you right on the sand. All the while, money never changed hands. We had an account, and I learned to add a tip when I signed my name to the check, and I barely thought about how Gigi must've received bills and paid them.

"But this year I only set foot on the sand once," I said. "And that was to run to the barn."

The breeze kicked up, and Charlie's hair fell in front of his face even more than usual. He pushed it back.

"Can I ask you something?" I said.

"Sure."

"How come you don't want to get a haircut?"

"Because my mom wants me to get one," he said. "She's pretty particular about the pictures she wants out in the world. If my hair's long, she's less inclined to want me next to her on the campaign trail."

"Don't they take pictures of you whether you're with your mom or not?"

"You mean the Shelby pictures."

"Yeah, those," I said. I felt myself blush again and I looked down at the sand. "And others, too. You're in a lot of pictures."

"Yeah." He paused. "You have no idea what it's like to have people thinking they know all these things about you. But really they just know the magazine version."

I sat down in the sand just above the waterline and patted the ground next to me. "Sit with me. Tell me things I wouldn't know from the magazines."

He sat next to me, so close I could see two pimples rising between the coarse hairs of his left eyebrow, and somehow that made him more appealing to me, because I knew those pimples would be airbrushed out of the magazines. This was real, Charlie beside me.

"What do you want to know?" he asked.

I wanted to know if he missed Shelby. And I wanted to know he wouldn't care if he knew the truth about who I really was. But I didn't ask those questions, because I was afraid to know the answers.

"Do you have a best friend?"

"As a matter of fact, I do. His name's Sebastian Martin."

"They say you should never trust a person with two first names," I said, and immediately I felt bad about saying it. "I'm sure Sebastian's the exception."

"I trust him with everything—almost," Charlie told me.

"Like Lennox and me."

"You trust her with everything?"

"Almost."

"I told Sebastian about you."

Charlie had talked about me—to his best friend? "Really? What did you say?"

"I said I'd never seen anyone with eyes the color of yours."

He was staring at me, and I stared back. His eyes were light brown, and they were like looking into something endless. Or at least something deep enough that the bottom was beyond the limit of my sight. He raised a single eyebrow.

"I like when you do that," I said.

"I know you do." Charlie cupped my chin in his hands.

My body tensed. "I'm a little nervous," I admitted.

"Why?"

I didn't know how to answer that question.

"You don't have to be," Charlie said, moving even closer. I could feel his words as he spoke them, and then his lips were on mine. He slipped his tongue into my mouth, soft and warm.

"How was that?" Charlie asked. We were cheek to cheek, and his breath grazed my ear. "Okay?"

"Mmm-hmm," I said. It was more than okay. It was the best thing I'd ever felt. I could almost forget who I was and why I shouldn't be with him. If I could've paused time right then and there, I would've; I would've stayed forever on that patch of sand with the waves breaking and my heart pounding in my ears and Charlie so close to me. This time I was the one who pressed my lips against his. He was the one kissing back. I felt out of breath, except instead of needing more air, I needed more of Charlie.

"Charles," a deep voice intoned. "I heard you'd come out here."

Charlie scooted back from me and stood to face Victor Underhill. I stood, too, and my heartbeat transitioned from throbs of excitement to throbs of panic. I wasn't sure why; there was just something about Underhill that made me nervous.

"Aren't you going to introduce me to your friend?" he asked Charlie.

"Lorrie, this is Mr. Underhill. He's helping out with my mother's campaign."

I held out a hand, and Victor Underhill gave one brisk, firm shake. "It's nice to meet you," I said.

"Nice to meet you. Lorrie, was it?"

"Yes."

"Lorrie what?"

I glanced toward Charlie. "H-Hall," I said.

"Lorrie *Hall*?"

"That's what she said," Charlie told him.

"You live in the area?"

I nodded.

"Whereabouts?"

I waved a hand toward the road. "Down a bit on Break Run," I said.

"I didn't know you lived that close," Charlie said.

"Break Run's got the best real estate in eastern Long Island," Victor Underhill said. "Don't you think?"

"Sure," I said.

"It's a shame how that one house affects the view."

I knew I wasn't imagining the fact that his gaze had changed and his eyes had narrowed. Charlie was wrong: I did have some idea what it was like to have people thinking they knew things about me.

"Do you go to school around here?" Underhill asked.

"She goes to Hillyer," Charlie answered for me. He reached for my hand. "Are there any other inane questions you need answered, because we were kind of in the middle of something."

"I came to tell you that you're needed inside."

"I already talked to Brock about the Riverhead event."

"Your father called from DC."

DC? I thought Charlie said his father was in New York.

"He wants you to call him back," Underhill said.

I wondered what Lennox would think about this nugget of information: Underhill was fielding phone calls from the senator, who might be in DC, or might be in New York, or might be hiding out somewhere in the Compound again. Anything was possible.

"Now," Underhill added.

"All right," Charlie said. "Give me a minute."

Victor Underhill nodded good-bye, then turned to head back to the house. Charlie and I followed. He was still holding my hand, but it had stopped feeling like a romantic gesture, since I knew he was just leading me someplace to say good-bye.

We walked around the side of the house to the edge of the path that led to the driveway. I didn't know I was the kind of girl who expected to at least be walked all the way to her car until I realized our walk was over. He lifted my hand to his lips and kissed it. "Good-bye, Lorrie."

"Good-bye," I said.

I walked away thinking that I'd said good-bye before with the expectation of seeing someone again. But for every person you meet, there will be a last time you'll say good-bye. And there's not always a way of knowing when that will be.

15

FOR RICHER, FOR POORER

LATE IN THE AFTERNOON THE NEXT DAY, ORION arrived back at Oceanfront. It was the first time since I'd owned him that he'd taken a significant journey without me there to prepare him for it—to wrap his legs in shipping boots and to sprinkle some familiar hay along the ramp up to the trailer so he wouldn't be scared. Equestrian Transport had picked him up from Woodscape and driven him nine hours across five states, which would be frustrating and exhausting for anyone, even under the best of circumstances. I'd been a bundle of nerves until Orion had finally backed down the trailer ramp, but he seemed no worse for the wear as I ran my hands along his sleek, beautiful body. "Welcome home, buddy," I told him. Orion snorted out what I thought of as an exhale of relief. "That's right," I said. "You're here and I'm here."

I led him to the empty stall Naomi had agreed to rent to me at the employee discount. That morning I'd hooked up his nameplate:

ORION

LOVED BY LORRIE H.

The words were spelled out in gleaming gold letters on the stall door. I'd also spread a fresh bed of cedar chips on the ground with a pitchfork, and Orion stepped in as if he owned the joint.

Since he was a boarder, attending to him was not only my responsibility, it was also my job. At least that's what I told myself so I wouldn't feel guilty about spending time with him. Especially since Naomi had taken Jeremy along with her to a show in Stony Brook, so the stable had fewer hands on deck. I brought out the currycomb, moving it in wide, circular motions over my horse's body to loosen up whatever dirt he'd picked up between Raleigh and New York. I took my time, and Orion leaned into the strokes. After that was the hard brush, quick motions around his coat. The debris rose from him like a mist. Then I used the soft brush and the leg curry. We were back together again, my horse and I. I always felt like we'd taken vows to be together, for better or worse, for richer or poorer. Whatever it was, we'd get through it together.

I brushed Orion's face, his mane, his tail. I lifted each of his legs to clean out any dirt from the grooves of his hooves. His front hooves needed new shoes, which shouldn't have been a surprise; it had been over a month. I'd have to call the farrier.

And just like that, I was pulled out of the moment, worrying about the future all over again. The farrier would be a hundred bucks. I couldn't afford that right now.

"Things have changed, boy," I told Orion softly, reaching for the soft patch of white fur on his neck, my favorite spot. "I don't even understand why, but they have. Gigi moved our money, and she won't tell me where. I've been looking—believe me. I made a list of every bank in the east end of Long Island, and I'm going to check them all. I started cleaning the house out, too. The answer is buried in there somewhere. I'm just taking it room by room, cleaning through the night because I can't sleep anyway. Last night I did the drawing room. Well, half of it, anyway. It's so big. And it's so . . . so suffocating. But if you squint when you're looking around, you can see a glimmer of what it once was. It's really hard, though. It's hard to see anything in Edgewater the way it's supposed to be."

When I paused, Orion nuzzled against me and snorted, as if answering me.

"And something else changed, too," I told him. "I think I met someone. Someone I really like. All this time, I told Lennox I didn't mind being alone, and it was the truth. I really didn't. It was so much easier not having someone I needed to explain things to."

Orion pawed at the floor, the signal that I'd been in there a while and he was wondering where his treat was. I'd found a box of sugar cubes at Edgewater. Gigi added a half dozen cubes to her tea each morning. But since I was sure they'd been purchased with money from my trust, and since she was the reason I didn't have cash to buy my own, I'd taken the box with me so I'd have treats on hand. Now I produced a cube from my pocket, and Orion's lips smacked against my palm.

"I wasn't lonely *until* I met this guy—his name is Charlie. Now I want to be with him so much. But the thing is, he's a Copeland, so that's a fairly impossible order."

Orion pawed the floor again, and I gave him another cube.

"Everything I want seems so impossible right now, boy. Meeting a guy you like and thinking maybe he likes you back— it's supposed to be such a great thing. If I were any other girl in Idlewild, my big worry would be figuring out some long-distance thing at the end of the summer when I had to go back to school. But I don't know if we'll get back to Hillyer in the fall. I haven't even told Lennox. I can only tell you. God, Orion. I *missed* you."

The love of an animal is an amazing thing, because it's in the moment and unconditional. Orion didn't question me or resent me for the long drive he'd just had to take, nor judge me for the fact that our summer plans had changed abruptly. To him I was the same person I always was. I didn't need to try to be anything else to impress him—just give him another treat. He lowered his head toward mine. I could hear his breaths coming in short, even bursts, more calming than my mantra. In and out. In and out. This moment, as far as Orion knew, was just another good one between us. Maybe I should forget about the rest and be in it, too, the same way he was.

I heard footsteps coming down the corridor, and I stood and grabbed a brush back off the shelf to look busy. I didn't want to be seen as taking advantage of Naomi's kindness, slacking off and staring at a horse instead of doing the work she'd prepaid me to do.

"She's down at the end," I heard Altana say, her voice an octave higher than usual.

And then a voice—*that* voice—in reply: "Thank you so much."

Excitement rose up inside me, lighter than air. But just as quickly I was filled with dread, because I was so unprepared. My hair was pulled back in the same ponytail it'd been in since eight o'clock that morning and could only generously be called a ponytail now, with so many strands loosened up and falling around my face and with the hay and dirt stuck to it in different places like ornaments on a Christmas tree. You'd think I'd been rolling around in Orion's stall. I was never the girl to care about whether my hair was out of place or if my jeans were smudged with mud, particularly when I was at the barn. But all of that changed right then, with Charlie's footsteps echoing in the corridor. Closer, closer. I yanked the hairband out and ran Orion's mane comb through my own hair quickly—an act of pure desperation.

I ducked out of the stall and met Charlie in the corridor. "Hey," I said. "You didn't tell me you'd be coming by today."

"This is why I couldn't get a haircut," Charlie said. "I needed to see *you*."

My cheeks warmed, and I didn't know if it was because Charlie Copeland—*Charlie Copeland*—had just said the most romantic thing a guy had ever said to me, or if it was because he'd come here, just to see me, and I was such a mess. I dusted a patch of dirt off my jeans as surreptitiously as I could. "Really?"

"Really." His fingers reached for the collar of my shirt, and he pulled me to him. I hung on and breathed him in. There was something fresh and salty about him, as if he'd just bathed in the ocean.

Orion nickered from the stall door. "Hey, boy," I said.

"So, this is your guy," Charlie said.

"This is my guy. Charlie Copeland, I'd like you to meet Hunting Achievement."

"I thought he was Orion."

"His registered name is Hunting Achievement," I said. "Orion is what his friends call him."

"What do I have to do to get friend status?" Charlie asked.

"Give him one of these," I said, producing a sugar cube. "Just keep your palm open and flat. Don't worry. He won't bite."

"Of course he won't," Charlie said. He held his hand out, letting Orion lick whatever infinitesimal bits of sugar remained. "We're friends already."

"I wish I hadn't promised Naomi I'd stick around," I said. "She's coming back from a show, and I said I'd help her unload and get all the horses settled in. It may go pretty late."

Which meant I would get a nice wad of overtime pay—money I would've given up in retrospect to be able to have dinner with Charlie, foolish as that may have been.

"I didn't come here to invite you out," Charlie said.

"Oh, sorry." Why had I been so presumptuous? "I just . . . never mind."

"I came here to see what the Dynamic Duo can do."

"You want to watch me ride?"

"Yeah, of course."

"Well, okay," I said. "I have to get him ready first."

"Tack him, you mean? I know the lingo. I can even help."

I led Orion down the corridor to an empty set of crossties to get him ready. Altana, along with Jen, ducked into a nearby stall, carrying supplies to clean it out. They were taking much longer than what the task called for, especially since there were two of them. And anyway, mucking a stall was neither of their jobs; it was mine. Their conversation was muffled, but occasionally the word *Copeland* escaped. My cheeks blazed, and I wasn't sure why I was embarrassed, especially because Charlie seemed impervious. I grabbed Orion's lead line and walked him to an empty ring outside, where a small jumps course was already set up. The ground hadn't been raked since the last ride, so there were spots of dirt kicked up. But I'd paced these jumps on foot a hundred times and ridden them a hundred more. And so had Orion.

Charlie sat on the small set of bleachers outside the ring, and I mounted my horse. "That's him," I whispered to Orion. "That's the guy I was telling you about. Let's put on a good show." We cantered in a wide circle, and I pointed Orion toward the first jump, an ascending oxer. For a split second Beth-Ann Bracelee was in my head, but then Orion was in the air and hurdling over. "Good boy, good boy," I said.

I felt Charlie's eyes on me, but I made myself stay focused. When you're competing, you know you're being watched. But you can't look at the judges. You need to keep your vision trained on the space between your horse's ears.

Orion jumped a couple of small verticals—easy-peasy, as

natural as breathing. I turned him toward a parallel oxer. He tucked his legs neatly under his body, and we soared over. I eased him into a trot, and only then did I let myself look up at Charlie, who was standing at his seat, shielding his eyes with one hand. A part of me wanted to impress him further, take Orion over to the advanced course and really show off his skills. Unlike Beth-Ann's horse, my Orion could practically jump the moon. But he'd been traveling all day, and even with Charlie Copeland in the audience, my horse's well-being came first.

Orion walked around the outer ring, nodding his head. I patted the back of his neck. "Good boy, good boy."

We slowed to a stop in front of Charlie. "Well done, team!" he said.

"Thanks," I said. I dismounted on the left; you always mount and dismount on the left—part tradition and part safety measure. Then I came around to face Charlie. "I have to untack and shower him now," I said somewhat apologetically.

A lot of girls I knew would pass their horses off the instant they dismounted, but I never minded the follow-up tasks. Until now, when suddenly my love for Orion had to compete with my desire to stay longer with Charlie. And just when I no longer had a choice; it was my job to do those things not only for Orion, but for other people's horses, too.

"I'll help you," Charlie said.

"You want to help shower my horse?"

"Is that all right with you?"

"Do you always answer a question with a question?"

"Do you like if I do?"

"That depends," I said.

"On what?"

"On what the question is."

"What if the question is, are you glad I'm here?"

I blushed. "Yeah."

"What question are you answering right now?"

"Either," I said. "Both."

I was so happy, in a way I would've thought impossible when I came back to Idlewild for the summer. We headed back to the barn, Orion between Charlie and me. I clipped him into cross-ties in the shower stall and removed his sweaty tack. Charlie put it aside for me, and I turned on the hose. Per usual, Orion tried to kick me away when the spray hit.

"Easy," Charlie said uneasily.

"He's okay," I said. I turned the water pressure down slightly. "This just isn't his favorite activity."

"Has he ever hurt you?"

"Not in the shower," I said. "But yeah, I've gotten pretty banged up over the years. The worst was when I first got him. It was the third or fourth time I was riding him, and this huge horsefly went right for his backside. Orion took off, and I was like a hood ornament, just along for the ride. I fell off and broke my arm."

"You could've been killed."

I shrugged. "It's the risk you take," I told him.

"You say that so casually, like it's no big deal if you live or die. Death is a big deal, you know."

I hesitated. Orion whinnied and stamped his foot. I patted his rump, right where the fly had gotten him all those years ago.

"You're almost done," I said, and then I turned back to Charlie. "I just meant, you know what you're getting into when you ride. At some point you're going to fall off, and you know in advance how dangerous it is. But there are lots of precautions to take. My arm healed, and I got back on the horse."

"Literally."

I was pretty sure he said *literally* because of what I'd told him about Nathan, so now we had an inside joke between us. I grinned. "Literally," I repeated.

After the shower, we walked Orion out to pasture. Knowing him, there was a fifty percent chance he'd roll around in the dirt. But I'd groom him before our next ride, and we'd begin again. The cycle of life as a horse owner. Charlie came with me to the tack room to put the supplies away. When I stood up from the trunk, he was right behind me, and he pulled me in for a kiss.

"Wait, Charlie," I said.

"What?"

I shook my head. I knew that the further I let myself go, the more it was going to hurt down the line when he left— which he inevitably would. I could feel the warmth of him all through my body, even though we weren't touching. Every part of me trembled, from the top of my head to the tips of my fingers and toes. Even though I couldn't understand why Charlie wanted anything to do with me, even though I wanted to protect myself, I wanted him more. I tipped my head up, and my eyes met his gaze.

He leaned in and kissed me, closing the gap between us. I felt his face on my face, his chest against mine. He held me tightly against him. I'd never wanted to be so close to another person.

And then there were voices in the corridor. I heard my name, and Charlie's name, and I broke away.

"It's okay," Charlie said.

"They're talking about us," I told him.

"I know," he said softly, so that his words seemed part of his breaths. "When I was little, I called them the Copeland birds. For the noises they make. They think they're being so discreet that you can't hear them, but of course you can. Chirp, chirp, chirp, like little birds."

"Doesn't it bother you?" I asked. "Or distract you?"

"I've never known it to be any other way." Which, of course, didn't answer the question.

"Excuse me?" Altana called. "Lorrie? Are you in there?"

I moved toward the stall door, but Charlie gripped my hand. "I'm here," I called back.

"Oh." There was a pause, as if she hadn't thought through what to ask me when I answered. "Did Galaxy get her Farrier's Formula today?"

"She did," I said. Charlie raised an eyebrow. "It's for hoof growth," I told him.

I heard footsteps, more than just one pair, and then Altana was peeking her head into the doorway, along with Jen and Claire Glidewell. As far as I knew, Claire had never before stuck around the barn to hang out with Altana and Jen.

"Sorry to bother you," Altana said. She was looking at Charlie, not me. "We were waiting for you guys to come out."

"Is everything all right?" I asked.

"Yeah, of course."

"I'm Claire," Claire said, stepping forward and thrusting a hand toward Charlie. "I'm an old friend of Lorrie's."

"Good to meet you," Charlie said.

"It's great to meet you," Claire said. She turned to me. "And, Lorrie—I heard you're *working* here."

I nodded stiffly.

"But you were supposed to be at Woodscape all summer."

"There was a change of plans," I said.

"So you're living at home, then?"

"Yup."

"That's got to be . . . interesting," she said.

"Uh-huh."

"I mean, I haven't been to your house in years. Not since your—what was it? Your ninth birthday party?" She didn't pause for me to reply. "When your aunt said we could each take a kitten home as a party favor? She let me take two, because I couldn't decide between a white one and a gray one."

My cheeks blazed as she recounted the story. I hadn't had a birthday party since.

"My mom would've gone mad if I'd brought home a kitten, let alone two of them," Jen said.

"Oh, my mom did," Claire told her. "I cried for a week when my mom said I couldn't keep them." She turned to me. "I wasn't allowed to play at your house anymore. Not that you've invited me."

I could feel judgment all around me, like the dust and grime of Edgewater. The blissful feeling of having Charlie there had been popped like a bubble. I wished I could blink him away from my side. Or blink and make myself disappear. It certainly wasn't the first time I'd wished to disappear. Instead, I stood there, completely visible, and praying that Claire wouldn't say any further incriminating things about me.

Jen started giggling, and my cheeks went hotter and redder, knowing the joke was on me. "What?" Claire asked.

"I'm sorry," Jen said. "It's just that you look exactly like you do in your pictures."

"Well, of course he does," Altana said.

Oh, good. They were back on Charlie.

"I think you're even cuter in person," Claire told him. "Can I get a picture?" She didn't wait for a response before she pushed herself against him and held out her phone to take a selfie. Then of course Jen and Altana wanted pictures, too.

"Listen," Claire said. "I'm meeting a bunch of people at Crescent for dinner. You guys should come."

"Oh, I can't," I said.

"I heard your membership lapsed," she told me. "But it's not a problem. You can be my guests. All of you." She swept her arm in a gesture of generosity.

Altana and Jen were nodding in assent, thrilled for the chance to have dinner with Charlie. But my heart was racing, and I couldn't get enough air. It was bad enough to be here with Charlie and these girls who knew too much about me. But to have to stay behind here and work while he went out with them—who knew what stories they'd spill in my absence? Certainly I'd never see him again. Or, worse, he'd fall for Claire, who didn't live a life of land mines, and I'd see him when he came to the barn to watch *her* ride.

Every time I played the movie in my head of what might happen if Charlie found out the truth about me, it never ended well.

Charlie checked the time on his cell phone. "Thanks for the invite, but I've got to get going," he said.

A whiplash of relief slammed my body.

"But I'll come by again soon, if it's okay with you."

"Yeah. It's okay with me," I said.

He gave me a last peck on the lips. I was too shell-shocked from leftover fear to appreciate the looks of jealousy from the other girls. For one brief, flickering moment, they might have even wanted to switch places with me. "See you around," Charlie said. "Soon." And then he was gone.

16

GHOST EYES

HOURS LATER I PUSHED OPEN THE FRONT DOOR AT Edgewater, accidentally knocking it into Prince Valiant, a geriatric, one-eyed orange tabby. "Sorry, old guy," I said. I reached down to pick him up, something I rarely did with my sister's creatures, and stroked his fur. Prince Valiant slowly blinked his remaining eye, which Susannah had once told me was a sign that he liked me. A kitty kiss.

I walked to the floor lamp in the corner, but when I turned the switch, it didn't go on. I hoped we had extra bulbs, though I suspected not. But I could always switch it out with a lightbulb from a less important lamp in a less important room. I moved deeper into the house, flipping light switches along the way. But the house remained dark.

I found Gigi in the library at the end of the hall, sitting in a club chair by one of Edgewater's nine nonworking fireplaces.

The room smelled the way just about every other room in the house did. But different, as if each room had been sprayed with a different scent of a line of perfumes. Eau de Decay, I'd call the line. Here in the library you could get a whiff of Decay Number Five: Book Mold.

I flipped one last switch, by the door. Nothing happened.

"Gigi," I said.

At the sound of my raised voice, Prince Valiant clawed to be put down, and when I did so, he tore out of the room. My aunt turned to me. Above her hung an oil painting of my mother as a child. My grandfather had commissioned somber-looking portraits of all the family members. They were hung around the room in custom-made gilt frames, each under its own spotlight. In the darkness Mom's childhood brown eyes looked like holes cut out of the portrait. It might as well have been a portrait of a ghost.

"Oh, Lorrie," Gigi said. "I thought you were out with Susannah and Brian."

"When have I ever been out with Susannah and Brian?"

"They said they were going to a carnival. I remember taking you when you were small. You insisted on playing ring toss until you'd won enough times to trade up for the exact prize you wanted. Now I bet you don't even know where that stuffed unicorn is, but I do."

"You've got to tell me where the money is, Gigi. We've got to take care of these bills."

"Look at what's out there." Gigi stood and stepped toward a window. Her voice was soft, as if it was coming from across a distance.

"What?"

"A hundred years ago, we would've been living off the fruits of our land. No reason we can't do it now. We have everything we need right in front of us."

"Listen to yourself," I said. "You sound crazy. This isn't a hundred years ago, and nothing grows on our land besides dandelions."

"I do love a good gazpacho," she said. "I'll plant some bell peppers—red or yellow ones but not green."

"Of course not green," I said. This was insane.

Gigi stood and pressed her hands against the glass pane. She looked out across the land she intended to conquer. I turned away in disgust and thundered up the darkened back stairwell to my room.

SLEEP ELUDED ME ALL NIGHT LONG, AND I WAS awake when the sun rose and the birds began chirping like it was any other day. I went into the bathroom and turned on the sink, twisting the knob around more than usual to get the water running. Finally I smacked my hand against the faucet, giving up. Either Gigi hadn't paid our water bill, or the water pressure was tied to the electricity, or both. I brushed my teeth with just toothpaste and the spit in my mouth. A shower was clearly out of the question. After I got dressed, I retrieved the brown paper bag that I'd hidden in the back of my closet and dumped its contents out onto my bed, surveying the collection. I fingered each piece of my grandmother's silver, wondering which utensil was the first she'd acquired. This spoon? That knife? The little fork to get the lobster out of a claw?

And which of them were among those bought in bulk once Grandpa had hit it big?

The pieces were no longer tarnished; at least Brian was good for something. I used the end of my nightshirt to get little remnants of polish out from in between some of the tongs on the forks and in the teeny-tiny petals of the flower at the ends of the handles. Then I gathered it all back up, put it into the bag, and headed out to Oceanfront.

ORION MUST HAVE HEARD ME OPEN THE DOOR AT the end of the corridor, because when I got to his stall, he was waiting for me, his sleek Hershey-bar-brown neck hanging over the door. It was still early; no one else was there, nor would they be for a while longer, so I didn't have to feel even vaguely conflicted about spending the next hour with my horse.

Orion knew what the sound of my undoing the latch meant, and he stepped back to let me enter. Chivalry was not dead, not even if you were a horse. I hugged him hello, and he lowered his muzzle to match my affection. I led him to the corridor and tacked him up. Ten minutes later we started out on the path behind the barn that went down toward the ocean, the path Orion and I had been riding together for years. We walked to a clearing where deer were grazing. They raised their heads and regarded Orion and me. We stood silently. Orion didn't so much as flick an ear. I think he was as mesmerized as I was.

When the rustle of wind in the trees sent the deer running, I gave Orion a little kick, and we were off. My horse's hooves beat against the ground. I felt his power as if it were my own—my own energy, my own strength, my own fury, pounding and pounding. We flew over a tree that had fallen across the path as if it was nothing. Branches arched above us, a few low enough that I had to duck my head to the space between Orion's ears. He cantered along the bend that led to a view of the water. From the vantage point of the top of a horse, it felt like being on the edge of a cliff. I couldn't see the ground in front of me, just the roaring ocean below. Once, I read that humans have a natural urge to jump off bridges and cliffs and other high places, as if something is pulling them in the direction of disaster. I wondered if that was what the freak was feeling when he stood at the Point that night—a surge of excitement and adrenaline at the realization that it would be so easy. Just one more step.

Would Orion do it, if I kicked him in the side and pressed forward? Did horses have the same urge that humans did? Even if Orion didn't, he wasn't green anymore. He trusted me, followed my lead. Would he follow me over the edge, if that was where I led him?

As if he'd sensed the thoughts in my head, Orion took a few tentative steps backward. I let out a deep breath and pulled to turn him around and head home.

Orion was more subdued on the walk back to Oceanfront, and so was I. Once at the barn, I clipped him into crossties, removed his sweaty tack, and hosed him down to cool him off. Then I used the sweat brush to sweep off the excess water and set him out to pasture. After he was settled, I headed into the bathroom, closed myself into one of the shower stalls, turned the dial, and marveled at the miracle of actual water pressure. Hot water! Cold water! As much water as I wanted! It's true what they say: You never realize how much you love something until it's gone. And I loved that shower. I stayed in extra long, letting the shower stall steam up around me. I hadn't felt so good since Charlie had showed up unannounced, and without even thinking about it, I wrote his name in the condensation. I traced the letters again and again as the water pounded around me.

CHARLIE COPELAND. And then I palmed out his name so no one else would see it.

WHEN I WAS DONE AND DRESSED, IT WAS JUST about nine o'clock and time to get on with the chores of the day—the ones I was paid to do. I turned out a half dozen horses and cleaned out their stalls. I was feeding a blue-black mare, Cobalt, a flake of hay when Lennox stopped by.

"Hey," I said, ducking out of the stall.

"'Hey'? That's all you have to say?"

"What do you mean?"

"Claire said she met Charlie here yesterday—because he was visiting you."

"She did, indeed."

"Holy shit, Lorrie! I can't believe you didn't tell me!"

"I don't have a phone," I reminded her.

She shook her head. "I know. It's really cramping my style."

"Yours and mine both," I said glumly.

"Okay, listen. I don't have much time, because I have to meet Claire for lunch."

Lunch. The word made my gut twist. I'd scoped out the

break room that morning and found an apple. Probably meant for someone's horse, but I ate it anyway. I was hungry again.

"But I need to be brought up to speed on this."

"He came here yesterday to meet Orion and watch me ride."

"And?"

"And not much else happened, on account of Claire interrupting us—and Altana and Jen, too." Lennox gave a sympathetic eye roll. "But a little more happened the other night."

"Whoa, whoa, whoa," Lennox said. "The other night? You've seen Charlie *twice* since the Fourth of July? I'm sorry, but this is essential information, and there are a thousand ways you could've gotten in touch to tell me. Brian's phone." I made a face. "Or the phone in Naomi's office. Or you could've stopped by the house. Or sent a carrier pigeon."

"Next time I'll definitely send a carrier pigeon," I told her.

"Good. That's settled," she said. "Now spill."

"He called me at the barn a couple days ago, and I went over to his house."

"You went to *his house?*"

"You've been there, too," I reminded her.

"That was different. There were a thousand people there, and I happen to know there wasn't another campaign party, because Julia's out in the district. I've been following along online."

"Of course you have."

"I haven't seen much about the senator, though. Kind of a double standard, don't you think? Julia was always at his side when he was the one campaigning. But anyway, we're way off-topic here—back to you and Charlie at his house. How'd you end up there, anyway?"

"He called me here and invited me over for dinner," I said. "The chef made a quiche. It was unlike anything I'd ever tasted before—there were shrimp in it that must've been marinated in some sort of pepper-lemon concoction."

"Who cares about the shrimp?" Lennox said. "Did he kiss you during dinner?"

"No, we just talked," I said. "And here's a Copeland snippet you'll like. Charlie asked what the best thing was about my day. He said his dad used to ask him that. The weirdest thing is, my mom used to ask us that, too."

"I didn't know that."

"Well, it's been a long time." I leaned back against Cobalt's stall door. The mare hung her head out next to me.

"You okay?" Lennox asked.

"Yeah, of course. Anyway, after dinner we walked down to the beach and took our shoes off and sat in the sand."

"And then he kissed you?" I nodded. "God, this story is such a cliché. And if it wasn't you, I'd be so jealous right now."

"Yeah, but—"

"But what?" Lennox asked. "Are you going to tell me that Charlie Copeland is a sloppy kisser?"

"Not sloppy at all," I said. "He's sort of gentle and strong at the same time."

Lennox let out an involuntary *ah*.

"But then Victor Underhill interrupted us and started asking me a bunch of questions."

"God, that guy," Lennox said. "I'm so dying to know what his story is."

"My impression of him is that he's not a hornet's nest you'd want to kick," I said. "And it was like he knew I had things to hide. About my family."

"I'm sure you're being paranoid," Lennox said. "The way you always are about your family."

"Something he said was strange." I shook my head.

"What?"

"Charlie told me his dad's doctor's appointment was in New York, and then when Victor came up to us on the beach, he said the senator was calling Charlie from DC. And Charlie jumped up like it was a code."

"Code for what?"

"I don't know. Maybe: Get away from this girl."

"Oh, come on, Lor. Clearly that's not the code. He showed up here to see you *after* you went there for dinner." She paused. "And there's something else you'll want to know, too."

"What's that?"

"He called my house this morning to get information on you."

I did a double take. "Charlie called your house? Now who isn't telling who things?"

"Serves you right," she said. "But it turns out that Charlie Copeland went online to find my blog, and then he found out my last name, and he called me."

"What kind of information did he want?"

"He asked me if I knew whether you'd be home tonight,"

she said. "And he asked for your address so he could stop by."

My stomach was a fist. "Oh God," I said. "You didn't tell him where I live, did you?"

"Of course not. I didn't give him your address or your phone number or even your last name—Lorrie *Hall*."

"Thank you." I paused. "I just want to keep the fantasy going for a little bit longer."

"It doesn't have to be a fantasy, Lorrie," she said. "You need to face your fear that this could actually go right."

I shook my head. "I'm not afraid of that. It's just . . . everything is so hard right now."

"Well, I made this part easier for you," Lennox said. "I told him you definitely wouldn't be at your house tonight because you were coming to a barbecue at mine, and I invited him to join us. So I scored you a date, and you'll be miles away from Edgewater."

"Plus, you'll get to see Charlie and pump him for further Copeland info."

"I got a Google Alert this morning—a blogger claiming that Charlie's dad has a drinking problem."

"Really? My dad had a drinking problem," I said.

"You don't corner the market on alcoholic dads," Lennox said. "But I don't buy it, because if it was true about Franklin Copeland, it would've been uncovered before, and this guy didn't even offer up any evidence of it, other than that some unnamed source saw the senator laughing loudly and carrying on in a restaurant. My guess—it was probably some political opponent trying to start a rumor."

"You're not going to ask Charlie about it, are you?"

"No, don't worry," she said. "Unless it comes up. Then all bets are off."

"Fair enough," I said. "And you won't blog about me and Charlie?"

"I swear, your love life will never appear under my byline," Lennox said. "Listen, I'm late to meet Claire. She said there's a new Theory store on Main, and obviously I need the perfect thing to wear tonight. You should come with."

"I have a job," I reminded her. "Some of us need to work for a living."

"Just for now you do," she said. "Just until the trust fund gets sorted out. And I can't wait until it does, because I don't get to see you nearly enough." She paused. "But at least you love it here. You've always loved it more than I do."

I was pretty sure she'd said that last part to make herself feel better. She pulled out her phone and mumbled as she texted: *If you beat me to the resto, order me the La Scala salad.*

The La Scala salad was twenty-six dollars on Declan's lunch menu. Chopped iceberg lettuce with salami, provolone, tomato, and garbanzo beans. Hardly worth the price tag. I'd started cataloging things that were wastes of money and thinking what I could do if I had that cash. With nearly thirty bucks I could eat for a week. My stomach grumbled at the thought. "Sorry," I told Lennox, cheeks reddening.

"Guess it's lunchtime for you, too."

"I forgot to bring any today."

"Granola bar?" she asked, pulling one out of her purse.

"Thanks," I said. "You're a lifesaver."

"It's the least I can do," she said. She reached out and tapped Cobalt on the nose. "I told Charlie seven o'clock, because I figured that would give you time to come over first and clean up."

"Yeah, I'm off at five," I said. "I just have to run an errand first, and then I'll be there."

"Cool. I'm going to say hi to Pepper. I'll see you later."

She headed down the corridor. I wolfed down my granola bar and then continued with my chores, feeding who needed to be fed. When I got to Pepper's stall, Lennox had gone. But there was a pile of fresh manure in a corner.

Jeremy was in the feed room measuring grain when I arrived to retrieve the wheelbarrow and pitchfork. "Do you ever wish you could just hit the pause button for a bit, for like a half hour or so, so that everything you cleaned up would stay cleaned up?" I asked him.

"Let me guess: dump duty."

"Yeah, Pepper. Major Code Brown."

"I thought I just saw Lennox," he said. "Second time in one week. I figured she'd be here more this summer with you around."

"She just came by to say hello." I paused. "She hasn't ridden Pepper much this summer, has she?"

"Nah," he said. "But I don't mind. Gives me an excuse to take Pepper out now and then. He's a great horse."

"Do you get tired of it?" I asked. "I don't mean Lennox, but just generally: Do you get tired of riders who have horses here not because they actually like horses, but because they like the idea of having them? And they have us to clean up after them?"

Jeremy dropped the grain scooper into the bin and shrugged.

"I don't really get caught up in it," he said. "The truth is, people make careers off of doing things other people don't want to do or don't know how to do themselves. I don't know how to give myself a tetanus shot or wire my house for cable, but I do know how to train a horse. We all do different things. It's what makes the world go 'round."

I heard Beth-Ann Bracelee in my head: *It takes all kinds of people for the world to function.* But she'd meant it in a different way.

"Listen," he said. "It's no secret that I can't afford a horse of my own. So here I get to ride some pretty quality ones, and love them, and sometimes even show them. And cleaning up horse shit isn't that big of a deal to me."

"I don't think Lennox knew about it," I told him.

I didn't want to think that Lennox had left it there for someone else to clean up. Though, truthfully, I'd done the same thing myself in the past; that's what you paid for when you boarded your horse at a barn like Oceanfront. And though Lennox knew I was working here, if she had seen it, she probably hadn't made the connection that I'd be the one to clean it up, right?

And what did I care anyway, cleaning up Pepper's shit, after everything Lennox had done for me?

I took the wheelbarrow and pitchfork and made my way back down to Pepper's stall.

17

IT SEEMED LIKE A GOOD IDEA AT THE TIME

I DROVE ACROSS TOWN TO THE AREA BY THE RAIL-road tracks where Brian Beecher's parents lived. Searching for the trust had been fruitless so far. We were drowning in unpaid bills, and so it had come to this. I got out of the car and clutched the brown bag of my grandmother's silver to my chest as if it was a baby, glancing to either side of the road. A black sedan with dark tinted windows passed by and stopped right in front of me. My heart was pounding, and I held the bag tighter, as if whoever was in the car was about to reach out and grab it from me.

But then I noticed the stop sign. Of course. That was why the car had stopped. After a moment it turned right. I took a deep breath and crossed the street to the Scully Farms Pawn-shop.

Inside the store were dozens of glass cases showcasing rings and vases and other flotsam and jetsam that was surely once treasured by its former owners. I walked down the center aisle to the counter in the back, where a bald man with a lit cigarette dangling from his mouth told me to dump the silver out onto the counter. He reached out with thick, dirt-smudged fingers, gruffly spreading the pieces around.

"They're from Tiffany's," I said. I had to ball my fingers into fists to resist the urge to swat his away. "My grandmother started the collection right after she got married."

The man grunted in response. He'd waited too long to flick his cigarette, and flecks of ash fell onto the silver. "Two thousand," he said.

I knew that two thousand dollars was a lot of money. More than I'd ever held in my hands at once. But then I started my list in my head: the phone bill, the electric bill, the credit card bills, Orion's shoes, his food, his board. Two grand wouldn't even stretch the month, and it certainly wouldn't get me back to Hillyer in the fall.

The man opened up a lockbox and began to count out the amount in hundred-dollar bills.

"Wait," I told him. "This set is antique. It's got to be worth more than two grand."

"It would be if you had the full set," he said. "But there are quite a number of pieces missing, and this one"—he held out a dinner knife—"isn't even silver. Feel it. It's too light."

I picked it up and picked up another knife to compare; he was right.

"Eighteen hundred is the best I can do."

"You said two thousand."

The man was picking up serving pieces and putting them down, picking up and putting down, to check the weights. "You got a couple of fakes in here."

"My grandmother spent years acquiring this set," I said, my voice just above a whisper. I cleared my throat and went on. "Brian—my sister's boyfriend—I think maybe he sold some of the pieces already. Maybe to you?"

The man shrugged. "I couldn't tell you."

"Maybe he sold them to someone else, then, and replaced the sold pieces with fakes. It wouldn't be the first time he pulled something like that. But he had no right—"

I cut myself off. Why was I telling the pawnshop guy? He didn't care. He probably heard a ton of stories just like this—a wedding ring with initials engraved, a grandmother's Limoges box, baseball cards. It didn't matter to him how I or anyone else had acquired anything or why we'd ended up at his store. For him, this was simply business. Give me your treasures, and I'll give you some cash. And we'll both move on.

He exhaled a line of smoke out of the corner of his mouth. "I'll give you twenty-five hundred if you want to throw in the Rolex," he said.

I looked at my left wrist. I'd worn that watch for over a decade. It had been my grandfather's, and Mom had worn it ever since he'd died. The night she left, when I was crying on the stairs, asking her to please stay home, she'd taken it off her wrist and put it on mine. "You can stay up a half hour later," she'd said. It was meant to be a way for me to keep track of my bedtime, but maybe she'd also meant it as a tangible reminder that she was with me even when she was gone.

What a crock of shit.

It was an inanimate object, not a mom stand-in. Besides which, I was never sentimental about her; no reason to start being so now.

"Take it or leave it," the man said. "Makes no difference to me."

But it made a difference to me, of course. That's why I was there. My eyes itched from the smoke, and I blinked a thousand times as I undid the clasp. A watch was just a single-function device anyway, as the senator had said. Immediately following this transaction, I'd pay our cell-phone bill, and the phone would tell the time. I'd pay our electric bill, and we'd get the house clocks back. I'd have absolutely no use for the watch, and I wouldn't miss it.

"You have a deal," I told him, handing it over.

He counted out the money in hundred-dollar bills, and I stuffed them deep into my front pocket.

Outside, I ran across the street back to my car. Double-parked at the end of the block was the same black sedan. My heart was pumping hard. The windows of the sedan were too darkened for me to see who was behind the wheel. But I couldn't help thinking it was someone watching me. I fumbled with my keys and got into the car, locking the doors again quickly.

I turned the ignition and sped in the opposite direction. On the drive home, the wad of money seemed to be buzzing from inside my pocket. I kept glancing into the rearview mirror, but as far as I could tell, no one was behind me. Twenty minutes later I pulled into the driveway at Edgewater and stopped with a screech. My goal was to pay the bills and get my phone in working order so I could give Charlie my number when I got to Lennox's, and then have electricity to see my way to my room when I got home. I banged my way into the house and ran upstairs for my phone—this time I'd press one to be connected to AT&T. But when I tried to power it on, it was dead, and of course without electricity, I had no way to charge it.

New plan. "Brian!" I called. "Are you here? Susannah! Brian! I need your phone!"

Susannah's bedroom door was closed. I was this close to barging in. On principle, I didn't give a shit what they were doing on the other side. But truly, there were some things I didn't want to see. So I knocked first, three hard, loud raps. I waited a few seconds for an answer, and then I pushed open the door.

Two kittens, one white and one black, immediately ran out. The room smelled musty and sour, and the sheets on the bed were twisted in the aftermath of I didn't even want to know what. Four more cats were sprawled out on top of them. But there was no Susannah, no Brian. And no phone.

"Goddamn it," I said as another cat slunk past me.

"Lorrie?" Susannah called.

I turned back to the hallway, in the direction of her voice. She was coming up the stairs with two large buckets. Her arms were extended from their weight, and she was walking carefully, but still water sloshed around and dripped onto the faded orange Oriental carpet runner.

"What's up?" she asked.

"I need Brian's phone."

"He went out," she said.

"Where?"

She stopped in front of me and put the buckets down with a thump, which sent more water splashing onto the floor. Not that a little bit of water would matter; the carpets were already saturated with cat piss. I made it a point never to go barefoot outside my bedroom. "I'm sure he'll be back soon."

I shook my head. On second thought, I didn't even need Brian's phone yet. After all, I only had cash on me, and it wasn't as if I could send hundred-dollar bills through a cell phone. I needed to deposit the money and then write checks.

But then there was the problem of our checking account being overdrawn. I was guessing that meant we owed the bank money and that they'd take their share out of whatever I deposited. Suddenly everything seemed so difficult, all over again.

A black cat jumped up onto the side of the bucket and started lapping up water. "You thirsty, Pickles? Not too much. That's for Lorrie." She turned to me. "I figured you'd need some, too."

"What for?"

"To flush your toilet," she said.

"Oh God, Susannah," I said. "Do you see what it's come to? We can't even flush the toilets."

"I know. I was upset this morning."

I nodded. "Finally."

"But now we have a solution," she said. "I washed my clothes this morning, too."

"And what are you going to do when you want to shower? Bathe in the stream?"

"Go to Brian's house," she said.

"I didn't know Brian had a house."

"Oh, stop. I'm sure he'd let you come, too."

"I'd rather stick needles into my eyes."

"Do you have to be so down on him all the time? He's the one who figured out we could use stream water to flush the toilets."

Another cat joined Pickles at the bucket. When she jumped up, the whole thing tipped over. Water everywhere. The cats skittered off.

"I can't take it," I said. And then I shouted: "I can't take it!"

Susannah bent to turn the bucket upright again. "Jesus, Lorrie, it's no big deal," she said. "There's plenty of water in the stream. We'll just get more."

When she stood back up, I gripped her shoulder. "Listen to yourself," I said. "Do you hear what you're saying? Or have you lost the ability to think straight?"

Susannah shook me off. "I'm not crazy. Things just don't bother me the way they bother you."

When we were really young, Susannah used to come into my room in the mornings to see what I was wearing. Only then would she get dressed herself—in the closest approximation to my outfit that she could manage. "She's copying me again," I'd whine to Gigi. I'd race back upstairs to change my clothes so I didn't show up at school dressed like my little sister.

If I'd known then what I knew now, I would've let her keep copying me. I would have dressed her in a matching outfit each day myself. Because having my sister end up as someone who was so *not* like me was the real frustration, the real loss.

Susannah had turned away from me and was headed to her room. I followed behind. "All day I've been blaming Gigi for what's happening right now," I told her, speaking to her back. "But the more I think about it, the more I think it's actually Mom's fault. She knew Gigi was a mess. She was always on her about being hopelessly, recklessly disorganized. They fought about it all the time."

We were in Susannah's bathroom, where pebbles from the litter boxes peppered the floor. On the windowsill, higher than the cats could jump, was a cage that housed a couple of mice she'd rescued from her cats' jaws. One was missing an ear, the other a tail. "Hey, Farley, hey, Whiskers," she said, tapping the wire mesh of the cage. The mice jumped toward her fingers, as if high-fiving her.

"Susannah, are you even listening to me?"

She turned back to me. "I am," she said. "And I don't remember them fighting."

She grabbed a crumpled towel off the rack and headed back out to the hall.

"Of course you don't," I said, following her. "You were so little, and now, well, now you've just acclimated to the crazy. We learned about this in Developmental Psych at Hillyer—how the first six years of your life are the most formative. You spent half of those years in this house, with Gigi as your primary role model. You don't even realize how crazy things are, because as far back as you can remember, they've never been any other way."

I'd always wondered why Susannah and I were so different, and it was making sense now: Those two years between us made all the difference. I had memories that predated this crazy life, and Susannah did not.

Susannah was on her knees, blotting at the carpet where the water had spilled. As if we needed to worry about spilled water. "But my point is, Mom *did* know better," I told her. "What was she doing, giving Gigi that kind of responsibility? She should've known that Gigi couldn't handle it. It's a wonder it all didn't go to shit earlier. Did Mom care about that? No, she did not. She just wanted to run off with her boyfriend. But we didn't choose to be born. She chose to have us. And that means she chose to make our lives her priority. And, I'm sorry, but you can't just change your mind about that." I paused, shaking my head in disgust. "I'm sure it seemed like a good idea to her at the time. She had a new boyfriend, and she didn't want to be saddled with two kids, so she basically paid someone to take them off her hands. It was practically a get-out-of-jail-free card."

Susannah stood and threw the towel over her shoulder. "She gave us a trust fund," she told me. "That's not free."

"So you're totally okay with her putting a price tag on her kids," I said. "And that she left us in Aunt Gigi's incompetent hands. Look at us, Susannah! We're living in the dark. Things are only getting worse."

"We have flashlights," she said.

I stamped my foot on the floor, like a child. I couldn't help it. "The batteries don't work." I knew I could buy new ones now, but that only seemed like adding insult to injury. "If we had a mother at home, she'd remember to buy new batteries. She'd remember to pay the electric bill."

"It hasn't been all bad," Susannah said softly. "Like you said, Mom chose to have kids. She chose to have *us*. So maybe we're just supposed to be grateful to her that we get to be here."

Out of habit, I glanced down at my wrist, but of course I didn't have a watch anymore. "It's gotta be late in London," I said. "Mom could be taking a midnight stroll with Nigel. Meanwhile we're here in the dark. That doesn't piss you off?"

"Mom's not with Nigel anymore," Susannah said.

"What? What are you talking about?"

"They broke up."

"She broke up with Nigel, and she's still not here?" Susannah nodded, tentatively. "How do you know?"

"There was a letter from Nigel's dad at some point. He said Nigel wasn't back in London, and he was trying to track him down here."

"That doesn't mean anything," I said. "Maybe they had some sort of deal—I'll abandon my family if you abandon yours."

Susannah shrugged, seemingly uninterested. "I guess it's possible."

"When did you see the letter?"

"I don't know," Susannah said, more forcefully this time. "It was a while ago. In a pile of stuff."

"I brought everything that had to do with Mom up to the attic a few years ago," I said. "All the cards and letters she ever sent us. Letters come in envelopes, and envelopes have postage stamps, even if they don't have return addresses. I'm going to find them."

"Why?"

"So we can find *her*."

"I thought you never wanted to see Mom again."

"I don't want to see her," I said. "I want to sue her. She's like our father. A deadbeat parent. Even worse than that, actually."

"Why are you angrier at her, when he was the one who left first?"

"You're angrier at him?"

"I'm not angry at anyone."

"Well, you should be. Especially her. Dad was a drunk who admitted he didn't want kids, but Mom—she made us love her first, and then she disappeared. Maybe you don't remember, but I do. When we were little, she'd sing us songs and tell us stories and go around saying we were the Three Musketeers. You just—" I broke off, and Susannah reached out, but I shook her off. "You just can't go around doing that and then leave your kids behind. Actions have consequences."

I left my sister standing in the hallway and headed to the small staircase at the end of the house that accessed the attic. It had been God-only-knew how many years since anyone had walked these particular halls, and they smelled old and musty. Eau de Decay, Number Eight: Abandoned Rooms.

The couch and love seat in the sitting room at the base of the stairs had layers of dust on them as thick as blankets. Cobwebs stretched between them. I spotted a spider, big as a baby's fist. My heart started to pound, but I wouldn't let myself acknowledge that I was scared as I put a hand on the banister. The dust on it was like a film. I crept up the stairs to the attic door and turned the knob. The door was stuck from being closed for so long. I pushed my whole body against it to make it open.

The stench on the other side was like nothing I'd ever

smelled before, and I pulled the collar of my T-shirt up over my nose. Things must have died up here for it to smell like this. In my head I cursed my mother one last time before I stepped in. The attic was one enormous room, as big as the footprint of the entire house, with a low ceiling and small dormer windows like the lookout windows on a ship. I squinted in the darkness and panned the room. Boxes were everywhere, with corners chewed off and things spilling out onto the floor—old bills, photographs, sheets, clothes. And there was the tent we'd used once, when I was seven and wanted to camp in the backyard. (We lasted for about a half hour before coming inside to sleep in our beds.) And there was Susannah's old dollhouse. And my first saddle. And stacks and stacks and stacks of books.

Something flew across the room—holy shit! A bat! I ducked and covered my head with my hands. My heart was racing, but I knew I had a job to do and just about a half hour left before the attic fell into complete darkness and all the night creatures came out. Then not being able to see would be the least of my problems. I wanted to stay close to the door—to a means of escape—but I needed the light from the windows. I took a deep breath inside my shirt and moved forward. I sat on a box by a window and pulled a stack of papers onto my lap to read by the diminishing rays of sunlight.

If we were all dead, I thought to myself, and I started a pile of things to dump: yellowed magazines and crumbling newspapers, bills for credit cards long closed, scripts for plays Gigi was never in, recipes for meals she never made, and notes scribbled in handwriting I didn't recognize. A breeze swept through the cracks in the windowpanes and sent the papers scattering across the floor again. For a split second I actually welcomed the fresh air, clearing out the smell of decomposing animals. But then *SLAM!* went the attic door, and my heart pounded like Orion's hooves.

Yim, yim, yim, yim, yim, yim, I repeated to myself, as quick as the heartbeats in my chest. But my mantra did nothing to calm me. As I moved across the room to the door, I couldn't get rid of the feeling that I was in another horror movie: Girl goes up into the attic, where no human has set foot in years. While rifling through items long discarded and forgotten, she gets locked in, and then she—

Oh, thank God. The knob turned, and the door opened. I wedged one of the heavier boxes against it so that even a gale-force gust wouldn't close it again. Now, back to work.

I needed to find the more recent piles. I spotted one of Susannah's coloring books on the top of a box, her name spelled out in messy capital letters, and I pulled the whole thing toward the window for optimum light. I flipped through old report cards, moldy stuffed animals, and pages ripped out of the phone book, scanning for clues of . . . what, I wasn't sure. Everything went into the toss pile.

I went faster and faster, so fast that I almost missed the drawings stuck in the middle of it all—my horse drawings. I'd been so little back then. I didn't know anything. I traced the lines with my fingers, remembering how hard I'd tried to get them just right. But this was no time to be sentimental. I crumpled them into a ball and tossed them toward the throwaway pile and turned back to the box. Nothing seemed remarkable until I found the red leather notebook. It was one of those fancy date books you can get from a bank. I opened it to the first page and recognized Mom's handwriting.

I just want to have a place to document the things I'm thinking and feeling, because there's no one who is safe to tell.

Oh my God. A diary.

She'd kept a diary. To write about whatever secrets she felt she couldn't tell anyone else. Maybe to write about how she didn't love her kids enough. Maybe to write about her plans to leave us.

My palms started to sweat, and my heartbeat, which had barely returned to a regular resting rate, started pounding as fast as hoofbeats once again. I felt like I was invading Mom's privacy, reading her diary. Not that she deserved any privacy. She'd left Susannah and me and never looked back.

And so I kept going.

I didn't mean for this to happen. I suppose that's how it always starts. No one says they want to be a bank robber or a drug dealer when they grow up. And no one says they want to have an affair.

Questions rushed into my brain faster than I could read the answers. Mom had had an affair before Dad left? With whom? And how did she meet him? How long did it last?

I wanted to have a normal life, and on paper I have one—a husband, a child.

A husband. Okay, it *was* when Dad was still around.

So my sister is a little messed up. At least she has character.

Oh, sure, Gigi had a lot of "character." I wondered if that was what Mom told herself when she left Susannah and me in her care.

I should be perfectly happy. I was mostly happy. Except for the times I'd wake up in the middle of the night with an inexplicable sense of loss, and I'd resent Keith next to me, sleeping the sleep of the dead. He'd worked hard to get where he was, from the rockiness of his childhood, to the rebellion and addiction of his young adulthood, to this normal life, and he never seemed to want any more than we had. The mornings after those sleepless nights, I'd come back to understanding his contentment. It seemed crazy—that I'd been so upset, and that I'd resented him for nothing I could even explain. I'd put on the coffee, and he'd shuffle papers into his briefcase, and we'd kiss the baby good-bye, and it all seemed to be the way it was supposed to be. And I was happy.

But things happen. A particular set of circumstances lead you to a particular place. A restaurant on the corner of Forty-ninth and Third. Your friend's late for dinner. A man sits alone at the next table. And suddenly your life is split in two. One life is your apartment and your husband and your kid. And the other life is just this man and nothing else. Everything else falls away. You tell yourself it doesn't mean anything. But then you keep going back—even though you know you shouldn't. It feels so good. So you go back again. And again and again.

I decided I wasn't surprised that my mom had betrayed her family for something that felt good for a moment. That kind of impulse was the same kind as the one that got her to leave her children for good. I flipped the page, but it was stuck to a clump of others. My fingers fumbled to pull them apart. "Shit," I said as I tore them instead of separating them. I pushed past the ruined pages to the next section.

I said I had a business trip, and then I got on a plane to meet him. Of course I called home to check in. Lorrie got on the phone to tell me about her day. Then she told me I had to say hi to each of her stuffed animals.

I thought back to the deepest recesses of my brain, to remember a phone call with my mom and a line of stuffed animals I'd made her greet. But I couldn't remember any of it. I couldn't even remember caring about my stuffed animals like that. That was Susannah's kind of thing.

Junior came into the room as I was greeting the hippo and the pig and the donkey.

Junior? What kind of a name was Junior?

I don't know why I was self-conscious. He's a parent, too. Up until now we've had an unspoken rule not to talk about our families. The names of our spouses and our children are verboten. But suddenly he wanted to know about other things I did with Lorrie. I told him all of our little traditions, but I left out any mention of Keith. As if we were a family of two and not three.

I felt bad for the child version of myself, on the phone with Mom. Of course, I'd had no idea what Mom was really thinking at the time. I wondered if she'd rushed me off once her boyfriend walked into the room. I flipped the page again.

Junior and I had no fewer than a thousand conversations about it, and in the end he'd always come to the same conclusion: Telling the truth would be so messy.

But life is messy. That's what I kept telling him. You make messes, and you clean them up as best you can, and then you make more messes. And so it goes. I thought maybe if I made this particular mess first, we'd clean it up together. So I told Keith the baby wasn't his.

The baby? Did she mean Susannah? Was Susannah not my father's child? Oh God. My sister. My sister wasn't my sister. At least, not entirely.

It was the biggest revelation of my entire life, and I was learning about it alone in the barely lit attic surrounded by garbage. My heart was beating madly and erratically, my stomach was in knots, and a lone tear fell from all those welling in my eyes. *Plop*, onto the page. I smudged Mom's words as I wiped it away and kept on reading.

But afterward, it just didn't work out the way I thought it would. My plan was, I'd tell Keith and report back to Junior, and he'd finally be prompted to tell his wife. It would be a hard year of adjustments—getting divorces and becoming step-parents to each other's children. But other people have done it. We could do it, too. And in the end it would even be better than what we were living now. That's what I told him.

But he didn't leave his wife. He said he didn't want to. He said we were being selfish and this was something we shouldn't have started at all. And Keith. I can barely stand to think about what this did to him. He threw away years of sobriety in one night. He said he never wanted to see me again. I cried and begged, "What about Lorrie?" But he said she reminded him too much of me and all he'd lost. He said she'd be better off without him.

So now here I am—without my husband, without Junior. A single mom, with a new baby on the way.

Was I supposed to feel sorry for her—because her husband and her boyfriend left her? It was only because of her own self-ish choices, like Junior said.

But my heart did break for Susannah. Memories from our childhood suddenly flashed into my mind. Like how she would ask to sleep in my bed almost every night. It's so weird, being the older sister. Sometimes you're not in the mood to be fol-lowed around or copied or needed. You don't want a little sister. You want to be an only child again. And those nights I'd tell Susannah to get back to her own room. But then, sometimes, there's no better feeling than having your younger sibling lying right beside you. In the mornings Susannah would let me brush her hair. I had a book of different braids, and Susannah was the model I practiced on to learn a fishtail, a French braid, a Dutch braid. The last one was her favorite. "It's inside out!" she'd always squeal with delight.

I looked back down at the journal on my lap. The words were a blur on the page, but I read them anyway, as if this time they'd spell out a different truth. I didn't hear the footsteps behind me.

"Lorrie?" Susannah called, and I jumped in surprise. Startled, Susannah dropped the candle she was holding. Mom's diary fell to the floor, and I kicked it away so she wouldn't see it. Susannah cried out, and for a second the only thing that registered was that the room was suddenly brighter. Then I realized she was on fire. Whatever synthetic tag-sale skirt she was wearing had gone up in flames, which were spreading quickly, licking her skin.

"I'm burning!" she screamed.

Stop, drop, and roll. That firefighting lesson from childhood popped into my head.

Once, in a Hillyer science seminar we'd been taught that small animals like flies and hummingbirds experience time in slow motion. That's what it was like for me as I tackled Susannah to the ground. She was wailing in pain, and the words I yelled out sounded distended and strange: "Help! Fire! Help!"

18

WE HAVE A
PROBLEM

"LORRIE," SOMEONE WHISPERED. "LORRIE, WAKE UP."

A hand clamped down on my shoulder, and I screamed before I'd even opened my eyes.

"Shh," the voice said.

It took me several seconds to focus on the man standing in front of me, dressed from head to toe in teddy-bear scrubs. I was in a hospital, I remembered. I'd come screaming into the emergency room, barely two hours earlier: "My sister! My sister! Someone help her, please!"

Now Susannah was lying in the bed next to me, and a machine beeped rhythmically, tracking her vital signs. I wondered what had happened to the car after we'd been checked in and treated. I'd pulled up right outside the ER door, and orderlies had come with a gurney to get Susannah from the backseat. One of them noticed my hand and brought me inside, too. No one had asked me to move the Mercedes. I think the keys were even still in it.

"My car," I whispered to Teddy-Bear Scrubs.

"It's all right," he whispered back. "Someone parked it for you."

"The keys?"

"They're in the bag with your sister's clothes," he said. "Don't worry. Can you come with me now, please?"

I nodded, got up, and followed him into the hallway, where a woman was waiting. She was in a pantsuit that Lennox's moms would characterize as "smart," and she had a clipboard under her arm. Around her neck was a tag that read: C. HILLMAN.

She held out her hand to shake mine but then noticed my bandage and gave me a pat on the shoulder instead. "I'm Cheryl," she said.

First-name basis. So, she wasn't a doctor. I was pretty sure she wasn't a nurse, either.

"And you're Lorrie Hollander."

"Yes," I said.

"Of the Hollanders on Break Run?"

My cheeks warmed. "Yes," I said again.

"No kidding," Teddy-Bear Scrubs said. "I've driven by that place a hundred times. I've always wondered about the people who lived there."

I never knew what to say when my house's reputation preceded me. Per usual I looked at the ground and didn't say anything at all.

"Why don't we sit down?" Cheryl Hillman said. She beckoned me toward a set of chairs in bright primary colors.

"But Susannah—" I started.

"Dr. Cortes will be in soon," Cheryl said. "And George can wait with her until he comes. Right, George?"

"Yeah, sure," Teddy-Bear Scrubs said.

"All right, Lorrie?" Cheryl asked.

"Yeah, all right." I followed her to a blue plastic chair underneath a Winnie the Pooh decal. Cheryl pulled a cherry lollipop from her breast pocket and held it out to me. I didn't think it was possible to feel any more diminished than I did right then. "Aren't those for the little kids who come in here?" I asked.

"They're for anyone who needs a little pick-me-up," she said. "I hear you've had a rough night." I didn't move to take the lollipop from her, even though I was starving, and she left it on the table between us. There were a couple of gossip magazines on the table, too, I guess for parents to read while they were waiting for news of their children. The headline on the top one proclaimed: DATE NIGHT FOR SHELBY AND HAYDEN. EXCLUSIVE PICTURES! I wondered if Charlie had seen it—not the magazine in particular, but the news in general that Shelby Rhodes and Hayden O'Conner had apparently been out on a date. And I wondered how he felt about it and if he'd thought about me at all when he heard. Was he thinking of me now the way I was thinking of him? I wished I was next to him, instead of next to Cheryl Hillman. I was *supposed* to be next to him—at Lennox's for dinner. I wondered if they'd eaten without me, and what excuse Lennox had made up for not being able to get in touch with me, and if Charlie was worried.

"Dr. Cortes filled me in a bit on what happened," Cheryl Hillman said. "I just wanted to meet you and see how you're feeling."

"I'm fine," I said. "I mean, my hand hurts, but that's to be expected."

"We can get you something for the pain."

"That nurse who was just here? George? He gave me a little something."

"He told me you were very brave."

My burns were all superficial. The worst one was a fiery blister in the center of my palm. George had covered it in ointment, wrapped it up with gauze, and given me Tylenol. Meanwhile my sister was in a hospital bed with tubes running in and out of her.

"Not really that brave," I said.

"Being brave doesn't mean you can't also be scared." Cheryl Hillman had one of those soft, measured, teacher-ish voices, and I could tell it was a line she'd delivered a few hundred times. "This is the top-rated hospital in the area, and Dr. Cortes said you and your sister are expected to make complete recoveries."

I curled my right hand, my bandaged hand, into a ball and felt a sharp pain. I uncurled it, then curled it again. Pain.

"You're safe here, Lorrie. You know that, right?"

"Yeah, I know."

"And at home? Any problems there?"

I shook my head.

"Are you sure?"

I knew she was only asking because my home had a reputation. The crumbling house that was bringing down the value of all the other mansions lining the road by the ocean. Surely the girls who lived there weren't really fine at all.

And we weren't fine. Especially not now. We were in a

hospital, for God's sake. My sister had come up to the attic with a candle because it was getting dark and she knew I couldn't just switch on a light like a normal person. It struck me that I wouldn't have minded so much if the whole place had gone up in flames. But since my sister was the spark of the fire, I'd had to put it out. I'd thrown myself over her, and together we'd rolled on the floor until the flames died down. The tip of Susannah's braid was on fire, and I'd cinched it with my hand.

None of it would've happened if our mother hadn't left.

Cheryl Hillman leaned in close. "You can talk to me, Lorrie," she said.

The words were on the tip of my tongue, and the tears were welling in my eyes, and I wondered how I'd possibly start this story. What words would I say? I never spoke the truth about my house. I only said things to cover it up.

But if I told her now, then what? It wasn't like Mom would come back, or that I'd get to go back to Hillyer. And if they managed to track down my alcoholic father, there was no way he'd sweep in and rescue us. He'd been off the scene for a decade and a half, and besides, I knew now that he wasn't even related to Susannah.

Instead, there'd be social workers dispatched, and Susannah and I would be taken out of Gigi's custody and put into foster care. They'd probably split us up. And foster parents don't necessarily sign up for being pet caretakers on top of caring for the kids they take in. I could practically hear my sister begging— screaming—to be able to take all her pets with her. The thought made me cringe.

I wouldn't be able to keep Orion, either. So maybe the

house of horrors that we knew was better than what we didn't.

I curled and uncurled my hand again. Ironically the pain turned off the tears. "No problems at home," I said.

"You really can tell me anything, Lorrie. It's my job to make sure you and Susannah are getting the care you need."

"We are," I said. "We're fine."

"With all due respect, Lorrie, you and your sister are in the hospital right now."

"We'll *be* fine," I clarified. "This was an accident. Accidents happen. You must see a lot of them."

"You're right, I do. And sometimes they're truly unavoidable. But you and your sister came in here alone. As I understand it, you drove yourself to the hospital."

"I was the only one home." I'd screamed and screamed for Gigi, but she hadn't come.

"Why didn't you call an ambulance?"

"I . . . I thought it'd be faster," I said. I couldn't bear to tell her we didn't have a phone.

"In these situations, we're often acting on adrenaline."

"Exactly."

"But if an adult had been present, perhaps he or she would have had the presence of mind to make the call for help. After all, I assume you're not trained for medical emergencies. Susannah could have gone into shock and needed attention while you were behind the wheel."

"But she didn't," I said, my voice low.

"It seems to me that you have a lot on your shoulders. Sometimes what happens is a sign that we should intervene before there's a next time."

"Listen, Ms. Hillman . . ." She looked back at me with eyebrows raised. "Or is it Dr. Hillman?"

"Lorrie, I'm Cheryl."

"Cheryl," I repeated.

And now I knew why she'd told me to call her by her first name. It had nothing to do with being a doctor or a nurse. It was to disarm me—to give the illusion of familiarity between us, so I'd feel comfortable telling her my family's deepest, darkest secrets.

"I know you're just doing your job, and I'm sure you've seen kids with terrible home lives who need your intervention. But my sister and I aren't two kindergartners who were left home alone and didn't know how to use the oven. I'm seventeen, and Susannah is fifteen. We do plenty of things on our own. And that's not because we're victims of neglect. It's simply because we're practically adults."

"All right, then," she said. She paused and looked down at her clipboard. I could tell she was just fake-reading, buying time before she said what came next. "Lorrie, I know you have a lot on your mind right now, but I just wanted to check—it says here that your insurance is Blue Cross."

"That's right. I don't know the policy number—the card is at home. But I know it's Blue Cross from when I've filled out my school insurance forms, and George said it wouldn't be a problem to call and get the policy number."

"You fill out your own medical forms for school?"

"Yes. Why?"

"No reason. It's just usually a thing a parent does."

"Our aunt is our guardian."

Cheryl nodded. "Yes, I know."

If she knew, then why did she mention the thing about a parent?

"So I'm going to be completely honest with you. We have a problem. We spoke to Blue Cross, and they said your family's insurance policy has been canceled."

My cheeks heated up as if the room was on fire. "I'm sure when my aunt gets here, she'll clear everything up," I said.

"But she wasn't home when this happened?"

Jesus. We'd been through this. "No."

"What makes you think she'll be home now?"

"I . . . I don't know . . ."

"She hasn't answered any of our calls. The phone just rings and rings."

"It's a big house," I said. "If you don't mind, I'd like to get back to Susannah now. I know George said he'd stay with her, and he seems like a really nice guy, but the truth is, he's virtually a stranger to us, and I think I should be there in case Susannah wakes up."

Cheryl Hillman stood and offered me a hand. But I shook my head; my legs worked just fine. I walked back down the hall, knowing she was watching. When I got to Susannah's room, George gave up the bedside chair to me.

Susannah was still sleeping. She looked so precious and so vulnerable lying there. A sheet had been pulled over her legs, and her torso was wrapped up in mummy-white gauze, like my hand. The singed end of her braid hung off the end of the pillow. She made a small sound when she inhaled, barely a squeak. Except for the machines, it was the only sound in the room.

Once, Lennox's mom Allyson had told us that when Lennox

and Harper had each been newborns, she'd go into their rooms in the middle of the night to check that they were still breathing. She'd watch their chests moving up and down, up and down. And if they seemed too still for a second too long, she'd wake them. Their cries were a relief.

At that moment I felt like I was Susannah's mother, consumed with the responsibility of her life, hanging on her every breath.

I wasn't Susannah's mom. I was her sister. She would never know she wasn't my full sister. I would never tell anyone.

I had no idea how much time had passed before I heard the *clack, clack, clack* of tap shoes in the hallway. Then the door opened, and Gigi came sweeping in, Brian right behind her. Her hair and clothes were wet. Brian took off his baseball cap, shook the rain off onto the floor, and put it back on.

"Darlings!" Gigi said.

"Shh, Gigi," I said. "She's sleeping."

But Susannah's eyes had popped open. "You're here," she said. "Why are you all wet?"

"It started raining," Brian told her.

"Cats and dogs out there," Gigi said. "But not to worry. I love extreme weather. It makes me feel more alive."

"I don't think anyone was worried about *you*," I said.

Gigi ran a dripping finger along Susannah's pale cheek, leaving droplets that looked like tears. "Are you all right, my angel? What am I saying? Of course you're not. Just look at you. Your poor little body."

"I'm all right," Susannah said. "The doctor said I won't even have bad scars."

"That's because she's tough as nails," Brian said. He reached out to hold the hand that wasn't tethered to an IV pole. I had to hand it to Brian. In the past few hours, he'd really come through. He had a working cell phone, which he'd answered when I'd called. He'd offered to track down Gigi, and now here they both were.

"You do look like shit, though, babe," he said. "If I'm being completely honest."

Now, there was the Brian we all knew and loved.

"Oh, Susannah," Gigi said. And then she started to sing softly. "Oh, Susannah, now don't you cry for me."

The door swung open again. Cheryl Hillman with her smart suit and clipboard. "Excuse me," she said. "Ms. Hollander, may I borrow you for a couple of minutes? We have some loose ends to tie up."

"I can't think about all that while my niece is lying here helpless."

"I assure you, Susannah is receiving the help she needs," Cheryl said. "There are just a few forms for you to fill out."

Gigi waved her away. "I should've had Brian drive me by the house so I could've picked up that afghan you like," she told Susannah.

"She wasn't home?" I asked Brian.

"Nope. I found her walking on Break Run, by that senator's place."

"What? The Compound?" I asked, raising my voice.

"Ms. Hollander," Cheryl said. "At the very least I need to get Susannah's insurance information. Lorrie said she thought you had a policy with Blue Cross, but we couldn't get a working policy number."

"We're between policies," Gigi said. "And Mercury is in retrograde right now, so I can't sign any new contracts."

Cheryl Hillman's eyes flicked to me for a second, but I looked away. I would not have her thinking that I was ready to confide in her about anything. "This is a private hospital, Ms. Hollander," she said to Gigi. "We won't turn away an emergent case for inability to pay, but for someone like Susannah, who is stable and simply requires observation—generally, in that situation, we order a transfer to the public hospital."

So this was how it went: Out in the hall, Cheryl had been full of concern. Now she was ready to ship us out. I was glad to not have trusted her, because I knew she didn't really give a shit, and that once we were out the doors, she would simply check us off her list and never think of us again.

But this was our life. My sister's life. "You said this hospital was the best in the area," I said.

"I'm so sorry about all this," Susannah said, her voice thick.

"There's nothing to be sorry about," I told her.

"Of course not, darling girl," Gigi agreed. She turned to Cheryl Hillman, looking her in the eye for the first time since she'd entered the room. "I insist on nothing but the best for my nieces. Just send me the bill."

"That's not how this works," Cheryl said.

"You were going to bill the insurance company. So send it to me instead."

"We're talking about an overnight stay, at the least."

"It's going to be so expensive," Susannah moaned.

"Oh, Susannah," Gigi said, her voice a song. "Don't worry your pretty little head about it."

Cheryl had her eyes locked on my aunt as if she was in a one-person staring contest. I saw her taking in Gigi's lace tunic, yellowed with age, her cloche hat, her tap shoes. Tap shoes! God, what a first impression Gigi made. I could tell Cheryl was fed up. *I've put up with her for over a decade*, I wanted to tell her. *You've had five minutes.*

"I know Dr. Cortes wants to speak to you about the girls. I'll have him paged now."

She left, and Gigi, seemingly unaffected, flopped onto the edge of Susannah's bed. I saw Susannah wince slightly as the mattress shifted, but Gigi's voice was all excitement and bounce. "Remember those cocktail umbrellas you used to take from my drinks when you were young?"

"I wanted them for my hamsters," Susannah said. "They were the perfect beach umbrellas for Coco and Mr. Shivers."

"Wouldn't they be a perfect touch at my party?" Gigi asked. "I'm hiring a mixologist to develop a special drink. We'll stick a little umbrella in each of the glasses, in honor of you, Susie. What do you think?"

"I think this isn't the time to talk about your party," I cut in.

"Nonsense," Gigi said. "This is the best time. We could all use a distraction, and what's better than a party?" She paused. "Party favors! The Copelands gave out tree ornaments for Christmas in July. Everyone got one to bring home."

"Was that why you were wandering by the Compound?" I asked. "To talk about party favors?"

"I had a little business to take care of. That's all," she said.

I felt the adrenaline start to surge again. "You had business at the Compound?" I asked.

"Nothing you need to worry about."

"'Nothing to worry about' is your stock answer to everything," I told her. I felt myself panting as the words came out, as if I'd just been running. "And it's never true."

There were countless things to worry about whenever my aunt showed up anywhere. I pictured her at the base of the Compound driveway, in front of the massive iron gates. She must've looked ridiculous dressed up the way she was, with rain pelting down around her.

Oh God. What if Charlie had been there to see her? What if he somehow figured out she was my aunt? I shuddered at the thought.

"Did you talk to anyone?" I asked.

"Don't worry about it," my aunt said.

"How can I not worry when you won't give me an answer? Why were you at the Compound?"

"Lorrie, stop," Susannah said. Her voice was like a little kid's at bedtime, fighting the urge to fall asleep.

I clenched my fists, and my right one ached from my burn. "Just tell me one thing," I said to Gigi. "You didn't mention me to anyone, did you?"

"You don't want to get mixed up with the Copeland family," she said, not answering the question.

"Why? What the hell is going on?"

"Why do you care so much about the Copelands?" Brian asked.

I sat back in my chair and folded my arms across my chest, not answering. Gigi had turned away from me, toward Brian. "I've been thinking, maybe you can invite one of your friends to my party so Lorrie will finally have a date."

"Sure, I think Lorrie'd love that," he said.

"Hear that, Lorrie?" Gigi said.

Brian grinned at me.

"Don't look at me like that," I told him.

"You need to learn to lighten up," he said.

"Is that what I need? Because we're in Susannah's hospital room right now, and that seems rather heavy."

"What are your friends' names, Brian?" Gigi asked.

"Stop it," I protested. "I don't need Brian's help finding a date."

"Suit yourself."

Gigi went back to fawning over my sister. A few minutes later, Cheryl Hillman came back into the room with Dr. Cortes. He gave us the rundown on what I already knew about Susannah—the burns on her abdomen were first and second degree. They were keeping her overnight to make sure she didn't get an infection. "Just add it to my bill," Gigi said brightly.

"Let me call the billing department," Cheryl said. "If that's amenable to them, that's fine. If not, we can arrange a transfer, as we discussed."

I couldn't count on Mom's trust fund anymore—wherever it was, if it even still existed. But I could feel the lump of cash in my pocket. I'd planned to pay for so many other things. But none of them was as important as Susannah.

"I have money," I said, pulling the lump from my pocket. It was a small miracle it hadn't fallen out and gone up in flames. But there it was, and I could use it. If you could throw money at a problem, it wasn't a problem at all.

"Lorrie!" Gigi said.

"I got an advance from the barn."

"Shit," Brian said. "You make a lot at that barn."

Gigi jumped up to give me a hug. "I'll pay you back, of course."

"Of *course*," I said. Gigi didn't seem to notice my sarcasm.

Dr. Cortes gave Susannah another shot for the pain. "That had a little sedative in it. Why don't you all head out, and come back in the morning?"

"I have to meet the guys anyway," Brian said. "They're probably right where I left them, and I could use a beer, you know."

Oh, yes, *Brian* had had an especially hard night.

"I don't want Susannah to stay alone," I said.

"Of course we don't!" Gigi said. She flopped back onto Susannah's bed, and Susannah gave a little wince. "We'll stay over. It'll be like a slumber party."

"I think the patient needs to get some rest," Dr. Cortes said.

"You go," I told Gigi. "Brian can drop you at home. I'll stay here."

I waited for Cheryl Hillman to say I was still a minor and couldn't stay the night at my sister's bedside, but she stood there silently with her clipboard tucked under her arm.

"If you're sure, darling," Gigi said, leaning back toward Susannah.

"Mmm-hmm," Susannah said. She was already halfway to dreamland.

Naturally Gigi made a big show of kissing us both good-bye. Brian patted the top of Susannah's head. And then they were gone, and so was Dr. Cortes. Cheryl Hillman gave me a pillow and a blanket and pulled in another chair to push against the one I'd been sitting in so I could stretch out.

"George is on all night, and he'll check in on your sister," she told me. "And I'll be following up with you. All right, Lorrie?"

"All right."

The door closed behind her. I watched my sister's eyelids droop and close until she was sleeping. I stared at her, this child of light, thinking of the parts of Susannah that were like me, and the parts that weren't, and how those parts made a little bit more sense now.

But I'd still do anything for her. Anything. And I couldn't let her go back to Edgewater and live in the dark. My grandmother's silverware had brought in less than two grand from the pawnshop, and I probably wouldn't get much for a cracked set of antique dishes or busted lamps or once-priceless, now-moldy works of art. But there was one thing I owned that I knew was worth a significant amount.

I didn't want to wake up Susannah, so I crept out of the room. The hallway was eerily quiet. Even the lights had been dimmed for the night. I had the strangest feeling of being alone in a ghost story. I walked down the corridor. As I turned the corner, I saw a man standing at the end of the hallway, under a bright red EXIT sign. I stopped and focused my eyes. It was Victor Underhill.

I didn't move; I didn't even breathe. I just stood there and stared at him, like a deer in headlights.

"Lorrie, can I help you?" someone said.

The words came as if across an ocean.

"Lorrie?" It was George. I turned to face him. "Do you need anything?" he asked.

"Huh?"

"Is there anything I can do for you?"

I couldn't think straight to answer the question. I turned back, and Underhill was gone. It was as if he'd never been there in the first place.

But I had seen him. I was fairly certain hallucinations weren't a side effect of getting a minor burn or taking Tylenol. He was there. What the hell was he doing in the hospital? Could it have anything to do with why Gigi was at the Compound?

"Lorrie?" George said. "Are you all right?"

A hospital is as public as a bus stop, I told myself. Underhill probably had a reason for being there that had nothing to do with my family. This was just a coincidence. It had nothing to do with me. "I . . . I need to make a phone call."

George walked me to the nurses' station and pulled over a large corded phone. "Here, you can use this."

I picked up the receiver and dialed. Somewhere in North Carolina, I imagined the phone ringing. And ringing.

No one was picking up. Perhaps it was a sign to hang up.

"Hello?"

I turned away from George and faced the space in the hallway where Victor Underhill had been standing moments before. "Beth-Ann?" I asked. "It's Lorrie Hollander. I have a proposition for you."

19

LAST

THIS TIME I WAS THERE TO PREPARE ORION.

It was three days after Susannah had been released from
the hospital and was settled at home, and I got to Oceanfront
before sunrise. Orion's head hung over the stall door as if he'd
been expecting me. Down the dimly lit corridor, my footsteps
seemed to beat out: *last, last, last.* But to Orion, it was like any
other day, and he wanted his morning treat.

There weren't many sugar cubes left in the box. Not that I'd
need to buy more. I dug in for one and held my palm flat out to
him. His lips made their wonderful smacking sound. "I'm sorry
for what's going to happen today, boy," I told him. "I'm sorry
for so many things—for you having to stay behind at Woodscape when I came home, and then for you to have to come
back here, just to be shipped out again." My voice cracked. For

better or worse, for richer or poorer. But people don't always keep their vows.

Orion pawed the floor of his stall, hoping for another cube. I obliged, and then I opened his stall door and stepped inside to be with him. He moved aside to give me room. He'd grown up to be a gentleman, my Orion. I reached up to embrace him, pressing my face into that fuzzy white spot on his neck. The scent of him made me weak in the knees. This horse, the love of my life.

I was losing the thing that mattered most all over again.

The morning after Mom and Nigel had left, Gigi had gathered Susannah and me in her bed to tell us that we wouldn't be going back to the city after the weekend, that we'd be living with her from then on. Mom's watch was dangling from my wrist. I shook my hand, trying to get the band to circle my wrist like a hula hoop. But at five years old, it was just as hard to get a watch to circle around my wrist as it was to get an actual hula hoop to circle my middle.

"We're going to have so much fun, girls," Gigi said. "Starting right now. We'll have chocolate for breakfast, and tonight you won't have to eat your broccoli before you get dessert. How does that sound?"

But the truth was, it didn't matter how it sounded, because I was five years old, and I didn't have a choice. Now I did. The decision was mine. Sure, I could rationalize that there wasn't anything else to do, that this was the only thing. But at the end of the day, I had to live with the fact that I'd been the one to pick up the phone and call Beth-Ann.

I'd been the one who decided that Orion was expendable.

"I'm sorry, I'm sorry, I'm sorry," I said, tracing a finger along the contours of his face to the bridle path between his forelock and mane. Orion pawed the ground again, hoping for another treat. Nothing I'd said had any meaning to him, and perhaps that was better. Humans spend so much time analyzing words and coping with changes. But my horse would simply wake up the next morning in a different stall, in a different state, under the care of a different owner.

I swallowed the lump in my throat. "What do you say to a last ride?" I asked.

Horses are such mysterious creatures. They don't wag their tails when you say "ride," the way dogs do when they hear "walk." But Orion knew my voice and my smell, and I imagined they soothed him as I groomed him and tacked him up. I led him down the trail I'd come to think of as our favorite, the one that sloped steeply down toward the ocean. Just in case it mattered, he would have one final memory of this place. I held the reins loosely, letting Orion pick our pace. He broke into an easy canter, and just then I thought, maybe we can go on like this forever, away and away and away. We'll live off the land, like Gigi said, and the reality of my crazy family won't affect us ever again.

Orion stopped on his own at the break in the path by the cliff, and we stood together watching the sun rise over the Atlantic. Pink sky, yellow sun. The ocean was a mirror, so you could fold the sky and the sea in on each other and they'd match up perfectly. It seemed implausible that something so beautiful could also be real.

I would remember this, always, and it was heartbreaking not to know if Orion could capture the same image and hold it in his brain for tomorrow and the next day and the day after that. Maybe it was better if he didn't, so it wasn't something he would miss, but the truth was, I wanted him to miss me, too. I wanted him to love me. No matter how well Beth-Ann could treat him, I wanted him to yearn for me the way I would surely yearn for him. The way I already was.

It was the height of selfishness to think that way—to put my own feelings and ego ahead of this creature that I claimed to love above all others. But I guess I was my mother's daughter, after all. I just couldn't help myself.

A seagull dipped in front of us and flew on toward the horizon. I watched it until I couldn't see it anymore. Then I turned Orion toward the barn. I wanted him to have ample time to cool down, to be fed, and to go to the bathroom. It was still my responsibility to look out for his best interests for a few hours more. When we got to the barn, I clipped him into crossties and removed his tack for the last time, hosed him off for the last time, and swiped the sweat brush in short, quick strokes around his beautiful body for the very last time.

Word must have gotten out that today was the day my horse was leaving, because even after it got later and the barn began to buzz with activity, no one came looking for me to ask for help with chores. I sat on an overturned bucket in Orion's stall and watched him while he ate. He bent his head to the bucket of oats, then lifted it to chew, and his neck rippled. Every inch of him was fascinating and magnificent. I had my cell phone with me—thanks to an advance payment from Beth-Ann, it was back in service, and we had electricity at home for me to charge it up. When I powered it on, it lit up with notifications for a hundred unread texts and unheard voice mails. But I didn't have time for any of them. I clicked over to the camera and pointed the phone toward Orion, filling up the memory card with pictures of his neck ripples, his legs, the back of his mane. I didn't stop until I heard my name.

"Hey, Lorrie. Hey there, Orion."

Charlie.

It was surreal that Charlie Copeland was someone who knew my name and knew my horse. It was surreal that my horse wouldn't be *my* horse for much longer. I felt like I wasn't actually in my life, living it. I was just hovering on the outskirts and watching it happen.

Orion lifted his head to investigate the source of the voice calling him, and, seeing Charlie there, he decided his oats were far more interesting.

I stepped over to the stall door. "Hey, Charlie," I said.

"I thought I would start making this a habit—surprising you at the barn. Especially when you're so hard to contact." He leaned forward to kiss me. I was reserved, kissing him back. "I meant to come by sooner," he said.

"It's fine," I said. "I figured you'd be busy. You know . . . with all your mom's campaign stuff."

"You're a good distraction," he said. He had his arm still draped over the stall door, and he fingered my face with the lightest touch.

"It's really sweet that you came, but I'm working." I took the pitchfork that was leaning against the wall and pushed around the floor shavings, like a little kid moving her broccoli around her plate to feign eating.

"Oh God. What happened to your hand?"

In just a few days, the burn on my palm had blistered and peeled off to reveal new skin underneath, soft and tender as a baby's. Per Dr. Cortes's instructions, I kept gauze on it when I was working at the barn.

"It's nothing," I told Charlie. "I got a blister from the reins."

"Well, I wanted to tell you we missed you at the barbecue the other night. Actually, we were pretty worried about you."

"I got wrapped up in something, and the time got away from me."

"Lennox said you weren't feeling well?"

That's what I'd told Lennox, when I finally got in touch with her. I'd called the barn to tell Naomi I wouldn't be able to come to work for a few days, until Susannah was settled back at home and fully on the mend, and she said she had about a dozen messages for me from Lennox. So then I called Lennox and said I'd had a sudden bout of nausea. It wasn't exactly a lie. I felt absolutely sick about everything in my life.

"Yeah, that's what I meant," I told Charlie. "I just wanted to spare you the details. I'm sorry if I made you worry."

"It's cool," Charlie said. "We managed to have fun, even though you weren't there. I like Lennox—I can see why you guys are friends."

"Yeah, she's great," I said, not really feeling it. I wasn't feeling anything for anyone right then. Orion finished his oats and gently butted my shoulder with his head. I reached out an arm to scratch under his chin. "Hey, boy, hey, boy," I said.

"Can I give him a treat?" Charlie asked.

I produced another sugar cube from the box and handed it

over. Charlie held it flat on his palm, just the way I'd showed him the last time. "Thanks for stopping by," I said. "But I really have a lot of work to do."

"Of course," Charlie said. "I'll let you get back to it. But are you free for dinner later on? I can pick you up at your place."

I clenched in fear. It still mattered to me, Charlie knowing the truth. "You know where I live?" I asked.

"As soon as you give me the address, I will," he said. "There's a new restaurant on Main that's supposedly impossible to get into. They have a six-course tasting menu."

"But it's impossible to get into."

"Oh, we'll get in," he said. He paused. "Unless you're not in the mood for that kind of thing. In which case we could just get a pizza. And champagne, of course."

"No, thanks," I said.

"No, thanks, you don't like pizza?"

"I can't."

"Are you afraid to be in a car with me? I promise I won't drive too fast."

I shook my head. "Tonight's not a good night."

"Tomorrow, then?"

"Yeah, maybe," I said noncommittally. Behind me Orion exhaled, and his breath on my neck made my eyes well.

"Are you all right?"

I blinked quickly. "Yeah, I'm fine."

He nodded toward the phone in my hand. "Will you give me your number? Or, at least, will you take mine?"

"Are you doing this because Shelby Rhodes was on a date with Hayden O'Conner?" I asked.

Charlie looked wounded, and my gut twisted with guilt. I knew I'd been rude; I knew I'd been downright awful. But I couldn't bring myself to apologize. I couldn't take care of anyone else's feelings. There were footsteps at the end of the corridor, and I turned to see Jeremy walking toward us. I kept my eyes on him, because it was easier to look at Jeremy than to look at Charlie.

"I'm sorry to interrupt," he said when he reached us.

"No, it's fine," I said. I turned back to Charlie, finally. "I've got to get back to work."

"Yeah, all right. I'll see you around, Lorrie." Charlie turned and briskly walked away.

Jeremy waited until Charlie had walked down the length of the corridor before speaking. "Naomi asked me to get you," he said. "She said the transport people are here. They're parked behind the barn. You've got to tack Orion up for the ride."

"Yes. Okay."

"Do you need help?"

"No."

"All right. If you do, I won't be far away."

He left me alone with Orion, for the last time. I Velcro-ed fleece around his halter and fastened shipping boots around his legs. After I'd unclipped him from the crossties, I noticed that his right front boot was twisted, and I bent in front of him to fix it, something I'd been taught never to do. If you bend in front of a horse and it gets spooked, it can run you over. But Orion rested his chin on my back, and I could feel the whole weight of his head in perfect repose.

Freezing time was the superpower I wished for the most.

The clock was ticking, and people were waiting. I stood and led Orion through the corridor for the last time. My voice was thick as I said things to soothe myself as much as to soothe him: "You're going to be fine. Better than fine. It's going to be great. You're going to love riding with Beth-Ann Bracelee. She's wanted you for so long, and her family isn't a mess like mine is, so she'll be able to take better care of you. She'll never make you wear an old bit or have to duct-tape your shoes back on."

Outside, the sun was too bright, the day all wrong. Naomi was standing with the guy who was going to be driving Orion back down to North Carolina. He said his name, but I didn't hear it. He opened the back of the trailer, and Orion walked in without protest. I went through the motions as if on autopilot, fastening the butt bar behind Orion before tying him up. He kept nudging me, nuzzling me. I knew he sensed I was upset, and I was trying so hard not to cry, to spare him my tears. The act of not crying felt like a physical thing, like someone had me in a choke hold.

Once Orion was secure, I pressed my hands to him for the last time, memorizing the sensation of him under my palms, the way I could feel his warmth and his breath and the beats of his heart. "I love you," I told my horse, in a whisper that was just his to hear. His ears flicked at my words. "I love you. I love you, I love you."

Naomi finally called to me, and I walked back outside, but I couldn't bring myself to close the trailer door. Since coming back from Woodscape, I had spent so much time trying to fit the pieces of my life back together to make things look the same as before. But now that was over. I was letting go. Closing the door on Orion and life as I knew it. The symbolism was so obvious it would've been amusing if my heart hadn't been breaking.

So Naomi closed the door for me, and that was it; I'd had my last glimpse of my horse. The driver got into the cab, and I watched the trailer snake down the driveway until I couldn't see it anymore. From this moment forward, it would just be me imagining where, exactly, Orion was for the rest of my life. Just like I imagined Mom.

"Why don't you go home?" Naomi asked. She had her hand on my back and she was moving it in circles, like a currycomb to a horse. "We can survive without you today. I'll still pay you."

"No, I can work today. I'm going to be thinking about Orion wherever I am, so I might as well be doing something productive."

I THREW MYSELF INTO AS MANY PHYSICAL TASKS AS I could for the rest of the day—the kinds of things you can't do without utter concentration. But the barn wasn't the distraction it'd always been, and all I wanted to do was weep. People were still giving me space, so I didn't have to interact with anyone. But that wouldn't go on forever. Sooner or later I'd have to have conversations, I'd have to deal with the girls who boarded their trophy horses, who didn't love them nearly as much as I'd loved mine. And I knew I couldn't take it. With the money from Orion's sale, I could afford something I hadn't had all summer: time to figure things out. I'd leave Oceanfront, keep up with the bills, and continue cleaning things out at home. And when I was ready, I'd find another job—a job that didn't come with so many memories.

I'd been able to avoid Orion's corridor for the entire afternoon, but at the end of the day, it was time to leave, and I steeled myself to walk past it. I wanted to get his nameplate—ORION. LOVED BY LORRIE H.—before someone else took it down and threw it away.

Lorrie H. I hadn't put my full name on it because I didn't want to burden Orion with what it meant to be a Hollander in this town.

His stall door was still open. It took every ounce of bravery I had to step inside and close myself in. There were indentations in the cedar chips where he'd stepped. I sat down in a corner of the stall, just wafting in the lingering scent of Orion. I wanted to absorb it, so a part of him would always be a part of me.

This is what it's like when someone you love disappears on you: You try to find the pieces to hold on to, the things no one can take away. The tears came hot and fast, and I made no effort to stop them.

I looked up when Jeremy opened the stall door. "Sorry," he said. "I just wanted to check on you."

I sniffled and swiped at my face. "I'm fine." All evidence to the contrary.

"This is tough," Jeremy said. "I know it is. I remember when I sold Triumph. That was my old horse—I don't know if you remember him."

I nodded, because I did remember Triumph, a brown horse with white markings like large splashes of paint.

"I didn't even want to ride for months after that. It took me so long to come back here, and when I did, there was Atherton. The Crystals acted super-grateful to me when I stepped in to train and ride him. I competed with him. We were doing incredible things together. I loved that horse. And then, without warning, they sold him out from under me. I know it wasn't my horse, but still. It had been easy to pretend. I'd worked hard with him, which I'm sure increased his value, and it hurt. It still does. Anyway, what I'm trying to say is, I know what you're going through. If that's any consolation."

I shook my head. It wasn't any consolation. I didn't feel better because Jeremy had been in pain, too. My eyes welled with more tears for us both.

"Orion's a great horse. I'm gonna miss having him around."

"Me, too," I said, and, despite my best efforts to keep it together in front of him, my voice cracked. "The thing is, I know that over the course of a lifetime people can have multiple horses. But I think there's always that horse who feels the most yours, your one-and-only. That was Orion for me. I miss him so much. It hasn't even been a day, and I miss him. And pretty soon there's going to be another horse in this stall. It's not like I was expecting Naomi to make it a shrine to Orion or anything. But it'll be like he was never here. And that makes it seem like he didn't even count. It's not fair."

The tears spilled over, and Jeremy was at my side in two strides. He wrapped his Gumby arms around me. To look at him, he was such a slight guy. I never imagined how big his hug would feel, the kind you could sink your whole body into. I sank in, burying my face in his shoulder, and I let myself weep.

"It still smells like him in here," I said. I could feel Jeremy's T-shirt against my skin, wet from my tears. "Can you smell it?"

"A horse's scent is the only cologne I've ever worn," he said.

I clutched Jeremy tightly, hanging on as if my life depended on it. He lowered his head so that his cheek was against mine. The wisps of his beard were soft.

"Lorrie," he said softly. I could feel his breath, and I knew all I had to do was turn my head an inch or two and he'd kiss me. And maybe I should—maybe all this time, Jeremy was the one I was supposed to be with. My body didn't buzz at the thought of him, the way it did when Charlie was around; still, there were certain things about me that only Jeremy could understand. He felt so safe.

I turned my head, so slowly, so slowly.

"Lorrie!" Lennox's voice broke Jeremy and me apart like the snap of fingers breaking a spell.

I stumbled back. Jeremy's face was suddenly as bright as a beet. Apparently he blushed just like I did.

"I was just about to go," he said.

"You don't have to," I told him.

Jeremy took my hand and squeezed it, and I felt my face flush when he did—not because there was any spark between us, but because there wasn't. Lately everything I did left me with an emptiness that could be filled only with regret.

"God, Lennox. What has gotten into you?" I asked once he'd left.

"What's gotten into *me*?" she asked incredulously. "What's gotten into you? You've totally been avoiding me—and don't tell me it's because you don't have a phone, because Charlie told me you do."

"So you and Charlie talk about me now?" I asked defensively.

"He called because he said you seemed upset."

I took a deep breath and said the words for the first time. "Orion's gone."

"Gone?"

"I needed money, so I sold him," I told her.

"Oh my God. I can't believe you—" She cut herself off and started again. "There must've been something else you could've done."

"You sound like Claire," I told her. "You want to tell me how you would've done this any better?"

"No, of course not. I'm sorry. Honestly, I don't know how you do it."

Hearing her say that just made me seethe all the more— saying you don't know how someone does something is just the socially acceptable way of saying you're so glad you're not in the other person's shitty situation.

"And I wish you'd told me," she went on. "I could've helped. You know I would've. When you needed someone to buy your plane ticket, I bought it. You needed to be picked up from the airport, I picked you up. You needed cash to pay Charlie back, I gave it to you."

"Nice to know you're cataloging my emergencies," I said.

"Stop it. I'm just saying I would've been there, and, frankly, I don't know why you turned to Gumby Gummer instead."

"Is that what this is about—you're pissed that I didn't include you in yet another emergency?"

Lennox pulled a piece of paper out of her pocket and handed it to me.

Dear Ms. Sackler and Ms. Kandell:

This letter is to inform you of your daughter, Lennox's, dorm and roommate assignment.

Eulberg Hall

Room 2-112B

Violet Tabachnick

"Obviously, I thought it was a mistake," Lennox said. "I called the housing office, and they put me through to Ms. Strafford. She said you'd withdrawn. Without telling me!"

"I was going to."

"When? I get that you have a lot on your mind. But really. We're supposed to be best friends."

"You see? That's it," I said. "You're pissed because you didn't know and didn't get to swoop in and save the day." I'd never thought of Lennox that way before, but suddenly it was all I thought of her.

"Are you kidding me? Any time I helped you, Lorrie, it wasn't for me—it was because I care about you."

"I'm just a project for you in between getting manicures and massages. You don't have to work."

"You didn't used to, either!"

"You only visit your horse when you feel like it," I went on. "You never have any responsibility."

Lennox shook her head. "I feel like I don't even know you anymore."

"You never knew me," I told her. "Not like you thought you did."

"What's that supposed to mean?"

"People don't always stay best friends. I don't think we have enough in common anymore."

Lennox's eyes grew as big and round as saucers. She didn't even bother to say good-bye. She just turned and walked down the corridor. I listened to her footsteps walking away. Then I finally emerged from the stall and slipped Orion's nameplate from the holder. ORION. LOVED BY LORRIE H.

Zeus had placed the great hunter among the stars so he'd never be forgotten, or so the story went. As if I could ever forget Orion.

NAOMI INTERCEPTED ME AS I WALKED ACROSS THE parking lot to my car. "I just got a wire for Orion's board for the rest of the summer. I can sign it over to you."

"What? My aunt paid for him?" I asked. Did the trust still exist, after all? Why did she wait until the moment after my horse had left to finally access it?

"No," Naomi said.

"There must be some kind of mistake."

She held out a piece of paper, and my heart skipped a beat when I read the words at the top: UNDERHILL ENTERPRISES.

20

YOU KNOW
THIS GIRL

THE DRIVE TO THE COMPOUND TOOK UNDER TEN minutes. I didn't even realize that I'd actually have the guts to go there until I was pulling my car up over the sensors at the entrance. I rolled down my window to announce myself. But this time the gates opened without a voice first demanding I state my name and my business.

There was nothing coincidental about this. Underhill was somehow connected to my family, and I needed to know why. I pressed the gas and tried to channel Lennox's journalistic mind as I went over the questions I had for Victor Underhill: Why had he been so interested in me on the beach with Charlie? Why had he followed me to the pawnshop? What had he been doing at the hospital the night Susannah was burned? Why had Underhill Enterprises made a payment for the board of my horse?

But as I came up the final stretch to the Main, my plan to confront Victor Underhill seemed absurd. There was no guarantee that he'd even be there. And so what if he was? It didn't mean he'd answer my questions. I'd probably be turned away at the front door or perhaps even escorted off the property by a security guard.

I'd stopped in front of the house, and I moved my hand to the gearshift, unsure if I was going to slide it into park or into reverse. Should I go up to the house or get the hell out of there? I pressed my palm to the gearshift. The burn didn't actually hurt anymore, but I hadn't yet dropped the habit of pressing against it as if to test that it was still there, like when you're a little kid and you lose a tooth and your tongue can't help but find the hole over and over again.

I had nothing left to lose, and I shifted into park, got out of the car, and ran up the steps to the house before I had a chance to change my mind. I was poised to ring the bell, preparing myself to face Victor Underhill's glare, when the door opened. And there, in the flesh, was Senator Franklin Copeland.

"It's you," he said. The surprise in his voice matched the shock that had been on his face that night in the tree house.

Me?

Tentatively, the senator reached out toward me. I took a step back, like a reflex. "Why are you backing away?" It seemed like a strange question; then again, it was probably the first time in history someone had avoided the touch of Franklin Copeland.

"Sorry," I said. "You just startled me."

"You startled *me*." At the word *me*, he brought his hand to his chest. "I thought I'd never see you again."

Why would the senator care if he ever saw me again? We didn't know each other. We'd never even spoken.

"Please don't be mad," he went on. "I didn't want it to be like this, but Victor said—"

I cut him off. "Victor Underhill?"

"Uh-huh," he said. "Julia hired him back, even though I told her not to. No one listens to me anymore!"

"I'm . . . I'm s-sorry?" I stammered.

The senator smiled. "But Victor's not here right now." His voice was a loud whisper. "Julia wanted him to interview campaign managers."

"Do you know when he'll be back?"

"Friday," the senator said with a smile. Friday was two days away. "We're so lucky," he went on, "because there's no way Victor would let me talk to you. He said if I stayed with you, I'd never get to be president."

"Stay with me? Sir, I don't think . . ."

"The voters don't like cheaters—that's what he said. The voters, the voters, the voters." Senator Copeland nodded his head to the beat of the words. "Did you ever notice that if you say the same thing a bunch of times in a row, it starts to sound strange—like it doesn't mean anything at all?"

"Sure, I guess," I said.

"I don't care about the voters anymore. I only care about you."

He reached a hand out again. I stood frozen in place. It was riveting and terrifying all at once. His fingers, as dry as paper, just like his son's, grazed my arm. He let them linger a second, two seconds, five. My heart was pounding.

"Did you get the flowers?" he asked. I shook my head and stepped away, breaking the touch between us. "Please don't be this way," he said.

"Senator," I said. "Senator Copeland. You have the wrong person. I'm sorry."

"I'm the one who's sorry," he said. "It was an accident! An accident! You've got to believe me, Danielle!"

"Danielle?" I repeated. My mother's name. "Do you mean Danielle Hollander? I'm Lorrie. I'm her *daughter*."

The senator blinked and shook his head. "Of course you are. Of course you are," he said, more to himself than to me.

"But you know her . . . my mom? Danielle?"

I tried to wrap my brain around everything I knew about my mom—she'd been married, she'd had an affair. She raised her kids alone after Dad left. She'd been the kind of mom who would sing us James Taylor songs in the car and put her watch on my wrist so I could keep track of the time till lights-out. And then she'd left without saying good-bye. She never called or visited. She just sent shitty letters, and then those stopped, too.

Now it turned out she'd known Senator Copeland. Could they also have had an affair? The walls seemed to be spinning around me. *Yim, yim,* I said in my head. It wasn't working. You're not supposed to say your mantra out loud, but I did: "Yim, yim, yim."

"I don't know what that means," the senator said.

"She's been gone for years," I said. "My mother. Danielle. She left my sister and me."

"Your sister?"

I nodded. "Susannah," I said. "She doesn't even remember our mother. She was too young when she left." The senator pressed his hands to the sides of his head.

"Please," I went on. "You said you sent her flowers. I don't care if anything happened between you guys, but I need to know where she is. I have a right to know."

"I . . . I'm sorry. I can't help you. I was mistaken. It's time for you to go."

"Dad?" The senator and I both turned to see Charlie walking across the foyer toward us. "Lorrie? What are you doing here?"

"You know this girl?" the senator asked.

"She's a friend of mine," Charlie said. He turned to me. "I thought you were busy tonight."

"I was just . . ." I shook my head. "I don't know what I'm doing here."

"She was just leaving," the senator said.

"Easy, Dad," Charlie told him.

"I don't know her. And I don't know anything about Danielle."

"Who's Danielle?" Charlie asked.

"My mother," I croaked out. "I think your dad knows her. He knew her name."

"He gets confused sometimes," Charlie told me. "He's been . . . he's been working really hard."

"I'm not confused!" the senator said loudly. "I didn't know her. Now your friend needs to leave!"

Charlie moved toward the door. "Listen, Lorrie," he said, "I think tonight's not going to be a good night. Can I get a rain check?"

I shook my head. "But he said things, Charlie. He knows where she is, and I don't."

"I don't know anything," the senator insisted. "Make her leave, Charlie!" The senator's face registered the distress of a child's. I had to look away from him.

"Charlie, I—"

But he cut me off. "It's just a misunderstanding," Charlie told me, practically pushing me toward the door. "Do me a favor, okay? Don't say anything to anyone. About this."

Before I could say another word, the door shut behind me. I left the Compound with more questions than I'd had when I'd arrived.

21

WIDE AWAKE

IT WAS JUST AFTER MIDNIGHT WHEN MY CELL PHONE started to vibrate against my bedside table. I startled awake and saw the illuminated screen, Lennox's name flashing. If she was calling to explain things, to yell at me, to forgive me, it certainly wouldn't be at this hour. I grabbed the phone and clicked to answer. "What's wrong?"

"Something's happened," she said. "I'm on Break Run, and I'm coming over."

I could've sworn there were sirens going off behind her words, and my body tightened in fear. "Is everything all right?"

"No," she said. "It's not."

I WAITED FOR LENNOX OUTSIDE. THE PORCH LIGHT HAD long since burned out, and the night's darkness muted the decay of the house—thank God for small favors. She pulled up in front. I watched as she reached over to grab her bag from the passenger seat and got out of the car.

Never before in our entire friendship had I not known how to act around Lennox. But right then, I needed a cue from her, so I didn't make a move closer to her. I waited until she'd climbed the porch steps and reached me. And when she did, I was holding my body still and rigid, as if I were afraid she was about to hit me. Instead, she threw her arms around me, and I sank into her. Her body was shaking. Something awful had happened. Someone had died. I just knew it. I rubbed her back in circles, the way Naomi had rubbed mine, imagining all the possible scenarios, each one unthinkable, each one worse than the one before: One of the moms? Both of them? Harper?

God forbid.

"I'm so sorry, Len. I really am. And I swear, whatever is going on right now, I'm going to be there for you. Because you've always been there for me."

Lennox pulled away. She'd been the one to initiate the hug, but now, looking at her face, I couldn't tell whether or not she was angry. She gathered her breath to speak, and I braced myself. "There's been an accident. I think Charlie might be dead."

"What?" I took a step back in shock and hit the wrong plank on the porch. It splintered under my weight. I fell back and cried out.

"Are you all right?"

I bent to rub my ankle, where a piece of broken wood had sprung up and scraped it. "He can't be dead," I said. "It's just not possible."

"I saw it online."

"You know you can't believe anything you read online," I told her. "Especially about the Copelands." But even as I said it, I could feel my heart in my throat. "What exactly did you see?"

"I got a Copeland Google Alert a little while ago. There was an unconfirmed report that a car matching the description of the senator's Porsche was in an accident on Break Run." She paused to take a breath, and when she started again, there was an apologetic tone to her voice. "I know this is going to sound bad, but I had to go see for myself. I didn't even tell the moms I was leaving. I just got into my car and drove. When I got there, there were all these flashing lights, and the guardrail by the Point was gone. He must've smashed right into it."

"Lots of people have Porsches around here," I said softly. "It could've been anyone."

"I saw the car," she said. "It was dredged up from the ocean by a crane, and it barely looked like a car anymore. But still, I could tell—it was that old Porsche Charlie's been driving all summer. A collector's item. Not the kind of car that lots of people have."

"I just saw him," I said. My heart was in full gallop. I could feel my whole body pulsing with the beats. "Maybe someone else was driving. The Copelands have so many people working for them, plus Julia's campaign staff."

I was saying these words, but the voice in my head was saying: *You never know when you're saying good-bye for the last time. You never know when someone is going to leave your life.*

"I doubt they would have let someone working for them take that car."

"Someone could have stolen it," I said. "When I was at the Compound today, the gates just opened when I drove up—that's gotta be a security risk. If someone else got onto the property that way, he could've taken the car for a joy ride."

Lennox nodded, trying to believe me. "You're right. A car thief probably would've taken the curve around the Point too fast—trying to get away."

"That's just the way Charlie drives," I said. I felt myself slipping down, and I clutched Lennox. "Oh God, Len. What if it *was* Charlie?"

She shook her head.

"I really wanted to be with him. It was the first time I felt like that, you know?"

"I know," she said.

"I don't have his number," I said, shaking my head. Why had I said what I'd said that afternoon in the barn? Why hadn't I taken his number? "Can you call him?"

"I did," she said. "Before I even drove out. I called his phone, and he didn't answer."

We were both crying. "Call him again," I said. Lennox pulled her phone from her bag. I watched her hit the button for recent contacts and press to dial Charlie. She held it to her ear, and I pressed my head against hers. We heard his voice mail pick up together.

"I don't want to be alone right now," I told Lennox.

"Me, either."

"Come in?" I said.

✳✳✳

WHEN WE WERE KIDS, LENNOX AND I USED TO TRADE off playdates at each other's houses. But things at my house were always a bit strange, and we ended up at her house most of the time, until we ended up at her house all the time. I wondered what it felt like for her now, to be back in this place for the first time in years. I'd worked so hard to clean it, but looking at it fresh, the way Lennox was, it seemed I'd barely made a dent. It seemed worse than ever before. We sat at the kitchen table, which was piled high with the usual dirty plates and glasses and unopened mail. I pushed aside a dried-up bowl of water mixed with flour, plus strips of newspaper, deflating balloons, and pipe cleaners. "What's all that for?" Lennox asked.

"Gigi's latest project," I said. "She wants to make decoupage favors for her forty-second birthday party."

"She's having a party?"

"In her imagination she is."

"Where is she now?"

"Upstairs. Asleep."

"Susannah, too?"

"Yup. With Brian."

Lennox nodded and pulled out her phone. "I'm gonna try Charlie again." A few seconds later she shook her head. "Straight to voice mail."

"Text him, too," I said.

"I did. I'll do it again." Her thumbs clicked over the keys. "I guess I should call the moms. If they wake up and I'm not there, they'll freak. Even worse than they'd freak to know I snuck out past curfew."

"What's it like?" I asked her.

"What?"

"To have parents who care about you that much?"

"Gigi cares about you in her own way."

"She'd never even think to set a curfew for me, or to worry if I broke it."

"Maybe because she knows you wouldn't listen to her," Lennox said.

"Because the things she says don't make any sense."

"If you want a system to change, you should change it," Lennox suggested.

I shrugged. "It doesn't matter right now."

Lennox made the call to her moms. Listening to her end, I could tell they weren't thrilled with her, but she didn't seem to be in major trouble, either. "Yes, fine. Fine, I promise," she said. I pulled open the freezer, which was no longer a cryobank for dead birds. After the power outage, Susannah had buried them in the pet cemetery beside Wren. In their place were new tubs of ice cream. I wasn't hungry, but I took them out anyway and put them on the kitchen table in front of Lennox. "Here," I said, handing her a spoon. "Fresh ice cream from a working freezer. Courtesy of the Beth-Ann Bracelee Scholarship Fund."

"She's the one who bought Orion?"

I nodded.

"Your roommate from Woodscape?"

I nodded again.

"That bitch."

"No, she did me a favor. I couldn't have a horse anymore. I have a different kind of life now."

"Oh, Lorrie."

"It's okay," I said. "I mean, it's not okay. I mean . . ."

"I know what you mean."

"But can I tell you something really strange?"

"Of course."

"It feels weird to talk about all this now, with Charlie . . ." Reflexively, Lennox looked down at her phone. "Anything?" I asked.

"No," she said. She paused. "Say what you were going to say," she said.

"Okay," I said. "Right after Orion got picked up, Naomi came out and said his board had been paid for the rest of the summer. And you know who'd paid it? Underhill Enterprises."

"As in Victor Underhill?"

"I think so. I mean, I don't know any other Underhills. And I told you how he basically interrogated me when he caught Charlie and me on the beach." Lennox nodded. "I also saw him at the hospital when Susannah had to spend the night."

"Hold up. Susannah was in the hospital?"

"She got burned."

Lennox sucked in her breath.

"She's okay now," I said quickly. A few thousand dollars later, she was nearly as good as new.

"Thank God. I feel awful that I didn't know about it."

"Don't," I said. "It was my fault for not telling you."

"But I know you—I should've known something was really wrong."

"I don't think knowing someone is anyone else's responsibility. I'm not even sure I think it's possible to really know anyone anymore."

"Even a best friend?"

I shook my head. "I just felt like I wasn't good for anyone to be around—you, Charlie."

I winced when I said his name, and Lennox's face was a mirror—the same pain, the same grimace.

I went on. "My life is so crazy, so unreliable. You and Charlie, you have so much more in common with each other than with me."

I paused and dipped into the pint of vanilla bean. But my stomach was in knots. I left the bite uneaten on the spoon.

"I was jealous," I said. "And it made me feel so bad—what kind of friend was I, being angry that things came easily to you? It made me feel like you were better off without me. Charlie, too."

"Oh, Lorrie," Lennox said.

"But I don't want to lose you," I said.

We were both quiet for a few seconds. Something was nipping at my ankle, and I reached down for the kitten—one of Wren's siblings, probably—and pulled her into my lap.

"You're not losing me," Lennox said finally.

"I'm sorry, Len. I'm sorry for the things I said, and for what I didn't say."

"You know, this is the first time you actually owe me an apology."

"Do you accept?"

"Of course I do," she said.

"I just—" I began, but my voice cracked. Lennox put her hand on mine. "I hope I get to apologize to Charlie, too."

She nodded. "Now, tell me about Susannah."

I brought her up to speed as best I could—about the electricity being out, and my sudden need to find my mom, and the darkness, and the candle. "I found my mom's old journal," I said. "She was having an affair with someone named Junior. That's why my dad left her. He started drinking again and he left. And Susannah—" I cut myself off.

"What?"

"Nothing," I said. "It doesn't matter. The point is, I haven't found her yet."

Lennox shook her head. "Your mom doesn't deserve you," she said. "But at least now you can get Orion back."

"I can't," I said miserably. Now it was past one o'clock in the morning. At that very moment Orion was spending the night at a rest-stop barn midway between New York and North Carolina. In just a few hours he'd be reloaded into the trailer and driven the last two hundred miles or so to Beth-Ann Bracelee. "Board expenses don't solve all our other bills—I used Beth-Ann's money to pay them. Besides, I can't take anything from Underhill without knowing why I'm getting it in the first place, or if any more is coming. I used to just spend money based on faith that I had a trust and there'd always be more, but that didn't really work out for me."

"So, what are you going to do?"

"I went over to the Copelands' to confront Underhill, but he wasn't there." I paused. "But the senator answered the door, and he recognized me."

"From the tree house? That's kind of incredible, don't you think? He only saw you for what—two, three seconds, tops?"

"I don't think that was it, Len."

"Explain, please."

"Charlie asked me not to," I told her. "But I guess all bets are off now, huh?"

Lennox looked at her phone again and shook her head.

"Nothing?" I asked.

"Nothing," she said.

The kitten was teething, and I balled my fist to let her chew on my knuckles. "Have you ever known anyone who died before?" I asked.

"My grandmother," she said. "You?"

I shook my head. "No."

We were quiet for a few seconds. I stroked the kitten's back. Her gray fur was as soft and light as the puffer flowers we used to wish on. Susannah must've named her, and she'd probably told me the name, but I couldn't recall it if my life depended on it.

"I know sometimes you think you can't," Lennox ventured. "But the truth is, you can tell me anything."

"The senator knew my mom," I said. "He thought that's who I was, and he went on about how much he wanted to be with her. He said Underhill tried to keep them apart—maybe that was the rift between the two of them? But he said he sent her flowers, and he was sorry; it was all an accident. It was so strange, and then Charlie came in and told me that his father gets confused sometimes and that I needed to leave. It really seemed like there was something very wrong with the senator. But, Len, I don't think Junior was the only person my mom had an affair with. I think she had one with Senator Copeland, too."

There's a silence that comes after a revelation. I stared at the melting cartons of ice cream between us. We'd finally had our ice-cream talk, though neither Lennox nor I had managed more than one bite. I picked up my spoon and let the little nameless kitten lick off the remnants.

Lennox picked up her phone and gasped. "There's another Copeland alert," she said.

"Tell me Charlie's okay," I said.

Lennox was holding the phone away from herself, staring at it as if she'd forgotten what it was. "It wasn't Charlie," she said. Her face had drained of color, like it had been emptied. "It was the senator. He's dead."

22
CULPABILITY

WE WENT UPSTAIRS—THERE WASN'T EVEN A DISCUS-
sion about whether or not Lennox would spend the night. She
was crying, and I don't think she noticed the wallpaper hanging in shreds off the walls, or the patches of cat urine squish-
ing under our footsteps. I very nearly forgot to be embarrassed
by them myself. Inside my room we sat on my bed, Mom's
antique lace quilt pulled up over our legs. That blogger must've
been right, Lennox said through tears. It wasn't just a political
opponent's smear tactic; the senator really did have a drinking problem, just like my dad did, and maybe even worse. It
explained everything: why Franklin Copeland had been hidden
behind the scenes at the Fourth of July party, and why Charlie and Underhill had contradicted each other about his trip to
New York or DC. It was why the senator had acted so strangely

earlier in the day and confused me with my mother, why Charlie had quickly ushered me out the door, and why his dad had driven so recklessly and ended up at the bottom of the ocean.

"Charlie was trying to protect him," Lennox said. "He's probably been doing it for years. That's why he told you not to say anything."

My trusty journalist had figured it out. But I couldn't shake the vague feeling of culpability. I had just seen Senator Copeland. Presumably I'd been one of the last people to see him. And I'd upset him. Even if it wasn't my fault, for the rest of my life I would have to know that. And Charlie would know it, too. My relief that Charlie himself was okay and I'd get to see him again was shadowed by the fact that he'd always connect me to this tragedy.

"I still can't figure out how the Underhill payment fits in," Lennox said. She reached for a tissue and blew her nose loudly.

"That seems like the least important thing right now."

"Do you think it's okay if I text Charlie again?" she asked. "You know, now that we know about his father? Just to tell him we're thinking of him?"

"Yeah," I said. "Tell him you're here with me, and tell him . . . tell him I don't know what to say, except that I'm sorry. I'm really, really sorry."

"I'll text him that from us both."

I don't remember what we talked about after that, or if we talked at all. Lennox fell asleep, improbably, and I lay there thinking about everything that had happened that day. It was the day Senator Copeland had died, and the day I found out he'd known my mother. It was the day Lennox came inside my house for the first time in years. And it was the day I'd lost Orion.

And to think there were other days where nothing remarkable happened at all.

Silently, perhaps out of habit, perhaps to pass the time, I began repeating my mantra in my head: *yim, yim, yim, yim.* And then the word began to transform in my head, to the rhythm of my breaths: *Ori-yim, Ori-yim, Ori-yim.* And then it was just: *Orion, Orion, Orion.*

Yim was a nonsense word to begin with, but the senator had been wrong; the more I said it, the more it sounded like it meant something, something dear to me.

I don't remember falling asleep myself; not that the moment of falling asleep is ever something you remember. It's more like an inexplicable miracle that happens each night. The kind that, the next time around, when you're tossing and turning, seems impossible to duplicate. But I must've been sleeping, because I woke to the sound of Lennox insistently calling my name. "Lorrie, Lorrie. Get up."

It had somehow become morning, and a stream of light was cast across the floor. "What's the matter?" I asked.

What else could possibly have gone wrong?

"I got a text from Charlie," she said. "He wants us to come over."

I took the phone to text him back myself. I wanted to write how happy I was that he was okay, how sorry I was for what had happened, and especially how bad I felt about yesterday. But instead I wrote: *Yes, of course. When?*

It was just past seven in the morning. He wrote back within seconds: *As soon as possible.*

LENNOX AND I EACH WASHED UP AND GOT DRESSED. I looked in the mirror and started brushing my hair, but then I felt self-conscious to be worrying about looking pretty, and I left the room with a few knots remaining.

A couple of cats were lounging on the stairs as we made our way down, but it seemed that most of the creatures of Edge-water—human and otherwise—were still sleeping. I pulled the front door open.

"Hold up," Lennox said. "You should write a note and say where you're going."

"No one will be worried," I assured her.

"But this is the thing I was getting at before," she said. "Maybe it's up to you to change the system."

I took an empty envelope out of the money drawer and bor-rowed a pen from Lennox's purse.

Senator Copeland died. Went to the Compound with Lennox. Home later.
    x L

We took Lennox's car, and we didn't talk much as she drove alongside the ocean. There was a lot of traffic, and a detour set up well before we got to the Point, so we couldn't see the accident site. Lennox made a right onto Eastern Road and a left onto Breezy Drive, which snaked around and brought us back to Break Run, but on the far end, so we approached the

Compound from the other direction. The street was already choked with news vans, their antennas shooting into the air like church steeples. On the side of the road, men and women in suits were holding microphones, and guys in jeans were pointing cameras at them. Then there were dozens of others, presumably regular people, who didn't have a job to do there but had simply come out to the Compound to be a little closer to the tragedy. A roadside memorial of flowers and candles had been started. Some people were crying, and some were praying. And the ones in suits were talking into microphones, and the guys with cameras were filming it all.

The space just in front of the Compound gates was guarded by a police officer. A flock of butterflies took flight in my abdomen as Lennox pulled up and rolled down her window.

"I'm going to have to ask you to leave," the officer said. I was almost relieved to hear him say it. Being here now felt like a mistake.

"Charlie asked us to come," Lennox said. She brought out her phone to show it as proof. "I'm Lennox, and this is Lorrie."

The officer said something into a walkie-talkie. Outside, the cameramen had pointed their cameras toward us, recording our riveting experience of sitting in a car and waiting. It felt like a glacier could've melted in the time we spent there. "I'm going to text Charlie that we're trying to get in," Lennox said.

A few minutes later a staticky voice came over the officer's radio. The gates opened, and he waved us in. The crowd surged toward us, and the reporters shouted out questions, but the gates closed behind the car, and we continued up toward the Main.

"I have a bad feeling about this," I admitted to Lennox.

"The worst has already happened," she said. "And I think it's really important that we're here. I don't think Charlie has friends besides us to call."

"He has a best friend," I told her. For some reason, that was what made me feel choked up. "Sebastian."

"I mean in Idlewild," Lennox said. "His family has been away for so long."

"I just think maybe I'm not supposed to be here," I said. "There's some connection to my family, and, frankly, it's scaring the shit out of me. What if Victor Underhill sees me?"

"Then he sees you. You can ask him about the Oceanfront payment."

"I couldn't do that today."

"You're not doing anything wrong, being here."

"But yesterday," I said. "He was so . . . I don't know how to explain it. Agitated to see me. The senator, I mean."

"I know who you mean," Lennox said. "But he was messed up before you got there, so you didn't drive him to drink or anything. Besides, Charlie asked you to come."

"I know."

"Listen to me, Lorrie," Lennox said. "I'm your best friend, so I say this with love: Being here today, it's not going to be about you or your family. The Copelands have a million other things to worry about right now. But if you want to turn around, I will."

"No," I said. "Keep going."

✳✳✳

CHARLIE WAS STANDING ON THE FRONT STEPS AS WE came up to the Main. I felt instant happiness at the sight of him, and then guilt for my own happiness. There were quick hugs hello, and Lennox and me both saying, "I'm so sorry." Lennox cried a little, and Charlie comforted her. "It's okay. It's going to be okay," he said.

She smiled sadly. "I'm sorry," she said. "I'm so awful. You shouldn't have to be comforting *me*."

"Come on, let's go inside," Charlie said.

"Charlie!" someone called—Brock, the guy from the campaign office—as Charlie closed the door behind us. The soles of his shoes made loud smacks against the marble floor as he rushed toward us. "Your mom has been looking for you."

Charlie turned to Lennox and me. "Sorry," he said. "This'll just take a minute."

Lennox and I stayed put as Charlie began to walk across the floor. But then he turned back to us. "Aren't you guys coming?"

"Oh," I said. "Sure."

And so we did, walking down the same hallway I'd followed Charlie down a couple of weeks—it felt like years—before. I guess I'd expected the house to be different, too, in mourning. But the rooms were light and airy and pulsing with life like a train station at rush hour. In the informal dining room, aka Julia Copeland for Congress Campaign Headquarters, Julia's team was assembled, everyone on their phones per usual—though now it was Franklin Copeland Funeral Headquarters. I caught snippets of "dignitary arrivals" and "Andrews Air Force Base."

There was a collective pause in the conversations just briefly as we walked past, and everyone turned to give Charlie looks that were equal parts sympathy and curiosity. Which was, frankly, how I felt about it, too: How awful and interesting it must be to be Charlie. I was glad Lennox was beside me. I wanted to reach out for her hand, but I felt too self-conscious to do so. After all, I wasn't the one who'd just lost a parent.

We found Julia Copeland in the library. She looked as polished as she had on the Fourth of July, except that she was in slacks instead of a dress and her hair was down around her face, the ends curled under and grazing her shoulders. Her assistant hovered over her shoulder with a glass of water.

"I said I didn't want any, Annette," Julia said sharply. "I need you to get this down—we need a motorcade into the city. Franklin attended the Church of the Heavenly Rest when he was a child, so I want the public viewing there. Then a flight down to DC, and another motorcade to the service at National Cathedral. I was up all night, and I've got fifteen hundred people on the guest list so far—"

"Mom?" Charlie said.

"Charlie. I wondered where you'd gone." She seemed about to say something else, but then she noticed Lennox and me hanging in the doorway. "May I help you?"

"This is Lorrie and Lennox," Charlie said. "You met them at the party. They just got here."

"I'm so sorry, Mrs. Copeland," Lennox said, her voice thick again.

"Me, too," I said.

"Thank you, girls," Julia Copeland said. "But I'm sure you understand that this is not the best time. Annette will show you out." She nodded toward her assistant.

"I've got it," Annette said.

"No," Charlie said. "I asked them to come. I want them to be here."

"Oh, Charlie, at a time like this? We're in the middle of making all the arrangements."

"I didn't think—" Charlie started, but then he cut himself off and tried again. "It's only been a few hours."

"There's so much to plan," Julia Copeland said. "It's good to plan." And for a split second she sounded vulnerable. But she recovered quickly. "There are fifty-six senators attending and nearly a hundred from the House. The Secretary of State, the President. I'm expecting you to speak."

"I'm not sure I want to," Charlie said.

"This is for your father," Julia Copeland said. "It's not about what you want." She turned to Annette. "What did Victor say his ETA was?"

My gut twisted at the mention of his name.

"An hour," Annette said. "And the senator's chief of staff and communications director are on their way."

"It's *not* a good time for guests," Julia told her son.

"You have your people here," Charlie told her. "I want mine."

I was embarrassed that I took pleasure in that: We were his people. Lennox stood beside me, her eyes wide at this unbelievable scene.

"They'll help me with my speech," he said.

Julia Copeland let out a deep breath, and I could tell she'd surrendered. "Where will you be?"

Charlie shrugged. "I don't know. Somewhere outside."

"The officers are working on securing the perimeter," Annette said.

"That's right," Julia said. "You can't go outside right now."

The phone in Annette's hand rang, and she answered it. A few seconds later she held it out toward her boss. "Julia, the President is on the line."

"Stay close," Julia told Charlie. Then she took the phone. "Hello, Mr. President," she said.

I half expected Charlie to grab our hands and say, "Now's our chance," and make a run for it. Instead, he only walked us up a flight of stairs to an atrium that looked out on the ocean. Charlie gestured toward the Point. "It was my dad's favorite place in Idlewild," he said. "He never said it quite like that. He wasn't the kind of guy to list his favorites. But he was always looking at it."

I looked out at the Point. There in the distance were specks of things that might have been a car and a crane. "We could go to another room," I offered.

"No, it's all right," Charlie said. "I want to look at it."

"Do you think that's why he was driving there?" Lennox asked. "To look at it up close?"

"I don't know," Charlie said. His phone pinged, and he pulled it out of his pocket. "Sebastian is in Rome, and he's been texting every twenty minutes like clockwork."

"I'm sure he feels bad that he's not here."

"He switched his ticket so he'll be back for the service," Charlie said. Then, to himself, he added, "More of a show than a service. It'll be such a spectacle."

I remembered the spectacle of his grandfather's funeral that we'd seen on TV. People lining the streets like spectators at a parade. Inside, the pews were packed with a couple thousand of the most important people in the country—in the world. And thirteen-year-old Charlie, in his black suit, sat in the front row beside his parents.

In this version of the spectacle, Charlie would be next to his mother. I pictured myself on his other side, comforting him.

God, what was wrong with me?

Charlie tapped out a message on his phone and pocketed it again. "I can call for breakfast if you guys want."

"We don't need anything," I said quickly.

"Yeah, we're not here to be fed," Lennox said. "We're just here for you. Whatever you need."

"I gotta eat anyway," Charlie said. He stood to pick up the house phone on a side table and asked whoever was on the other end—Annalise, I imagined—to send up a spread. He glanced back at me. "And a Coke," he added.

When he sat back down, he stared out at the Point, and I watched him. I wanted to reach out and touch him, but that seemed like the wrong thing to do. You can't help the thoughts you have in your head, but privately I admonished myself for having all the wrong ones. "I just want to say . . ." I started.

He turned to me. "What?"

"I'm really sorry about yesterday."

"It doesn't matter."

"It does," I said. "I was so rude to you at the barn. And then, when I came here afterward—"

He cut me off. "Let's not talk about it."

"Okay," I said.

He looked back out the window. In profile, he looked so much like his father.

"Do you want to work on the speech, then?" I asked.

"I was thinking about what we talked about on the Fourth," Lennox said. "How he said you can't ignore the past if you want to step boldly, confidently into the future. You could say something about that and maybe tie it to your dad's work and his legacy."

"That's a nice idea," Charlie said. "But my mom doesn't really want me to write it myself. The funeral is going to be a campaign event for her, so whatever I say will be written by her team and approved by Victor Underhill."

I felt the trademark Victor Underhill gut twist.

"Can I ask you something?" Lennox asked.

"Shoot," Charlie said.

"What's the name of Victor Underhill's company?"

"I don't know," Charlie said. "Why?"

"I just wondered what his job was."

"He's a political consultant."

"So, you call him if you're running for office?"

"Yeah, or if your dad suddenly drives off a cliff."

Lennox and I shifted uncomfortably.

"Sorry," Charlie said. "I just meant he's the go-to guy if

something goes wrong." He shook his head. "I don't know why my dad had to pick last night to drive, out of all nights," Charlie said quietly. "Given the state he was in."

"Was he not supposed to drive?" Lennox asked. I could see the wheels turning in her head: The senator would certainly have been advised not to drive if he had a drinking problem.

"Why? Are you going to blog about it?" Charlie asked. His voice had a sudden edge.

"No, of course not," Lennox said. "I'm here as a friend."

Charlie nodded.

I was flushed from head to toe. "I just need to say, if I did anything to upset him yesterday, I'm really sorry."

"He was having a hard time lately. It didn't have anything to do with you." Charlie paused. "I'm glad you guys are here. But can we just not talk for a little while?"

Lennox and I both mumbled our assent. A few minutes later a cart arrived full of bagels and croissants and various butters and jam, plus fresh-squeezed juice, and coffee, and of course the soda for me—which Annalise opened and poured, as if I couldn't do it myself. I didn't really want it, but I took a sip to be polite. Lennox grabbed a dry bagel, but she turned it over in her hands instead of eating it. Charlie didn't make a move for any of the food. His phone pinged on the table where he'd left it, presumably with the next text from Sebastian. But when Charlie picked it up to look at the screen, his voice came out awestruck. "Oh God, it's Shelby," he said, and he stood up. "She wants to come. I've got to . . . I'll be right back."

He walked out faster than you'd ever want the boy you liked to leave a room while you were still in it. I felt like an idiot. Of course he'd leave me in a room to go talk to Shelby. Maybe this tragedy would even bring them closer together. I felt bad for myself, and I felt bad for feeling bad, because this day and this house and the aftermath of everything that had happened were not about me.

"Lorrie," Lennox said, but I waved a hand to stop her. I didn't want to talk about it. So we sat in silence, looking out at the exact spot of the ocean where the senator had died.

"Maybe we should go," I said.

"If you think that's best. Whatever you want."

"I think it would be easier for him if we did."

"All right."

We walked downstairs very quietly, as if we were walking through a church. Down the hallway past the library, now empty. A crowd remained in the dining room, though it had thinned. But now there were more voices in the house, coming from the main foyer. They got louder as we drew closer. I hoped Victor Underhill's wasn't among them. Much as I wanted my questions answered, I didn't want the responsibility of having to deal with it right then. I stopped short, a couple of rooms away from the foyer, to brace myself, just in case.

"You all right?" Lennox asked.

"Yeah," I said.

I was about to step forward again, but then I heard one voice ring out over the din of the others: "Let me see my niece! Lorrie!"

Lennox and I looked at each other, eyes riveted. All at once I realized how foolish I'd been—worrying about Shelby, worrying about Underhill. When my biggest problem was a few yards away, in the main foyer of the Copeland Compound. I thought I might die there, in the hallway, with Lennox beside me. And, honestly, right then I wished it would happen. I wished the floor would open and swallow me whole. Or I wished a bomb would go off. Even if its casualties included people I loved, too. Anything to prevent what was about to happen.

Charlie appeared from around the corner. "I was just coming to get you," he said. "There's a woman here—she says she's your aunt, and, well, she's creating a scene. My mom just can't take it right now."

I nodded, speechless. I could still hear Gigi's voice. Now it was all I could hear.

"Can you come out?"

Lennox gently pushed me forward. Gigi was smack in the center of the room. She was wearing a new dress. But she was also in house slippers, she hadn't brushed her hair, and her right arm was in the tight grip of Officer Tim Blum.

Tim Blum, who was oh-so-familiar with my family because of all the calls he'd fielded over the years from our friendly neighbor Richard Deighton, railing against Edgewater. Susannah was standing on Gigi's other side. Brian was next to her, glancing around as if he was casing the joint. A dozen other people were observing the scene—Julia, Annette, Brock, some of the campaign workers, and staff members in uniform. Mouths gaped open at the sight of my aunt straining to break free of a police officer's grip.

"Lorrie," Susannah said. "You *are* here."

"I told you she was," Gigi said. Her eyes were wide and wild, like those of an animal in a trap. She made a move toward me, but Blum pulled her back.

"Don't hurt her," I said. "I'll get her out of here."

"Wait," Charlie said. "This *is* your aunt?"

"Yes," I said softly.

"Lorrie likes to pretend she doesn't know us," Brian said.

Lennox reached toward me. But I couldn't touch her. I could barely look her way. I felt bad for even having a best friend. If I'd stayed close to home and kept my life small, like Susannah, I wouldn't have to endure humiliation out in the world. Everyone in that room was looking back and forth among Gigi, Susannah, Brian, and me—the imposters. I was in the horror movie of my life all over again. My eyes filled, and I clenched my fists, just trying to hold it together, to get out of this scene.

"I thought the perimeter was secure, Officer," Annette said.

"She got in because she said her niece was here, but we have a larger team working the gate now."

"And what about these people?"

"We're leaving," I said. I stepped toward Gigi and grabbed her hand, yanking her from Tim Blum.

"You mean we're not getting a tour?" Brian asked.

I glared at him. "Shut up."

"Sorry, Lorrie," Susannah whispered. "Gigi said you left a note. She freaked out and made us come here. She said we needed to get you right away."

"Let's just go."

We would've made it out, but the front door opened and

Victor Underhill strode in. He surveyed the scene, and something registered in his face. I thought it was rage, but later I'd come to realize it was something else entirely: fear.

"Someone tell me what the hell is going on," he demanded.

Gigi dropped to her knees in front of him. On the polished floor of the Copeland house, at the entrance to the ballroom-size foyer, just hours after the senator had died. The people around us had multiplied, and she was the spectacle.

"She'll stay away," Gigi said. "You promise, right, Lorrie? He said if you stayed away, it would be taken care of."

"What would be taken care of?" Charlie asked.

"Ignore her," I told him. "She's not well. Please, Gigi." I pulled at her arm. "Come on."

Gigi rose to her feet, but she kept babbling. "We need the money. He gave me money every month, and then it stopped."

"That's enough," Victor Underhill said. "Let's everyone clear out."

"Who gave you money?" I asked.

"The senator. And now he's gone. Where will I get the money now?"

"No shit," Brian said. "You were getting kickbacks from Senator Copeland?"

"Are you saying my husband was paying you for something each month?" Julia asked.

"Don't concern yourself with this," Victor Underhill said. "This woman is clearly out of her mind."

"Because of the other car," Gigi said.

"What other car?" Julia asked.

"Julia, I'm taking care of this," Underhill said.

"There was another car," Gigi said.

"That's enough. It's time for you to leave. Security, please escort these people out immediately."

"Now, wait a minute," Tim Blum said. "There *was* another car found off the Point. The divers discovered it when they initially went down. It was pulled up twenty minutes ago. Said it looked like it'd been down there for quite a while."

"A white Mercedes," Gigi said.

"It was a Mercedes," he said. "The color was no longer apparent."

"I don't understand what's going on," Julia said.

"She saw the car on her way over," Victor said. "You heard the officer—they just pulled it up."

"Your husband," Gigi told Julia Copeland. "He drove us home one night. There'd been a party, and he insisted."

"My dad drove you home?" Charlie asked me.

"No," I said. "I've never been in a car with him in my life."

"Not Lorrie," Gigi said.

"Then who?"

Gigi didn't answer. Julia had crossed to Charlie's side and was holding on to his arm. I couldn't tell if it was to comfort him or if she felt she needed his protection.

"It doesn't matter," I said. I pulled on Gigi again, trying to urge her toward the door.

"Lorrie," Lennox said. She'd raised a finger the way she did when she was figuring things out. "He thought you were your mom," she said.

"He was confused," Charlie broke in.

"He told you he was sorry for the accident," Lennox went

on, to me. I felt Charlie looking at me, but I couldn't look back. Now he knew I'd told Lennox, even though he'd asked me not to tell anyone. My shame deepened. Every feeling I had deepened.

"What about the accident?" Susannah asked.

"I'm not supposed to say," Gigi said. She looked at Julia Copeland, imploring her with her eyes. "I won't say anything else. Please."

"Don't you see, Lorrie?" Lennox asked.

I held up a hand as if to stave off her words. I was afraid to hear what she had to say.

"Franklin Charles Copeland Junior," she said. *"Junior.* The one from your mom's diary."

"Oh God."

"Mom had a diary?" Susannah asked. I didn't respond. "Lorrie!" Susannah said. "Mom had a diary?"

"It was in the attic."

Lennox nodded to herself. "And that other car," she said. "I think maybe your mom was in it."

"Yes," Gigi said. Her voice was a wail. "Yes . . . she was."

"Was there someone in the second car?" Julia asked Tim Blum.

"There's not much to identify after so many years in the ocean," the officer said, "but we do have reason to believe there were people in the car."

"Not my mom," I said. "She's in London. She moved there with her boyfriend twelve years ago. It was my aunt's birthday. Mom left my sister and me with a babysitter, and she and Nigel and Gigi came to a party here at the Compound. She never came back."

The words echoed in my head: *She never came back.*

"Twelve years," Blum said. "That sounds about right."

"No," Susannah said. "We got cards on our birthdays. Holidays, too."

Gigi was back on her knees, not begging, just crying.

"Oh my God, it was *you*," I said. "It was you, this whole time. You knew she was dead, and you gave us those cards and said they were from her."

Gigi pressed her palms against her eyes. "She was my sister," she said. "I knew her handwriting as well as my own."

"But they had little drawings on them. A mom in the middle of two little kids, just like she drew on the notes she left in my lunchbox every day."

"The first note I wrote, you mentioned that the drawing was missing. From then on, I drew it."

Brian was shaking his head in wonder. "I don't believe this," he said.

"I did the best I could!" Gigi wailed. "I did the best I could."

"Oh my God," Lennox said. "Oh my God. I'm so sorry, Lorrie."

Mom had never taken the Eurostar to eat chocolate croissants in Paris.

She'd never strolled through Hyde Park in her Wellington boots, sharing a big umbrella with Nigel.

She'd never had breakfast in Piccadilly Circus or grabbed a bite to eat in a pub. She'd never watched the changing of the guard at Buckingham Palace.

She'd never even made it out of town.

"He told me this was for the best," Gigi cried. "He said he'd take care of me, and he'd take care of the girls. It'd be easier for them if they didn't have to grieve for their mom, and they'd want for nothing."

"Who?" Julia asked.

"The senator!"

"No. It can't be," Julia said.

"But, Mom," Charlie said, "yesterday Dad said—" His voice caught. "Lorrie said he told her that he knew her mother."

"Julia, I assure you, this has nothing to do with you," Victor Underhill said.

"I think the authorities need to make that determination," Tim Blum said. "I'm calling for backup. In the meantime, I'll take these folks in for questioning."

The voices were coming to me as if through a fog, so far away. I was breathing hard. I couldn't speak. I couldn't catch my breath. From somewhere far away, a deep wail filled the room. Lennox had stepped up to me, and her arms were around me, holding me up, holding me still.

23

TRUER THAN
THE TRUTH

IT TOOK THE POLICE A HALF DOZEN INTERVIEWS
with Aunt Gigi to piece it together, what had happened that
night.

There'd been a party at the Copeland Compound. The
Copelands had had parties before, of course. But Gigi herself
had never been invited. This time, she was. Practically all of
Idlewild had been. Mom had already made plans to celebrate
Gigi's thirtieth birthday at Edgewater with Susannah and me,
and she told Gigi she didn't want to go to the party. But since
Gigi was the birthday girl, it was her vote that mattered. So
Mom agreed to hire a babysitter. She brought her new boy-
friend, Nigel, to Idlewild for the first time. He'd be Mom's date
to the party.

Maybe Mom had wanted to make the senator jealous
because he wouldn't leave his wife for her; maybe she'd wanted

to show him that she'd finally moved on and there were no hard feelings. Likely it was something in between, but we'd never know, because the only person who could tell us had been dead for over a decade.

Gigi hadn't known anything about it at the time, because she hadn't known that Mom and the senator had had any kind of relationship. She hadn't even known they'd ever met before. All she knew was that there was a party at the Compound, on her birthday. A sign that the universe wanted her to have an extra-special celebration. She wore a new dress that she'd bought just for the occasion, and tucked her little poodle, Katie, into her bag, her date for the evening. There were passed hors d'oeuvres, and Katie got to taste duck confit and caviar and even a tiny sip of the specialty cocktail Gigi was drinking—champagne-infused Christmas punch. It was a Christmas-in-July party, and there were lights in the trees and ornaments everywhere. At the end of the party, guests were told they could choose an ornament to take home and put on their own trees on the real holiday.

The only part of the night that hadn't been perfect was that they hadn't had a chance to speak to the senator or his wife. Gigi didn't want to leave without thanking them for a wonderful night—it wasn't polite, she said. But the Copelands were nowhere in sight, and Mom insisted it was time to go.

They'd almost reached the front door when suddenly, like magic, the senator appeared in front of them. Mom didn't have much to say, but Gigi gushed enough for them both about what a spectacular evening it had been, even though she hadn't seen her cake at the dessert buffet. She'd worked so hard on it—

three-tiered with buttercream icing and, no doubt, delicious. But the drinks were amazing, Gigi said. She just loved specialty drinks at a party. She told the senator she'd lost count of how many she'd had.

Nigel had also had a lot to drink, and he slurred his words when the senator asked him if he, too, had enjoyed the party. That was when Franklin Copeland offered to drive them home. He said he could get them home safely because he'd had only two drinks over the course of the night. A claim that Julia Copeland, when she was called in for questioning, would corroborate: The senator had a two-drink rule for himself when it came to social events. He always wanted to maintain control. It was a rule he abided by until the day he died.

Mom said the ride home wasn't necessary—it wasn't far at all, and she had also limited herself to two drinks, and besides, what would they do about her car? The senator said he held his liquor better than my mother did. Gigi had no idea how he knew that, but it didn't matter to her. She brushed Mom off and said they'd love the ride and she'd come back in the morning for Mom's Volvo herself. The senator led them to his white Mercedes, and Gigi got to sit in the front passenger seat. Mom and Nigel were together in the back. They cruised down Break Run. Gigi had rolled her window down and let Katie out of her purse, because even a poodle should get to experience the pure, unadulterated joy of being in a car driven by Senator Franklin Copeland, with the sea breeze ruffling her fur and the ocean roaring in her ears.

But then . . .

But then Katie jumped across the divide, into the backseat.

Gigi twisted around to retrieve her. Katie was on Mom's lap, wagging her tail. Nigel had nodded off, though they'd only been in the car about five minutes. And Mom was sitting there, oblivious to Katie, her eyes lasered in on the rearview mirror.

Maybe it was because it was dark, and the curve in the road near the Point was too hard to see. Maybe it was because Katie jumped back, and when Gigi reached around to get her, she knocked the senator's elbow on the gearshift.

Maybe it was because he was returning Mom's fixed gaze.

There was a smash, metal on metal, harder and louder than anything Gigi even knew was possible. They went through the guardrail and hit the water with the same force, the same sound. Water rushed in, and the car filled up fast. The water was as cold as ice, and Gigi tried to keep her head up, where there was air, but she was sinking down, freezing. The senator grabbed her hand and pushed her through a window. The headlights of the car flickered off, and the ocean was as dark as a cave. Gigi kicked and kicked but couldn't tell if she was moving up or down. Finally her head broke the surface, and she could breathe again. And the senator helped her swim to shore.

He went back under and tried to get Mom and Nigel—and Katie, too. But it was too late. So he sent Gigi home with instructions to stay quiet. Not to tell Susannah or me what had happened to our mom. Not to tell anyone. He had a guy who could fix anything, he said. And his guy would repair the guardrail and arrange for it to look like Mom had moved away with Nigel. He'd get rid of Mom's car and clean out her apartment. He'd explain it all to whoever needed to know these things. He'd take care of everything.

Susannah and I wouldn't have to grieve the death of a parent. The senator told Gigi it'd be easier that way. And he said we'd always be taken care of. He wired the first payment into her account the next day.

Just before sunset on the day after Gigi's thirtieth birthday, she walked Susannah and me over to the Point. She told us to pick puffer flowers and blow wishes into the water. Gigi ran her hand along the rail. She couldn't find the part that was new. It looked the same as it always had.

"I think right then," Gigi said, sitting on an old, scraped-up wooden chair, at an old, scraped-up wooden table, in a back room of the Idlewild Police Precinct, "that's when I started to believe that the story was true. That this was actually Danielle's plan, to run off with Nigel and leave the girls behind with me. You tell yourself a story for long enough, it becomes truer than the truth itself."

Tim Blum wrote it all down and filed his report.

24

THE PARTY
FOR CERTAIN

GIGI HAD BEEN TAKEN STRAIGHT FROM THE POLICE
station to Idlewild General for psychiatric evaluation, where
she was promptly admitted for treatment of a host of things—
depression, anxiety, post-traumatic stress disorder. Mom had
been dead for well over a decade, but suddenly it seemed that
there was urgency to plan a funeral, and it was up to Susannah
and me. There were so many choices: venue, flowers, and if
anyone would speak. It made me think of Gigi and the details
of her birthday party that she wouldn't have after all—I guess
the only party you can be certain of is your own funeral.

Mom's funeral would be small, we decided. Just us, plus
Brian and Lennox and the moms, for moral support. More
people would increase the odds that someone would tip off
the press to the details, and we wanted to keep the press away.
Though they were everywhere. If you turned on the news, it

seemed as if Idlewild was the center of the universe. Members of the media, and regular people, too, had camped out in clusters at the bottom of the driveway to Edgewater, by the gates at the Compound, and at the Point. The roadside memorials had grown to gargantuan proportions. In the pictures I'd seen, I could barely make out the driveway to our house under the crush of flowers and candles and pictures and poems.

I was no stranger to stares and gossip, having been the girl in "that house" for so much of my life. But this was a whole different universe of notoriety. I was *famous*; my image was on television and all over the Internet—pictures lifted from my Facebook profile and candid shots from last year's Hillyer yearbook. People I would never know were getting magazines and newspapers delivered. They were reading about me, and saying my name out loud, in between bites of scrambled eggs and loads of laundry.

I'd been hiding out in Lennox's house for days. Allyson Sackler and Meeghan Kandell had been named emergency temporary guardians to Susannah and me, and it was a relief to be taken care of. There was plenty of toilet paper at their house; in fact, each bathroom was stocked with extra rolls, and you never saw the supply diminish, because the minute you put in the replacement roll, a replacement to the replacement appeared under the sink. The food in the fridge was always fresh. The electric bill had been paid, and every last light fixture worked. Susannah had wanted to stay back at Edgewater, which was crazy to me. Why choose Edgewater over a house of order? But of course Edgewater was where her menagerie was. So at night Susannah bunked with me in the guest suite, and in the morning one of the moms would drive her through the thicket of onlookers so she could visit with all her creatures—including Brian.

The morning of Gigi's birthday, the morning of Mom's funeral, Allyson dropped Susannah at Edgewater early so she could feed the cats. She said she'd shower and get ready over there. Brian would bring her to the cemetery. I hadn't thought ahead to funeral clothes when I'd shoved my jeans, a couple of T-shirts, underwear, and bras into my oversize Goyard bag to head over to Lennox's house, and I didn't have anything to wear to Mom's service. But Lennox procured something from the back of Harper's closet—a gray skirt and matching top. I was glad it wasn't mine, so I wouldn't have to put it back and see it in my closet between a sundress and my barn jacket.

I'd never have to see it again.

When I walked into the kitchen, Allyson was back. She folded up the newspaper she'd been reading at the counter and stuck it into a drawer, presumably to hide it from me. A point-less victory, because there was a desktop computer in the guest room, and I'd already seen a hundred articles about Franklin Copeland's secret accident twelve years earlier, his affair with the woman in the backseat, and the child that relationship had produced: Susannah.

Of everything that had happened, that was the worst thing—that Susannah had to learn the truth of her parentage. I didn't know how it had gotten out. I hadn't told a soul, and through all of Gigi's police interviews, she hadn't mentioned it, which meant she hadn't known or maybe even suspected it. The news outlet that broke that part of the story cited "an unnamed source close to the family." Brian was on Susannah to get genetic testing done, to give proof that the rumor was true. It was just a cheek swab, he said. And then she'd be entitled to some of the Copeland inheritance. But Susannah said she didn't care about the money; she never had cared about such things. I'd certainly never get a cheek swab to show anyone I was anything but a hundred percent Susannah's sister, and I had fantasies of tracking the unnamed source down and throttling him.

"How about something to eat before we go?" Meeghan asked me. "Anything you want—a waffle, an omelet?"

I had a feeling if I'd said what I was really in the mood for was a hard-shelled lobster garnished with beluga caviar, she'd dive into the ocean herself and wouldn't come up for air until she'd found them.

"I'm not hungry," I said.

"You've hardly been eating," she said. "And I'm a mom, so I know your mom would want you to eat today. Some fruit? Cereal? Milk or no milk, it's up to you."

"Leave her alone, Meegs," Lennox said. I offered Lennox a grateful smile, but when I sat down next to her, she nudged her toast slathered with fig jam over toward me. I took the smallest of conciliatory bites, and then I had to chew for about a full minute to get it down.

The phone rang, and Allyson picked it up and checked the caller ID. "Assholes," she said. She clicked the button to answer, then hung it straight back up. "God, those reporters. I turned the ringer on not two minutes ago, because Craig was supposed to be calling right back."

"I'm sorry," I told her.

"What are you apologizing for?"

"They wouldn't bother you if I wasn't staying here."

"So we'll turn off the ringer again." Meeghan shot Allyson a look. "It's no big deal."

"The calls aren't all bad," Lennox said. "Everyone from Hillyer has called to check in. I saved some of the messages on my cell. I can play them for you, if you'd like."

I shook my head. Kids from Hillyer, people I'd never even been friends with, were quoted in the articles, too, commenting on everything from what classes I took to how I never invited my family to Visiting Day. Anything to be a part of the story.

"Has Charlie called?" I asked.

"No, I'm sorry. He hasn't."

"I'm sure the entire Copeland family is thinking about you right now," Meeghan said. "Especially Charlie. But he has his own grief to deal with, too. Yesterday must've been a particularly hard day for him."

Yesterday had been Senator Copeland's funeral. Not the public spectacle Julia had been planning. Instead, a dozen family members sailed out a couple of miles on the Atlantic and scattered his ashes. I'd seen pictures on the Internet of that, too, captured by cameramen with telephoto lenses. But no other details were released.

"I don't want you to think for a second that you should be staying anywhere but here," Allyson told me. She'd come up behind me and squeezed my shoulders. "But we should get going. Are you ready?"

"Yes," I said. "I am."

✳ ✳ ✳

I SAT IN THE BACKSEAT OF THE MOMS' CAR, BESIDE LEN-
nox. There weren't any news vans outside the gates to Dream
Hollow, but once we made the turn onto Lamb Avenue, there
they were, lining both sides of the street.

"Don't run over anyone's toes," Meeghan said as Allyson
maneuvered slowly through the throng.

"I wouldn't mind if you did," I said.

"Oh, Lorrie," Allyson said, and I could tell by her voice that
she was smiling. "I'd do almost anything to please you right
now."

She drove through the cemetery gates. I spotted Tim Blum's
cruiser and Brian's red pickup beside it. He and Susannah got
out of the truck and walked toward us. Susannah was in a slate-
blue peasant dress. Her hair, which she'd cut herself after the
fire, was brushed out and damp at the ends. Brian was in his
good jeans, a button-down that looked like he'd rescued it from
the bottom of a pile of laundry, and a skinny tie. He was holding Susannah's hand, and I remembered the feeling of Charlie's
hand in mine. How strange that I'd lost my mother because
of his father; even so, I wanted him with me when we finally
buried her.

From a few yards away, I could hear the *click, click, click* of a
couple dozen camera shutters, capturing us in staccato move-
ments. We'd been found out, despite our best efforts to keep
things private. Tim Blum stood in front of us, as if his one body
could shield the six of us from the photographers.

We walked up the driveway together and entered the main
building, which was filled with fresh-cut flowers. Like the

flowers lining Break Run Road. It seemed a strange tradition, flowers to honor those who'd died. All I could think about
was how they'd be dead soon, too.

A man in a dark blue suit approached us. He introduced
himself as the funeral director, Ed Seeley. I nodded; I'd spoken
to him on the phone. He led us down a corridor to a room
filled with plush couches in pastel colors. There were boxes
of tissues on every surface. "I know this is hard," Ed Seeley
said. His mouth was set straight, but there was the warmth of
a smile behind his eyes. "I'm going to do what I can to help you
through this."

"The girls appreciate that," Meeghan said.

"Yes, thank you," Susannah said.

"No thanks required. I'm just doing my job, and as you
requested, we'll have a small graveside service. Your mother
will be buried on the far side of the cemetery."

There'd been no body to recover, as Tim Blum had said. Just
the remnants of jewelry she'd been wearing and what were
probably fillings from her teeth, or maybe Nigel's. Nigel's own
father had died, it turned out, but his extended family had been
notified. Across the ocean, perhaps he was being memorialized
in some way. The moms had suggested that Susannah and I put
the few things that remained in a casket so there'd be some part
of Mom to visit.

"It's quite private," Ed Seeley went on. "You can't see it
from the road, and there are oak trees right there, so it gets nice
shade."

"That sounds peaceful," Allyson said. She squeezed my
hand. "I think your mom would've liked that."

"Uh-huh." I nodded.

"And which one of you is speaking?" Ed Seeley asked.

"I am," I said.

That had been another suggestion from the moms. They'd pulled me aside a couple days ago and told me in confidence that they'd written a similar request into their living wills about wanting Harper and Lennox to speak at their funerals one day. Their daughters didn't know about it; the moms didn't want to upset them with thoughts of their eventual death. But when you go through something sad, everyone is more inclined to tell you their own sad stories—even those that haven't happened yet.

I agreed that it was a good idea, and I wrote down funeral words to say: *Perhaps there is a predetermined time for each person's life, and we should be grateful for the time we had.*

"I brought pictures," Susannah told Ed Seeley. "Brian went through the house the other day and found a few. I thought we could display them."

Brian's backpack was on the floor by his feet, and he leaned over to unzip it. I glanced around the room, at the Pepto-Bismol-colored carpeting and the matching floral couches. It was hard to believe this all was real; I felt distanced from myself, as if I was a girl in a movie. My gaze fell back on Brian, fumbling with his backpack, and I saw something red.

"What the hell?" I said. I stood up to peer closer. Without asking, I reached in for the journal.

"What do you think you're doing?" he said.

"This is my mother's diary."

"Mom's diary?" Susannah asked. "It didn't burn in the fire?"

"I never went back to check," I told her.

Now I was angry at myself—how could I have been so careless? How could I have not checked to make sure that thing was burned to a crisp?

But that paled in comparison to the rage I felt for Brian. I glared at him. "What are you doing with this?"

"I'm not doing anything with it. I found it when I was looking for pictures. I thought you might want to read from it when you give your speech or something."

"Bullshit," I said.

"It's all right, Lorrie," Meeghan said. She'd been sitting on a side chair, pink to match the carpet, but now she stood and gripped my shoulder.

"You're the one who told the press about Susannah. Aren't you, Brian? You're the source. No one else knew."

"You knew about this before?" Susannah asked me. "You knew all along we were just half sisters?"

"I only found out the day of the fire," I told her. "And I didn't tell you because it didn't matter. Nothing Mom did or wrote a dozen years ago does anything to change the fact that you're my sister—my whole sister." I turned to Brian, shaking my head. "God, I knew you were awful. I just didn't know you were this awful."

Susannah took a deep, shaky breath, and then another. We were all looking at her, even Ed Seeley. "I'm sure there's another explanation," she said finally, quietly. "Brian would never do that."

"He has the diary, Susannah."

"Did you ever think that maybe it was your father?" Brian said. "He knew. Maybe it was his final revenge."

I startled as if I'd been stung. I knew where my dad was now, because the press had tracked him down. But in the articles I'd read, he'd refused to give them a comment. Not that he was the model of a parental figure; still, I knew instinctively that he wasn't the source. "I could call the *Times* myself and ask for the name of their source in exchange for a quote," I told Brian.

"He didn't do it," Susannah said stubbornly.

"Is she right, Brian?" I asked.

"It bugs you so much that Susannah dares to disagree with you," Brian said. "You think you're right about everything."

"All right, Brian," Meeghan said. "That's enough."

But he went on. "I saw you at the Copeland house. I saw your face when you walked into the room and saw we were there. You were mortified. Of your own family."

"*You're* not my family," I said.

"This is not the place," Meeghan said.

"It's all right," Mr. Seeley said. "I've seen it all. People have this romantic notion that loss brings you together. But the truth is, we all grieve in different ways. I've done this a thousand times, and I can tell you that every single experience is its own. And none of them is wrong."

"Tell her," I said sternly to Brian, at the same time that Susannah said, her voice meek, "Tell her."

"You were at the Copelands' that day," Brian said to Susannah. "It was like being in a different universe. To think people live like—" He broke off.

Brian had lived around the wealthy Idlewilders his whole life. He'd probably logged hours, days, maybe weeks imagining what it would be like to live like them, and then, when he finally saw firsthand, it must have exceeded his wildest dreams. I felt the slightest twinge of empathy for him. But that feeling only lasted a millisecond.

Brian began again. "They think they're better than everyone else, but they're not. They don't deserve what they have. You deserve it, Susannah."

"No," Susannah said.

"That's why I did it—for you, babe. Even if the senator is dead, you can get tested and prove you have a right to his money. It should be *yours*."

"No," Susannah said again.

"But, babe . . ."

"What part of *no* don't you understand?" I asked.

"Of course *you* don't want her to get tested."

"What's that supposed to mean?"

"You think you're the special one. But your mother—"

"Don't you dare bring my mother into this."

"She'd want this for Susannah," he said.

"I'm sick to death of people saying what my mother would've liked, what she would've wanted. You did this for yourself, Brian. Not for Susannah. Certainly not for my mom." I pressed a hand to my eyes.

"It's okay," Lennox said, standing up from the couch to be beside me. "Lorrie, it's okay."

"Did you know people who drown don't actually die from drowning?" I said.

Lennox shook her head. "I didn't."

"I read it online. They have heart attacks first, and that's what kills them. Chances are, that's what happened to my mom, but we'll never know, because it's been too long. There's no body for an autopsy."

"It doesn't matter exactly how your mom died," Lennox said quietly.

"It matters to me," I said. "It's one more thing I don't know about her. I should've made myself remember her more, so the memories didn't drift away." Unconsciously, one of my hands waved in the air, like a seagull flying and fading out of sight. "I should've practiced her voice in my head, because I can't even remember how she sounded. And I should've told Susannah stories about her. Good stories. I don't think I've said a single nice thing about her in over a decade. I've been remembering her all wrong, this whole time."

For the first time ever, I started to cry for her—for the loss of my mom. Lennox wrapped herself around me, and then each of the moms came to hold me, too. Susannah was sitting on the couch, crying. "Oh, Susie, I'm sorry," I said. "I'm sorry." Through the thicket of Sackler-Kandell arms, I reached a hand out toward her. She rose and clutched me, and the group pulled her in. We stayed that way for a little while, until sobs turned to sniffles and Mr. Seeley passed around a box of tissues. We untangled ourselves and blew our noses. Everyone may experience grief in different ways, but no one looks or sounds glamorous while doing it.

Brian had been watching us from his spot next to Susannah on the couch. He reached a hand out, but she was still holding me with one hand, and she had a tissue in the other. There wasn't a hand for him to take. "You should go," she told him.

"Aw, come on," he said. "I'm sorry if I screwed up. But don't let Lorrie—"

She swiped at a corner of her eye with a knuckle. "This has nothing to do with her. You don't belong here."

Brian gave a hard nod. "All right, if that's how you feel. I'll see you at home later."

"It's not your home," I said.

"Lorrie, stop," Susannah said. I swear, a flicker of triumph crossed Brian's face; he actually thought he'd won this one. "I've got this." She turned to him. "It's not your home," she repeated. "You can't stay there anymore."

"Oh, come on, babe," he said. "I love you."

"I don't know if you do," Susannah told him. "And what's more, I don't know if I love you back. Not anymore. Please leave."

Brian picked up his backpack. I wanted to grab it from him and shake the contents out onto the floor, pick through them and make sure nothing else had been taken from Edgewater. But this was Susannah's battle, not mine.

Tim Blum had been standing in the corridor to give us some privacy, and Susannah went to him to tell him in no uncertain terms that Brian was not to be given admittance to Edgewater. "I'm on it," I heard him say from the hall.

Everything that had happened had served to delay the inevitable, but now we couldn't avoid it any longer: We had to bury Mom. Whatever was left of her. We walked out the back door of the funeral home. Susannah and I were holding hands, which we hadn't done since we were kids. She'd never felt so completely like my sister. In the distance, the cameras were *click, click*ing away, the sound as faint as the memory of a dream.

"I lied when I said I didn't love Brian anymore," she said. "I know I'm not supposed to after what he did. But I do."

"I know you do," I said.

"Are you going to give me a list of reasons why that's wrong?"

I shook my head. "You know what I love most about you?" I asked.

"What?"

"You always think the best of people. You're always ready to love them. I honestly don't want you to ever change."

Susannah gave my hand a squeeze. "Thank you."

"I love you," I told her. "And I understand not being able to shut feelings off. I keep thinking about Charlie. Even though I shouldn't. I mean, I've only known him for such a short time, and after what his dad did . . . I'm sorry. I just can't shut it off. And now we're at Mom's funeral, and I shouldn't even be talking about him."

"Please don't stop," Susannah said. "I like when you talk to me about your life. You never do." We made a left on the foot-path. I saw a hill of dirt on the ground, beside the open mouth of a grave, and a snow-white casket suspended above it.

"Oh, Susannah, I love you so much," I said. "I'm so proud you're my sister."

"Lor, Lor, I love you more," my sister said. "I'm trying to figure out what all of this means, and I think I might have to go away for a bit—leave Idlewild for the first time. But I don't want to leave you."

"I left you," I reminded her. "I was so mad at Mom for leaving us, and then I did the exact same thing."

"You always came back," she said, and I nodded. "I really thought Mom would, too."

"So did I. It's so much harder, isn't it? Knowing she never will?"

"Yeah, it is."

THE SKY WAS A PERFECT BLUE, AND THE GRASS WAS A perfect green, as if they'd been colored in that way. On a little table set up by the graveside, we placed the photos of Mom; moments in time, once captured, now gone: Mom and Gigi as young girls in matching dresses. Mom standing in between her parents, in a cap and gown, at high school graduation. Mom blowing a kiss to the camera. Mom holding me. Holding Susannah. And there were all three of us, the Three Musketeers, on the steps of Edgewater.

Mr. Seeley began: "Today we are gathered because, exactly twelve years ago, Danielle Rae Hollander left this earthly world. But she lives on—in her beloved daughters, Lorrie and Susannah, who are here today, and in her sister, Gabriella, who took over raising them."

The casket had beveled edges, just like the one in Charlie's drawing, and there was a spray of flowers on top of it. White and yellow roses, whose petals were already browning in the heat of the sun.

"Now, Lorrie, would you like to say a few words?"

I scrunched up the piece of paper that I'd brought to read from. "My mom played James Taylor on long car rides, and she called the three of us 'the Three Musketeers,' and she kept a packet of crayons in her purse so that when we were at a restaurant waiting for our food to come, she could keep Susannah and me entertained." I looked at Susannah. "You always wanted her to draw you a full zoo—lions and flamingos and giraffes and a dozen other animals."

"I don't remember that," Susannah said.

"She drew great giraffes," I said. "But I wanted her to draw horses. They weren't exactly her specialty. Once, I caught her practicing them, when we weren't even out to dinner. She was sitting at the counter in the kitchen of our apartment in the city. She had one of my horse picture books propped up, and she was working out the proportions so she'd be able to draw them better the next time I asked. I think that's why I started drawing them myself. To be like her. To be a little closer to having her back."

Ed Seeley gave us cards with the Hebrew words of the Kaddish written out phonetically, the Jewish prayer for the dead, and we recited it as best we could. A lever was pressed, and the casket was lowered into the ground. Susannah and I each shoveled eight times over Mom's casket. One time for every letter in *I love you*.

SUSANNAH AND I WALKED ARM IN ARM BACK TO THE parking lot. The photographers had been waiting for us, and I could hear the camera shutters start up again.

Across the parking lot, a car door opened, and someone stepped out. A silhouette of a square jaw and shaggy hair. Lennox raised her hand in a wave, but then she lowered it quickly. The Copeland birds were chirping, as loud as ever.

Charlie flipped his bangs out of his eyes, and then they settled back down again. I'd stopped in my tracks, and so had the rest of my group. We waited for him to reach us. The cameras were going crazy. Here was the money shot.

"Hi, Lorrie," he said.

"You're here," I said. My eyes filled, but then I fell into silence, not knowing what to say. What can you say to the first boy you ever loved, the only boy, whose father had been the reason you'd lost your mom, even if he'd loved her, too—too much but not enough, it turned out. It was like the plot of a movie, but in a movie, someone would've written the dialogue for us. In real life, there were really no words.

"You're Susannah," Charlie said.

"I am," I heard Susannah say. "And you're Charlie. I've heard a lot about you."

"I'm really sorry for your loss."

"I'm sorry for yours, too."

"Maybe one of these days, we could . . . I don't know, get coffee or something. I feel like we should get to know each other."

"I'd like that," Susannah said.

Charlie turned back to me. "I knew today was the funeral, and I wanted to pay my respects. But it took me all morning to be brave enough to actually get here. I started and turned back and started out again, like, a hundred times. By the time I got here, the service had already started, and I didn't want to interrupt. And then I thought you probably didn't want me here anyway. I'd be, like, the *last* person you'd want at your mom's grave. I am, aren't I?"

I shook my head, too stunned to find the words.

"You're not the last," Susannah told him.

Charlie gave her a small smile. "I don't want to make things harder by ambushing you. Today of all days. But I brought you something."

"You brought me something?" I repeated.

"Uh-huh." He pressed a small box into my hands. I started to lift the lid. "Can you do me a favor and wait to open it?"

"Okay," I said. "Thank you."

The paparazzi were shouting. "Charlie! Lorrie! Susannah! Over here!"

"They sound like they're hungry for blood," I said.

"I'll get you out of here," Tim Blum said. He was on his walkie-talkie, calling for backup. We were shuttled into our respective cars. I waited until Allyson had pulled through the gates before I opened the box. Lennox and Susannah were on either side of me.

"I don't believe it," I said.

25
EDGEWATER

WE PUT EDGEWATER ON THE MARKET A FEW DAYS after Mom's funeral. Not even twenty-four hours later, it was sold—to Richard Deighton. Apparently Deighton wanted to expand his Break Run empire. At first I didn't want to let him have our house. He'd spent so much time decrying the state of Edgewater, and now I felt protective of it. It seemed cheesy and clichéd to walk around thinking, *If these walls could talk*, but that's what I did. My family had laughed and wept and been together in this house. It was wild—it was nearly unfathomable—that after three generations, and so much work, and so much pain, it was about to be over. Just like that. All that time, and suddenly there'd be no more.

Susannah was the one who convinced me that it didn't matter who bought the house; the bottom line was, it wasn't going to be *our* house anymore. And maybe there was even some kind of poetic justice to Richard Deighton and his family walking the same halls we'd walked.

"He'll probably tear it down," I told her.

"Even better," Susannah said. "Richard Deighton doesn't deserve to live in Edgewater."

To sell it, we needed Gigi's approval. Susannah and I brought the papers to the hospital for her to sign, then got on with packing up our lives. Out front in the driveway was a dumpster the size of a small planet. I'd spent weeks that summer trying to clean the house. Susannah, Lennox, and the moms had pitched in recently, too, but of course it was a bigger job than we could handle. Allyson did some online research and found a cleaning crew willing to finish it up. Not an ordinary cleaning crew; this one specialized in crime scenes. Island Crime Decontamination boasted that they'd seen it all—blood, guts, and gore. But I did find it strangely satisfying when Dave Cooley of Island Crime Decontamination walked into the house with his associates for their first day on the job and admitted he'd never seen anything quite like Edgewater.

The dumpster was filled until it nearly overflowed. The rest would be donated or put in storage until Gigi was released from the hospital. She wasn't going to be prosecuted for anything connected to Mom's death. Yes, a crime had been committed, but Gigi had been under no legal obligation to report it. The fact that Gigi knew about the accident and kept quiet may not have been laudable, but it wasn't criminal. She herself didn't do anything to cover it up, and she never lied to the authorities, so there was no obstruction-of-justice charge.

However, she'd never paid taxes on all the money she'd

received from the senator, which was a crime—tax evasion. But very quickly a judge approved a settlement, to be paid with proceeds from the sale of the house. No one wanted to see Gigi sent to prison. After all, she was a victim, too.

The moms had scoped out a town-house development called Wildflower Hills in a neighboring town. Each unit had its own patch of grass out front, and in the back each had a patio. Brown and white cookie-cutter homes. My grandfather would be rolling over in his grave, or so the expression went.

But actually, I didn't think so. I thought about the dead all the time now, and I decided that even if they had some sort of inexplicable knowledge of what happened after they'd gone, I didn't think they'd care so much, at least not about all the stuff we tend to place value on during the course of our lives. Six feet under, what did it matter if my grandfather had designed a one-of-a-kind beachfront estate or if he'd lived out his days in a boxy apartment? The ones left behind honor the dead simply by doing the best they can.

And what I came to understand was, all that time she was raising us, Gigi really *was* doing the best she could. I'd softened to her, realizing how she'd tried to give us everything we wanted, and to teach us things, from meditation to power poses, to help us move through life. I think some of those lessons even worked. The moms kept saying that, despite some of the awful choices she'd made, Gigi had managed to raise two remarkable girls. I didn't feel so remarkable myself. But Susannah sure was. And as for me, I was doing the best I could, too.

I drove out to see Wildflower Hills, and I agreed that when Gigi got out, she should go live there, or someplace just like it. Of course, she'd remain under a doctor's care, too. Once a week the community gardener would come to water lawns and clip hedges, taking care of the outside. Susannah and I decided we'd hire a housekeeper to come in once a week to help Gigi with the inside of the town house. But neither of us would be living there with her.

Susannah had found a farm in upstate New York that hosted high school students. In exchange for helping with various chores, she'd get free room and board. Once September hit, she'd begin her sophomore year at the school a mile away.

I looked at the pictures of the farm Susannah showed me online. "I don't know," I told her. "You'll be sharing a bunk in a barn with three other strangers."

"And what did you do when you went to boarding school?" she asked. She had me there.

The moms drove Susannah up to visit and agreed to sign off on the arrangement, as long as her grade point average stayed steady. Before she moved, she made flyers to find homes for her dozens of cats, and she personally met with each of the new owners to be sure they'd be the right fit for her babies.

So Susannah left. And then so did Lennox, back to Hillyer for senior year. She had to go a couple of weeks before classes officially started, because months earlier she'd signed up for the advisor program for incoming freshmen. "Come with me," she'd said. We were in her room at Dream Hollow, and she was packing up the vintage presidential-campaign posters she'd ordered for her dorm-room walls: LET'S BACK JACK KENNEDY FOR PRESIDENT and ALL THE WAY WITH LBJ. She'd pull them out of their tubes, hold them up to admire them, then reroll them, put them back into their tubes, and gingerly place them in her big trunk, as if she was laying a baby in a crib.

"Kathleen Strafford filled my spot weeks ago," I reminded her. She unrolled a picture of an owl and held it up to show me. "The Wise Old Bird Says 'Hoo, Hoo, Hoo-Hoo-ver,'" I read aloud. "Definitely my favorite."

"You haven't even tried to see if Strafford is willing to squeeze you back in, so you don't know for sure that she wouldn't."

"True."

"Get on it, Hollander! You were at Hillyer for the last three years. Don't you want to finish up high school where you started it?"

I couldn't say money was the issue anymore, and Lennox knew it. Even with Gigi's tax settlement, there was still a nice chunk left over from the sale of Edgewater. Plus, the senator's will had been read, and Susannah and I were both named in it. There was a trust fund, a real one, with an executor chosen by the bank. All our expenses would be vetted through him—not Gigi. If I wanted to, and if Ms. Strafford could find a spot for me, I could go to the executor to approve my tuition payment.

"They all feel bad, you know."

I did know. Among the flowers that had arrived for me at the Sackler-Kandells' were two enormous arrangements from Hillyer. One from the headmaster, and one from Kathleen Strafford herself. Both made mention of "your Hillyer family."

"That's not it," I told Lennox. "For the first time in my life, I don't want to run away from home. I think that means I'm supposed to stick around for a while."

I'd made plans to live at the one place in Idlewild that still felt like home—Oceanfront. It had been Naomi's idea. She said there was plenty of room in the house, and she could use the company. I had no idea if she really meant it; Naomi didn't strike me as the type of person who ever got lonely. But I decided to take her up on her offer nonetheless. She had let me choose between two guest bedrooms at the top of the stairs. I picked the smaller one, painted yellow, with a bookshelf taking up the length of the longest wall and a window that looked out to the barn so that when Orion stuck his head out the back window of his stall, I could see him.

My Orion. He'd be living in Idlewild, too. Not because of Underhill's payment—I wouldn't have taken anything from Underhill Enterprises, even if the police hadn't frozen the company and all its assets. But I'd called Beth-Ann to see about buying him back myself. She'd flat-out refused, even though I offered ten percent over the purchase price, then twenty percent. "Name your price," I'd told her.

"He's not for sale," she said.

Those words were familiar. We hung up, and it wasn't even five minutes before I got a call from Clayton Bracelee, Beth-Ann's dad. I could have Orion back, and a refund of the sale price was just fine—no need to inflate it. He'd even take care of the shipping costs. He proceeded to give an interview about it—free press for the candy company. But I didn't care. My horse was coming home.

Lennox stuck the owl poster into the trunk, pouting. "I thought we were starting senior year together early this summer. I didn't know we wouldn't get it at all."

I knocked her in the ribs. "You'll have Nathan," I reminded her.

She rolled her eyes. "I don't know what I ever saw in him," she said. "And, regardless, he's no substitute for you."

"No, for that you have Violet Tabachnick."

When I said Violet's name, Lennox wrinkled her nose as if she'd drunk milk gone sour.

"Sorry. Is she that bad?"

"So far we've only e-mailed to work out which one of us is bringing the mini fridge and which one is bringing the throw rug. And I know you're going to tell me I should give her the benefit of the doubt until I meet her, but what kind of person do you think wouldn't have a roommate worked out for senior year?"

"Who has two thumbs and is holding an 'I Still Like Ike' poster?" I asked her.

"This girl," Lennox said softly. She looked at me, tears brimming in her eyes. "Aw, man, Lorrie. I'm really going to miss you."

My own eyes grew moist. "I'm going to miss you, too."

"What if I bag this advisor thing? There are plenty of people who want to be freshman advisors, and we'd get a couple more weeks of summer together."

I shook my head. "You should go," I said. "You'll be a great advisor, and October break will be here before we know it."

Lennox closed the trunk and pulled me into a hug. "This is the first time I'll be at Hillyer without you—or Pepper."

I squeezed her, too, tightly, and then broke away and wiped my eyes. "I hope I didn't pressure you into leaving him."

"No, you're right. Jeremy is a better rider for him. Pepper will get to show what he's made of, and the moms love the idea of owning a horse that might win big."

"You can always change your mind," I told her. Though for Jeremy's sake, I hoped she didn't. "And I'll look after him, too."

"I know you will. The truth is, I love Pepper, but I haven't loved riding in a long time. I never loved it as much as you did. I rode for you, you know. I rode him to stay close to you."

"That's an expensive pastime, just to hang out with your best friend."

"You were worth it."

CHARLIE CALLED TO SAY HE WANTED TO SEE ME.

"Not somewhere public," he said.

Because people would see. I understood. The last photo we'd been in together, standing in the center of the parking lot of the Idlewild Cemetery, had been in newspapers around the world. I imagined people in other countries picking up the paper. I imagined one particular person in one particular country— my mother—grabbing the morning's paper as she walked through King's Cross to catch a train. She'd find her seat, flip it open, and see me. Her long-lost daughter. Or rather, I wasn't lost; I'd been in the same place all these years. I wondered if she'd recognize the five-year-old she knew in the seventeen-year-old I'd become.

Of course I knew that Mom was dead, that she'd never been in England. But I still pictured her there. I couldn't help myself.

I had a few days to pack up what was left at Edgewater, and I told Charlie he could stop by the house. It was perfectly safe and private, save for the occasional car that would slow down at the bottom of the driveway just to gawk at the house. But the press had packed up their cameras and left a couple of days after Mom's funeral. I guess they'd finally taken enough pictures of the house where Mom no longer lived. The pile of flowers at the end of the driveway was also gone, courtesy of Island Crime Decontamination. Though before they disposed of them all, Susannah ran down to rescue a bouquet of pink sweetheart roses. She pressed them between the pages of a thick old book and brought them upstate.

IT WAS ANOTHER CHARACTERISTICALLY GORGEOUS Idlewild day, and I'd thrown open all the windows that I could reach. The house was flooded with natural light, and I felt like I was outdoors, but not in the way I used to. Instead of the outdoors creeping in unwanted through the floorboards and invading the sanctity of our home, it was all air and freshness. A breeze swept through, rustling the curtains and brushing my cheek like a kiss. It was wishful thinking—I knew that—but I hoped it was a sign from my mother, and it was the happiest moment I'd had in Edgewater since she'd been gone.

I had downloaded *James Taylor's Greatest Hits* onto my phone, but I hadn't been able to listen to it. Now I plugged it into a set of speakers and scrolled down to "How Sweet It Is."

Just after noon, I heard the car drive up. The James Taylor album was playing in a loop as I bubble-wrapped my grandmother's delft china. A bunch of the pieces had been broken and were now in the dumpster out front, but what was still intact was coming with me to Naomi's. She'd said I could bring a few things that felt like home, and the blue and white china had long been a favorite of mine. Decades ago, my grandmother had purchased the set for display, and part of me thought it was a little bit crazy to put them in the cabinets of the barn house and use them for everyday things like waffles and spaghetti. I heard a voice in my head that wasn't my mother's, couldn't be my mother's, but that sounded like hers all the same: *What are you saving them for? Just use them. Use them!*

Life lessons from a box full of plates.

I taped up the salt and pepper shakers with the peacocks on them and put them in the box. Then I headed downstairs. Charlie was coming up the steps of the porch when I opened the door. Behind him, in the driveway, was a navy-blue BMW. I wondered if it was another from his dad's collection.

"Hey," he said.

"Hi."

He gave me an air kiss on either cheek. There was his Julia Copeland training. Plus, he'd finally gotten that haircut his mom wanted so badly. No more bangs, just short hair all around, so thick that the strands stood up on their own like individual fibers of carpet. The new cut made his hair look darker, almost the color it was when it was wet. I could see the tops of his ears for the first time.

Other things seemed different about him, too. I regarded him, trying to put a finger on the features that had changed. I realized that he stood a bit stiffly, as if the effects of the haircut had trickled down all over him.

"I'm glad you came," I told him, feeling oddly formal myself. "I never got to properly thank you for the watch."

"It was nothing," he said. "It was the least I could do."

"How did you know where to find it?"

"I don't know if I should tell you."

"Oh, come on," I said. "I've been racking my brain these last few weeks, trying to remember if I ever told you about pawning it. I know I didn't, and Lennox swore up and down that *she* didn't tell you. She didn't even know herself until after you gave it to me, when I was obsessing about it."

"You were obsessing about it?"

My cheeks warmed. "It was nice to have a different kind of mystery to think about," I said. "Anyway, the only possible explanation I can think of is that you were following me."

"You're close," he said.

"Tell me."

"Victor Underhill was following you," he said.

I remembered the sedan that I'd seen on my way into the pawnshop and on my way out again. Underhill had been behind those tinted windows, no doubt.

"He wanted to keep tabs on your family," Charlie continued. "I'm sure you read about his involvement."

"Yeah, I did." The police had interviewed Underhill following Gigi's confession. He admitted he'd been the guy to step in and arrange a middle-of-the-night repair job on the guardrail. He'd come up with the story about Mom and Nigel moving to London and taken care of the details. But afterward, he'd had a crisis of conscience, or so he claimed, and he'd urged the senator to turn himself in. That was when the senator had ousted him from the inner circle.

Then, when Julia decided to run for Congress, he'd been called back. The senator had recently been diagnosed with

Pick's disease, a brain disease that causes dementia. It wasn't alcoholism the family was covering up. Julia was afraid that if news of his illness got out, she wouldn't be elected, and it was her turn, she maintained. After being the supportive political spouse all those years, she didn't want to have the public thinking she should stay home and care for her ailing husband.

Underhill said he hadn't known Gigi had been in the car all those years ago. It was the senator himself who started to make secret payments to Gigi to buy her continued silence. Who knew why he chose to keep that one detail a secret from his formerly trusted advisor? Maybe he was worried Underhill would do something to Gigi, or to Susannah and me. Or maybe he was just ashamed. Whatever the reason, due to his illness, he'd recently forgotten to make the promised payments. Underhill didn't learn the whole truth until Gigi showed up at the Compound the night Susannah was burned, and once he did, he told Gigi he'd take care of things, as long as she kept me away from Charlie. That was why the money for Orion's board had come in.

"Victor wasn't about to turn my dad in, because he was sick and all that," Charlie said. "But when he figured out who you were, he just wanted to be sure you wouldn't make any trouble for my mom." He shook his head. "I'm sorry. I just wanted you to have your mom's watch back. Even if the way I knew about it was totally sleazy. I guess I didn't really think through the fact that you'd ask me, or I would've come up with a better excuse."

"There have been a lot of secrets and lies between our families," I said. "I think we should stick to the truth from now on."

"Yeah," he said. "The truth sounds good to me, too."

"I used to pretend I didn't care about my mom's things," I said. "But I always wore the watch, and I'm happy to have it back, however you found it. So, thank you."

"You thanked me already."

"I mean it so much I said it twice," I told him, and I put a hand over the face of the watch and pressed down briefly. It was a new habit I'd developed, touching this thing that Mom had touched. I wondered, if you dusted for prints, whether her fingerprints were still on it. God, how I hoped so.

"Cool," Charlie said. He nodded, as if he was assuring himself. "Cool. So, this is your house."

"For another week it is," I said. "We just sold it. It's weird, though. I've lived here my whole life. Well, my whole life since my mom . . . you know. And even before then, this house has been in my family for decades. I'm going to miss it."

And that was true: I actually would.

"I like seeing the house where young Lorrie *Hollander* spent her days."

I gave a hard nod at the mention of my real last name. "I spent a lot more time at Lennox's house. I was always looking for excuses to get away from here."

Charlie regarded me. "Can I come in anyhow?"

"Oh, sorry, yes, you can," I said. I grinned and opened the door wider. "Yes, you can."

"You said it twice. I guess that means I'm *really* allowed to come in."

"You really are," I said. He stepped across the threshold. "I can't believe you're here," I told him. "I can't believe you're in my house."

Charlie Copeland, standing in the foyer of Edgewater. A cleaned and dusted version of the Edgewater foyer. But still, a few weeks ago I couldn't have imagined inviting anyone into my home.

Things change. Even when you think they couldn't possibly. It was an amazing thing to know.

"Why is it so hard to believe I'd come over?"

"It's not you. It's this house. I never let anyone come over. Not even Lennox. It was such a mess."

"I don't think your friends would care if your house was messy," Charlie said. "At least, I wouldn't."

"*Mess* isn't the right word for what it was," I said. "It was a disaster area, a health hazard. Have you ever seen the homes they have on those hoarder shows?" Charlie nodded. "It was like that, but on steroids."

"I'm sure it wasn't *that* bad."

"It was," I said. "But I don't care anymore. As a matter of fact, I feel like I deserve some kind of badge of honor for making it through twelve years."

"If I'd known that's what you wanted, I would've brought you one," Charlie said.

"I was so ashamed," I said. "I wasted a lot of time worrying that people would find out and think terrible things about me. You know, judge me because I lived here."

"When I think about what my dad did to your mom, and how he kept it a secret . . . I just . . ." Charlie shook his head.

"He was trying to control what people thought of him." It was strange to realize I had something in common with Franklin Copeland, but there it was. "There's a part of me that gets that," I said. "I mean, *I* wanted to control the story people had about me."

"But you didn't hurt anyone in the process," Charlie said. "I'm so sorry, Lorrie. I think I'll be sorry about it for the rest of my life."

I didn't know what to say back to him. I couldn't just say, *That's okay*. Because it wasn't, and it never would be. But it wasn't Charlie's fault. Just like Edgewater wasn't mine.

"People thought he was so good," Charlie said. "And now they think everything about him was a lie and that he was all bad. I guess it's easier to categorize things like that: white versus black, good versus bad." Charlie paused and shook his head. His hair stayed stiff and still, like it wasn't his own. "Sometimes . . ." he said. "Sometimes even I think of him as all bad. There's less to figure out that way."

I nodded. It was easier for me to think that way about the senator, too; the same way it had been easier for me to think that way about Mom. For years I thought the fact that she'd left was the only thing about her that mattered. It was the story I told myself, and my sister, and my friends. It was the story I put out into the world.

But it was *my* story, and it turned out it had very little to do with my mother. There are the stories people tell about your life, and then there's the truth about it, which is completely your own.

"I know what you mean," I told Charlie. "I know exactly what you mean."

James Taylor's voice wafted down from above. "My dad loved James Taylor," he said.

"My mom, too."

"I wonder if they listened to him together."

"I guess we'll never know," I said.

It was a long list of things I'd never know about my mother. I looked at Charlie's face, the lean nose and the square jaw and his eyes squinting in discomfort. Not for the first time, I wished my mom were around to talk to her about what I felt for him.

"You must be so angry," he said.

"Sometimes."

"Me, too. And it feels so weird, because I also miss the hell out of him. I dream about him. And during the day, basically anything and everything reminds me of him—the view of the Point, obviously, and also the sound of the waves, and the way the light hits a certain painting on the wall, and the stupid prize at the bottom of the box of cereal." He smiled sadly. "I just have so much to ask him. I found out so much I didn't know about him, and now I only have more questions. Isn't that crazy?"

I shook my head. People were like icebergs. There was so much more than you could see. Everyone had secrets below the surface. "You once told me that people are complicated," I said.

"I'm pretty wise." He paused. "When did I say that?"

"In the tree house, on the Fourth of July," I said. "You said it about Lennox and Nathan, and I think it's the truest thing you could say about anyone. Like, even my dad. I know where he is now, and clearly he knows where I am, but he hasn't reached out. I wonder if he's too mad to come back, or if he's too embarrassed. Or maybe he's still drinking. I don't know. But I think I'll send him a letter or something. Not today, but soon. I'm sure there's more to his story than I've been told, and I'd like to find out. I haven't told anyone else that. What do you think?"

"I think you should," Charlie said. "Maybe you'll be disappointed, but at least you would've tried. I wish I'd tried harder with my dad. When I was a kid, he wasn't around that much, but when he was home, he'd always grill me about what was going on in the news, and he'd get annoyed because I couldn't have cared less about any of it. I just wanted a dad who, I don't know, coached Little League or something. And then he started to change. It happened so slowly at first. You could barely tell anything was wrong, up until these last few weeks. My mom just wanted to wait until after her election to go public. And my dad, well, he'd stare out at the Point. For hours, he'd stare. This was a man who never used to stand still for anything. Once, he grabbed my hand and told me I had to go down there and bring flowers. He had a bouquet of flowers. I had no idea where he got them or why he wanted me to bring them, but there was something in his voice . . ." Charlie's own voice trailed off. "Anyway, I didn't question it. I just went."

So it was Charlie that Lennox and I had seen that day at the Point, my first day back in Idlewild. And it was Charlie who'd left the flowers. Of course it was. I wasn't even surprised.

"But even at the end he remembered your mom," Charlie said. "Writing you and Susannah into his will was probably the last sane thing he did before he got too sick." He shook his head. "I'm having the hardest time believing he's gone."

"Susannah used to have such a hard time saying good-bye to her pets," I told him. "Even saying good-bye to animals that weren't her pets. I didn't get it. I told her that once something was dead, it was dead. But now I understand her wanting to hold on a bit longer. It's funny, because she seems to be adjusting pretty well to everything now. She's going to school upstate. She made all the arrangements herself."

"And you," Charlie said. "You going back to school?"

"Not to Hillyer. It's a long story, but the bottom line is, I'm gonna do senior year here in Idlewild. Naomi has a spare room at Oceanfront. That way I can visit my aunt and be around Orion and the horses. What about you?"

"Correspondence school," he said. "I just have a few credits left. This way I can do them online from wherever I am."

"That's good," I said. I toed the floor. "And are you back with Shelby?" Charlie looked at me funny. "I mean, you said you guys were taking a break for the summer, and then she texted . . . that day."

"We're friends," he said. "But we're not right for each other. Not that way. Mostly I went out with her because it drove my mother crazy. But I was hoping . . ."

"What?" I asked. "What were you hoping?"

"I've wanted to tell you this for a while, but it's been so hard. There's only one person I've wanted to be with since the day I met you." He stuck out a finger and pressed it lightly into my breastbone. "You, Lorrie."

"Really?"

"Really. There was something about you at the gas station that day—not just that you were beautiful." I felt my cheeks warm. "But you were so . . . so self-possessed, and so unimpressed with me."

"That's not how I really was," I said. "Not on the inside."

"That's all right," he said. "I still want to be with you."

"Won't being with me drive your mother crazy, too?"

"Maybe," he said. He smiled again. "But that's not why I want to. Which may be a first for me, as relationships go." He paused and took a breath. "I think about you all the time. I think about you when I'm sad about everything that's happened, which is almost always. And I think about you in between the sad times, when I have these bursts of feeling okay again."

"That's when I think about you, too," I said. "All those times."

"So, what do you say, Lorrie? Do we get a fresh start?"

I glanced around at the front hall of my house—at the fountain, still dried up but now clean of dirt and grime, at the wood-paneled floors that had been stripped bare of their moldy rugs, and at the winding staircase that stretched up three stories—and I realized something: I didn't need a fresh start. It was all a part of me. It all mattered. And whatever else Senator Copeland had done wrong, he was right about one thing: You can't ignore the past if you want to step boldly, confidently into the future.

I shook my head. "No," I said.

Charlie's face fell.

"Let's just pick up where we left off."

Charlie pulled me toward him, wrapping himself around

me. I buried my head in his neck and kissed him, tasting him. My lips found his mouth. He was slow and gentle, and I wasn't scared of losing him. Of all the movies I'd played out in my head, the way it really happened was something I never could have imagined. But you can never know how the movie of your life will go. You just have to live it.

It was a long time before Charlie and I broke away from each other. "Come on, let's go," I said.

"Where are we going?"

"You owe me a pizza date," I told him. "And we're going to have to go out in public at some point."

"All right," he said. "You lead the way."

I took his hand and led him out the door of Edgewater, and we walked into the future, together.

ACKNOWLEDGMENTS

THANK YOU, THANK YOU, THANK YOU:

To Laura Schechter, for her generosity, her unwavering support, and most especially for the "spark" of this book—"Hey, you should write a *Grey Gardens* YA, with sisters!" Laura, I hope I produced something that makes you proud.

To the YA writing community, for inviting me into the fold long before I had my own official YA book on the shelf. And to one YA writer in particular, my dear, sweet friend Sarah Mlynowski, who opened up the "writers' lounge" to me in the spring of 2011 and who has welcomed me nearly every day since: Thank you for everything. Thanks also go to my fellow lounge regulars: Elizabeth Eulberg, Jennifer E. Smith, and Robin Wasserman; to the Type A Retreaters: Emily Heddleson, Lexa Hillyer, Jess Rothenberg, Leila Sales, Rebecca Serle, and of course Laura Schechter (look, Laura—you're in here twice!); to Adele Griffin and Erich Mauff, for the thousand ways they helped me get started; and to my Tuesday afternoon Writopia workshop students: You know who you are, and you are exceptional—infinite points to all.

To Altana Elings-Haynie, who introduced me to the real Orion; to her friends Rita and Chloe Callahan, who were the kindest hosts and the most patient teachers; and to the inimitable Regan Hofmann, who answered every last question I asked about horses.

To Isabella Carpi, Stephen Melzer and his son Jackson, Jennifer Michael, and Alyssa Siegel-Miles, whose anecdotes and expertise further informed the story.

To my friends who read the messy early chapters and helped me push through to the end of the book: Gracie Aaronson, Lindsay Aaronson, Samantha Aaronson, Fátima Ptacek, and Kai Williams. And to Meg Wolitzer, one of my all-time favorite writers: Thank you for reading every single version, for critiquing, for cheerleading, and mostly for being my friend.

To Arielle Warshall Katz, who is the model of the best friend in everything I write. To a few more essentials who put up with endless *Edgewater*-related discussions and who sometimes sent food: the Bressler/Shuffler family, Jen Calonita, Maria Crocitto, Erin Cummings, Jennifer Daly, Gitty Daneshvari, Julia DeVillers, Melissa Brown Eisenberg, Rachel Feld, the Fleischman/Tofsky family, Gayle Forman, Mary Gordon, Logan Levkoff, Melissa Losquadro, the Lucas family, Linda Mainquist, Wendy Mass, Lauren Myracle, Nina Nelson, Stacia

Robitaille, Jennie Rosenberg, Kieran Scott, Katie Stein, Bianca Turetsky, and Rebecca and Jeremy Wallace-Segall. And extra special thanks to Geralyn Lucas, whose generosity knows no bounds.

To Sam Droke-Dickinson, Liane Freed, Angela Mann, and Cristin Stickles, for their willingness to read and their extremely kind words.

To my family: my father, Joel Sheinmel (first-reader extraordinaire); my mother, Elaine Sheinmel, and my stepdad, Phil Getter; my sister, Alyssa Sheinmel, and my brother-in-law, JP Gravitt; and my stepsiblings, their spouses, and the littles who aren't so little anymore: Nicki, Andrew, Zach, Sara, and Tesa. If I had all the families in the world to choose from, I'd still pick you to be mine.

To Tamar Rydzinski at the Laura Dail Literary Agency, Inc., for her enthusiasm and her invaluable notes. And to the amazing Laura Dail herself, who knew instinctively the story I wanted to tell, who got behind the book in a major way, and who wouldn't rest until it was in the right hands.

Speaking of those right hands, to the brilliant, indefatigable Tamar Brazis, the editor of my dreams. And to everyone at Abrams/Amulet books, especially Orlando Dos Reis, Emily Dowdell, Jen Graham, Maria T. Middleton, and Nicole Russo. Thanks also to Kristen Barrett, Leslie Kazanjian, and Lauryn McSpadden for their careful reads of the manuscript.

To two women I never met, Edith Bouvier Beale and her mother, Edith Ewing Bouvier Beale, for being so staunchly themselves, and so inspiring.

Finally, enduring thanks to my grandmother, Doris V. Sheinmel, who was the most hardworking, uncomplaining, and extraordinary person I've ever known. Grammy, I miss you every day, and every day I try to live up to you. This book is for you. (I'm sorry about all the curses.)

With love,
Courtney

ABOUT THE AUTHOR

COURTNEY SHEINMEL is the author of *My So-Called Family*, *Positively*, *All the Things You Are*, *Sincerely*, and the Stella Batts series for young readers. She lives in New York City.

AN INTERVIEW WITH COURTNEY SHEINMEL BY HER SISTER, AND FELLOW NOVELIST, ALYSSA SHEINMEL

Alyssa: You've been my big sister for over three and a half DECADES! Do you think that has influenced how you write about sisters?

Courtney: Absolutely. Everything I know about being a sister I learned from being your sister.

Alyssa: So, does that mean I was the inspiration behind *Edgewater*?

Courtney: Actually, it was the writer (and our friend) Lauren Oliver, who knows that I love the documentary *Grey Gardens*. I think you've seen it, too, but in case you don't remember, it's about a mother and her daughter, Big Edie and Little Edie.

They'd once been very wealthy, but now they were confined to the ruins of their former lives, in a house overrun with cats and other critters, the walls crumbling down around them. And the Edies didn't make any apologies for it. They simply were who they were.

Like many of us, from the time I was young, I thought I needed to put on an act—to say the right things and wear the right things—in order to be accepted. When I was around eight, Mom took me shopping and I found a shirt I loved. It looked like a patchwork quilt, and it reminded me of Grizabella from the musical *Cats*. I looked in the mirror and thought: *I need this. I need this.* Mom said I could have it, and excitement swelled inside me. Then I started to cry. "No, I can't have it," I told her. "The other kids won't like it."

Alyssa: You never told me that story.

Courtney: It was one of those moments that doesn't feel important enough to share, yet it somehow gets to the heart of who I was back then. Here we are more than thirty years later, and I can still conjure the excitement and the dread I felt in that dressing room, so maybe it's also a bit of who I am now. But watching Little Edie on-screen, marching in her turban and makeshift skirt, I suspect that if she had wanted an oversized patchwork shirt, she would've gotten it, and she would've worn it proudly no matter what the other kids said. She was so staunchly herself. That's a hard thing to be, even in the best of circumstances, and it's something I greatly admire.

But, anyway, back to Lauren. She said, "You should write a *Grey Gardens*-y young adult book—with sisters!" From the moment I heard the idea, I thought it was magical. I loved thinking of sisters in that kind of house, sisters who were completely devoted to each other but who had very different feelings about their house—one of them, I decided, would go with the flow of the chaos and one would be itching to get out. I named the older sister, the narrator, Lorrie—in honor of Lauren.

But you, Alyssa, are the reason that my friends know I love writing sister stories.

Alyssa: I remember you saying this book was particularly hard to write . . .

Courtney: Every book is hard to write. When we were kids and I dreamed of being a novelist, I figured the first one would be the hardest, and then it would get easier and easier, like playing a song on the piano or doing a cartwheel—neither of which I can actually do, but I assume if I spent enough time trying to master them, I'd get there.

Alyssa: Practice makes perfect?

Courtney: Exactly. But what I came to realize is that when it comes to books, writing each one is an experience unto itself. What I'm practicing is telling that particular story. I suppose were I to try and write *Edgewater* again, the second time around would be markedly easier. But the first time, whoa, it was a doozy!

Alyssa: It was your first time writing an "official" young adult novel. Was that something you wanted to do?

Courtney: Oh, yes—I really wanted to write a YA novel. I had so many friends who were writing YA—not to mention you, my one and only little sister—and when we all hung out, I sometimes felt like an imposter because back then my books were all middle-grade and young-reader books. Not that I wasn't proud of those books; I was! But I desperately wanted to feel like I'd earned the title "YA writer," so *Edgewater* meant a lot to me. I was beyond thrilled when I found out Abrams would publish it. At that point, I'd written only a few chapters, so I needed to get on with finishing it.

As you know, since 2009 I've been mentoring teen writers at an amazing nonprofit in New York called Writopia. There are times when one of my students will share a particularly lovely piece and the other kids in the room will shower their peer with admiration and praise, and then, inevitably, when it comes time for them to turn back to their own work, they start to feel bad about it. I tell them not to compare themselves to others, and when that doesn't work, I tell them to use the moment as motivation to write their stories as best they can. "The story in your head is yours. It doesn't belong to anyone else, and you are worthy of telling it," I say.

But at times while I was writing *Edgewater*, it was hard to take my own advice. I loved the idea so much, but I worried that I wasn't worthy of writing it, that I wouldn't be able to do Lauren's idea justice. As long as something is in your head and not yet written, it has the potential to be perfect. I was scared of imperfection; actually, I was scared of making a giant mess of it. I remember thinking that if only she'd given the idea to someone else, one of our other friends, the book would be finished, and it would be brilliant.

Alyssa: One of my favorite quotes about writing—from the great Ann Patchett—speaks to that idea: In order to write a story, you have to be willing to give up the perfect story in your head and write the (imperfect) story you're capable of writing instead. How did you handle that?

Courtney: I got up every morning and got started on my word count goal for the day. That's my writing routine—a certain amount of words every day, and eventually a finished book. Lauren's idea no longer felt magical; it felt like I was wading through quicksand. It felt impossible. I thought up a mantra that I kept repeating to myself: "It's not impossible. It's just hard." Finally, I finished a first draft, got feedback, and went back in to fix things. Rinse and repeat.

Now that it's a real book that I can hold in my hands and you can hold in yours, the magic comes in again. There was nothing but a one sentence spark: "You should write a *Grey Gardens*-y book—with sisters!" And now there's a 300-something-page book with my name on the cover.

That's one of the things I love best about writing: the making something from nothing, from just the spark of an idea. We all have so many ideas, all day long, and most of them don't become anything. But sometimes we follow one through, and then it becomes something tangible that you can hold—that other people can hold. Usually the finished product doesn't sound anything like I first imagined it would, and certainly it's completely different than what someone else would've written. Writing isn't painting by numbers or making an Ikea shelf. It's so specific and personal, and when it's done, you get to share it. It's frightening and exhilarating, and it's what I always wanted to do. I am so grateful I get to do that.

Alyssa: I feel grateful I get to do it, too. You mentioned Writopia earlier—did being around teens help you write for teens?

Courtney: Oh, yes. Each week, in the ten minutes before class starts, the kids file in and chat. I always take notes. Plus, it's just inspiring whenever I think of all they juggle: six or seven classes, studying for quizzes and tests, writing papers, studying for SATs, applying to college, and then their own storywriting. Surely if they can do all of that, I can write my book.

Alyssa: Do you think you'll write more about sisters?

Courtney: You know the answer to that: Of course!

IN ADDITION TO BEING COURTNEY SHEINMEL'S KID sister, Alyssa Sheinmel is the *New York Times* bestselling author of several books for young adults, including *Faceless* and *R.I.P. Eliza Hart*. Visit her online at alyssasheinmel.com, or follow her on Instagram and Twitter @AlyssaSheinmel.